THE FRAGRANCE OF DEATH

Also by Leslie Karst

The Sally Solari Mysteries

DYING FOR A TASTE
A MEASURE OF MURDER
DEATH AL FRESCO
MURDER FROM SCRATCH

THE FRAGRANCE OF DEATH

Leslie Karst

SEVERN
HOUSE

First world edition published in Great Britain and the USA in 2022
by Severn House, an imprint of Canongate Books Ltd,
14 High Street, Edinburgh EH1 1TE.

Trade paperback edition first published in Great Britain and the USA in 2022
by Severn House, an imprint of Canongate Books Ltd.

severnhouse.com

British Library Cataloguing-in-Publication Data
A CIP catalogue record for this title is available from the British Library.

ISBN-13: 978-1-4483-0903-0 (cased)
ISBN-13: 978-1-4483-0928-3 (trade paper)
ISBN-13: 978-1-4483-0904-7 (e-book)

All Severn House titles are printed on acid-free paper.

Typeset by Palimpsest Book Production Ltd.,
Falkirk, Stirlingshire, Scotland.
Printed and bound in Great Britain by
TJ Books, Padstow, Cornwall.

To Laura, the sister Sally could only dream of having.

ONE

The moment I opened that cardboard to-go container I suspected something might be amiss. At lunch yesterday, the pizza's aroma of garlic had been so powerful that Allison and I had joked about waking up the next morning with the stink emanating from our pores. But now, as I held the box up to my nose, I detected no hint of garlic whatsoever.

Huh. Well, perhaps it simply needed reheating to unlock its pungent smell. I slid the cold pesto slice onto a plate and shoved it in the microwave, then set about brewing a pot of coffee. Java and leftover pizza – breakfast of champions. And given the day before me, I knew I'd be glad of the fortification provided by both.

At the ding of the machine, I pulled out the hot plate and set it on the counter. *Weird.* Still no whiff of garlic. *How could that be?*

Gingerly lifting the hot slice to my lips, I blew on it before taking a bite from its pointy end. Nothing. And I mean truly *nothing*: not only was there no smell, but the pizza was devoid of any flavor whatsoever. I could *feel* the texture of the crispy crust and gooey topping on the roof of my mouth and my tongue as I chewed and swallowed. But I couldn't taste a thing.

What the . . . ? I stared accusingly at the leftover pizza, trying to fathom how something which the day before had positively reeked of basil, garlic, and cheese could now taste like cardboard. *No,* I thought as I dropped the offending slice back onto the plate. *Cardboard has more flavor than this.*

And then I realized the horrible truth. I'd been down with a cold the previous week, which had been accompanied by a particularly vicious sinus infection. Yesterday, however, the pounding in my head had finally diminished and I'd started to feel a little better, so I'd celebrated by going out to lunch with my high school pal, Allison.

But I hadn't truly recovered, after all. Although the infection may have begun to subside, it had left in its wake something far worse.

I'd lost my sense of smell. And with it, the ability to taste food.

I'm a cook by trade, so I depend on my sense of smell – and taste – for my livelihood. Not to mention my happiness. After all, who can be truly content if they're unable to appreciate the flavor of a chicken slow-roasted with sage-and-onion stuffing or the fragrance of a tree-ripened peach?

Though right at this moment, I was primarily concerned about the next six hours. For today I'd be competing in the annual Artichoke Cook-Off out on the Santa Cruz Municipal Wharf, and I had no idea how I was going to make Artichoke Salad with Lemon Aïoli for two hundred people with no ability to smell or taste what I was preparing.

Not only that, but one of my fellow competitors was my father, who would love nothing better than to best his only daughter this afternoon and bring home the prized thistle-shaped plaque for first place.

With an oath that would have made my fellow Gauguin line cooks proud, I took another bite of pizza. Whether I could taste it or not, I'd need the sustenance for the day ahead.

At least I wouldn't be on my own at the booth. Each competitor was allowed one helper, and I'd enlisted the aid of our restaurant's trusty prep cook, Tomás, for the job. He'd proven himself to be both talented and reliable (this last trait perhaps the more important of the two), and I'd been thinking of moving him up to the Gauguin hot line sometime soon. I'd have to discuss the possibility with my co-owner, Javier, but I was fairly certain he'd agree. In any case, today would be a good test of the young cook's ability to stand the stress of working the line.

Tomás and I used a dolly to cart all our equipment and supplies from his battered pickup truck to our designated spot. It was a little too close to the walled-off enclosure housing the dumpsters and grease-trap for my liking, but at least we were upwind from the area. And the wind was indeed blowing. The organizers of the cook-off had erected canopies for all the contestants, and their canvas roofs were whipping about like the sails on a racing sloop. Good thing we'd thought to bring clamps to fasten down our tablecloths, or they'd have been immediately carried across the water all the way to the Boardwalk.

But I was thankful it wasn't raining. And in the moments of respite between the gusts of wind, it was actually fairly warm for the end of March.

While Tomás got started unpacking the ingredients for our salad, I set up the portable stove I'd borrowed from my dad that we'd use for making the aïoli. I'd chosen a simple dish for today – one that wouldn't be too difficult to pull off in a camp-style setting, yet which allowed the earthy flavor of the artichokes and the bright, tart notes of the lemony garlic-mayonnaise to shine through. *Not that I'd be tasting any of that today*, I thought with some chagrin as I screwed the stove's nozzle into the propane tank.

I had just unpacked our hand-press citrus juicer when a shadow fell across the crate of yellow lemons before me.

'Morning, Sally.'

I looked up in response to the familiar voice. 'Hi, Dad. You set up already?'

The contestants had from nine until ten o'clock to organize their booths, but no food prep or cooking was allowed until after that time. Then, at noon, the crowds would descend and the tastings commence.

'Uh-huh,' he said. 'I finished twenty minutes ago.'

'Yeah, well, you have a distinct advantage, given that Solari's is just across the street from your booth. Who'd ya have to bribe to get that spot, anyway?'

Dad merely smiled in response to my quip, which made me wonder if maybe he *had* bribed – or at least sweet-talked – someone. It certainly was a boon for him that our family's Italian seafood restaurant was only twenty paces from where he'd be cooking today. If he needed a different pot or ran out of an ingredient, it would take but a few minutes to fetch the item.

My restaurant, on the other hand – Gauguin, which I'd inherited from my aunt the previous April – was a good ten minutes' drive away. Which meant I didn't have the luxury of forgetting anything important for my cook-off dish.

'What'd you end up deciding to make, anyway?' I asked. I knew my dad had been vacillating between an artichoke, Parmesan cheese, and shallot dip and a soup prepared with artichokes, potatoes, and chicken stock.

'I went for the soup,' he said. 'It may not be what the deep-fried loving crowd goes for.' Dad nodded in the direction of the booth next to mine, where a woman in an Oakland A's baseball cap was setting several gallons of vegetable oil next to a portable deep fryer. 'But I made it last week and thought it was amazing. It's more of a subtle dish that I think the judges will appreciate.'

There would be two sets of prizes given out today: those for the Judges' Awards (decided via blind tasting by a panel of six tasters) and those for the People's Choice Awards (decided by popular vote). This being my first time out as a cook-off contestant, I'd be thrilled with a third place in either category, but Dad was gunning for number one in the judges' division. He'd now entered the contest for three years' running, with one second place and two wash-outs and had declared that this was going to be his year.

We'd see about that.

After my father left, I consulted my list and checked off the ingredients I'd need against what now stood on the long table: three cases baby artichokes, six bags arugula, two bags peeled garlic cloves, one crate eggs, one case lemons, two jars Dijon mustard, five pounds Pecorino cheese, two three-liter bottles olive oil, sea salt, and black pepper. Plus the two gallons of water we'd brought along for drinking and for thinning the sauce.

At five minutes to ten I was double-checking my equipment (knives, mandoline, mortar and pestle, pots, bowls, cutting boards, whisk, spoons, side towels, paper towels, serving plates and forks, napkins) when a voice called out from the booth next to mine, 'Sally Solari! I thought that was you.'

I turned to see a tall, stocky man sporting a white T-shirt with a bright green artichoke on its front. It took a moment, but then I remembered who he was.

'Neil Lerici. I didn't know you were still in town.'

He hefted a bag of artichokes onto his table with a grunt.

'I never left. After a couple years at Cabrillo I decided college wasn't for me and ended up working at the farm. That's where these come from,' he said, indicating the mesh bag before him.

I glanced again at his T-shirt and saw that it bore the same logo as on the produce bag. 'Lerici Brand Artichokes – Thistle Make You Hungry' was printed below the large green artichoke on the bag. 'Ah, so your folks still own that farm up the coast.'

'Yep. That's the reason I've been doing this competition the past few years – as advertisement for our produce. 'Cause, c'mon, let's face it,' he said. 'We *do* grow the very best arti-chokes in the tri-county area.' With a grin, Neil slapped the mesh bag affectionately, as if it were a beloved dog. 'And hey, it's worked, too. Nothing like winning the People's Choice Award two years in a row to drum up business.'

I nodded toward the woman in the A's cap helping him, who was now inspecting the baskets for the deep fryer. 'What are you guys making this year?'

'The same thing I've done the last two years – *Carciofi alla Giudia* – a recipe from my mom's *nonna*. It's pretty grungy dealing with all that oil, and prepping the suckers is a real pain in the butt. But people can't seem to resist anything that's deep-fried, so I figure why mess with something that ain't broke?'

'True.' I'd had the dish before – twice-fried artichokes that, if properly prepared, come out tender inside and crispy outside, with the pleasing appearance of tiny sunflowers. But a real pain, indeed, to make. 'So how's Grace these days?' I asked. 'She still in town, too?'

Grace was Neil's older sister, and she and I had been in the same year in high school and had hung out together freshman year. She'd owned a horse back then, and we used to spend afternoons taking turns riding the aged Pinto around a ramshackle ring her dad had constructed next to their fields of artichokes. But we'd drifted apart during our junior year and then, after I headed to Southern California for college, I'd lost track of her completely.

'Yeah, she is,' Neil said. 'She moved up to Chico after high school and was there for years, but then ended up getting involved with a plumber who was from Santa Cruz. She moved back down here just last year, after they got married, and works as the bookkeeper for his company, now. But hey,' he added, leaning down to grab a large, red-handled cleaver and a paring knife from a box at his feet, 'Grace said she'd come down here today, so you can ask her yourself what's going on with her these days.'

At the blast of an air horn – the signal that we could now begin our food prep and cooking – Neil reached for an artichoke and whacked off its spiky top with the giant cleaver. 'Good luck,' he said with a grin. 'Not that luck is gonna help you any, since there's no way I'm not winning again this year.'

With ten minutes left to go in the cooking period, I was frantically whisking a stream of olive oil into my mixture of egg yolks, garlic, lemon juice, and mustard. Tomás was plating up tasting-sized servings of arugula topped with thinly-sliced raw artichoke that had been marinated in olive oil and lemon, which would be drizzled with the lemon aïoli and scattered with shaved Pecorino cheese right before service.

'Hey, Tomás,' I called out to him, 'come here a sec, would ya?'

The prep cook wiped his hands on his side towel and walked over to where I stood.

'Could you taste this and tell me if you think it needs any more lemon?'

'Sure,' he said, dipping a spoon into the garlicky mayonnaise. 'But I doubt I'll know any better than you do.'

Should I tell him about my loss of smell? No, I decided, better he didn't know.

He tasted the sauce, then frowned. 'Actually, it could use a lot more lemon. As well as a little salt.' And then he smiled. 'You were just testing me, huh?'

'Right,' I said with a forced chuckle. 'And you passed with flying colors.'

I'd just whisked a half cup more of lemon juice and a handful of salt into the enormous pot of aïoli when the horn blasted once more, telling the hungry hoards milling about the wharf that they were now free to sample our goods. A line had already formed at Neil's stall next door, and before the horn had even ceased reverberating against the line of buildings facing us, people started pushing their way to the table, hands out for his crunchy delights.

Here we go, I thought as I drizzled aïoli onto the dozens of plates Tomás had set out along the long table. *Let's hope we didn't make too much.*

But I needn't have worried. Perhaps it was the overflow from Neil's booth, or perhaps word had gotten out that our salad was actually pretty darn tasty, but by one thirty I was starting to wonder if we'd made *enough* salads.

Tomás was plating up another twenty servings, and I was whisking the second batch of aïoli to smooth out any lumps that might have formed, when I heard my name called out once again. It was Grace, and, with the exception of a few lines about the eyes, she looked almost exactly as she had over twenty years ago, back in high school.

'Neil texted me that you were here,' she said, leaning over the row of salad plates to give me a hug and peck on the cheek. 'It's so great to see you after all this time!'

'I know!' I agreed. 'Though you don't look like much time has actually passed. What's your secret?'

Grace laughed. 'It comes in a little bottle I buy at the drug store,' she said, flipping back a lock of shiny, reddish-brown hair. 'And I do my best to keep my thighs and butt in shape by riding as often as I can.'

'So you still have a horse?'

'Two now, actually,' she said, moving aside to allow a trio of women to come up to the booth and accept the artichoke salads offered by Tomás. 'Since me and my husband both ride. A quarter horse gelding and an Arabian mare.'

Two more people lined up behind the threesome and Grace stepped even farther back. 'Look,' she said, 'I should let you do your thing. And I have to meet up with my parents and brother Ryan in a couple minutes, anyway. But we should get together sometime and catch up. Are you on Facebook?'

'I am. More often than I should be.'

Grace pulled out her phone. 'Cool. I'll friend you, and then we can figure out a time to meet up later.' With a wave of the

hand to me and then to her brother Neil next door, she made
her way through the crowd, eyes glued to her screen.

I checked the clock on my phone. It was a quarter to two,
five minutes before my scheduled time to bring a sample
to the judges' booth. Taking a paper plate from the stack
behind me, I made a bed of arugula, then lay slices of artichoke over the greens in such a way that it looked as if they'd
been simply 'scattered' on top, yet had a pleasing and artistic
design. Next I drizzled lines of aïoli back-and-forth over the
salad, and then finished the plate with five curls of Pecorino
cheese.

The man standing guard at the judges' booth accepted my
salad with a grunt. He tore a raffle ticket in two and placed one
half on the side of the plate (messing with my presentation,
but I wasn't about to complain) and gave me the other half. As
he wrote my name and number down in a spiral notebook, I
examined the ticket. Lucky number seventeen – or so I hoped.

A line had now formed behind me of other contestants
bearing their dishes, but the doorman was not making the
slightest attempt to hurry his pace. He leisurely tore another
ticket and accepted the next sample, then set it on a table
behind him next to mine.

As I headed away from the judges' booth, I passed the gal
from Neil's stall, standing at the end of the line and talking to
the tall, blond guy next to her. Neither looked terribly happy.
In her hands was a plate of fried artichokes, still steaming from
the hot oil they'd been fried in.

'Wow, those look delicious,' I said. 'I'm gonna have to stop
by and try some for myself.'

She turned to me with a harried look. 'Thanks. But I just
hope that with this long line, the judges get to taste them before
they're completely cold.'

'Well, no matter what, I'm sure you'll do great in the People's
Choice division. I can't believe the throngs that have been stop-
ping by your booth.'

'Yeah, they've been super popular,' she said with a shrug.
'Neil's already starting on our fifth batch.'

I headed back down the wharf toward my booth, but, when
I passed by my father's table, decided to stop and sample his

soup. 'Gotta check out the competition,' I said as Dad handed me a small cup garnished with crispy, frizzled artichokes. It was only when I took a sip that I remembered the malady that had struck that morning: I couldn't taste a thing.

'So what do you think?' Dad asked, his blue eyes eager with anticipation.

'Uh . . . I *love* the texture. Silky smooth, with that crispy garnish – it's perfect. And the flavor is great, too,' I improvised. 'Subtle but refined. Is there sherry in it?' I figured there was a good chance a soup like this would have some sort of wine or sherry.

He smiled. 'Close. It's white wine. Or maybe it's the shallots you're tasting.'

'Ah, right.' I tossed the cup into the wastebasket next to his booth. 'Well, good luck to you. Gotta get back to work.'

I threaded my way through the crowd and, once back at our stall, spelled Tomás so he could take a break and go check out the other competitors' dishes for himself.

A few minutes later, I heard a commotion from Neil's booth. 'What the hell?' a shrill voice yelled. It was his helper, who dashed to the deep fryer and pulled one of the baskets from the hot oil. The burnt remains of artichoke florets were visible within the mesh basket, now transformed into a shriveled and blackened mess.

She turned an accusing eye on me, as if to say, *Didn't you notice the smell?*

But, of course, I wouldn't have smelled anything even if the entire booth had gone up in flames. 'Oh, wow,' I said, coming over to inspect the charred mess. 'Sorry I wasn't here to catch it, but I only just got back, myself.'

'Where the hell could Neil have got to, anyway?' she said, and set the basket on its draining rack. 'He had no business leaving while a batch was in the deep fryer.'

A group of people had now gathered around the booth, some curious about the hubbub, others merely wanting a taste of its fried delicacies. 'It'll be a few minutes before I can get another batch going,' the woman called out to the crowd, then got to work draining and patting dry the prepped artichokes soaking in a tub of lemon water.

I returned to my own booth, but kept a curious eye on the goings-on next door. Once she'd dropped a fresh basket into the deep fryer, the woman pulled out her cell phone, typed a message, then shoved the device back in her pocket with an irritated shake of the head. 'Where on earth *are* you?' I heard her say as she dumped the now-drained basket of burnt sticks into the trash can.

Noticing that we had only ten salads on the table, I turned to check on our aïoli supply. There was less than a quarter pot left, and only one bag of arugula, but the People's Choice voting had closed at two o'clock, so it wasn't a big deal if we ran out before long. I plated up another dozen servings of salad, at which point I was joined again by Tomás.

'What's that smell?' he asked, waving a hand in front of his nose.

'The guy next door left his booth while a batch of artichokes was in the deep fryer, and they burned.' Glancing toward Neil's booth, I saw he still hadn't returned. The woman had pulled out her phone again and was typing furiously on the screen.

Tomás and I continued to pass out salads, all the while talking up Gauguin and its menu with the cook-off attendees – for that was, ultimately, the primary purpose of participating in events like this. After about a half an hour, the prep cook looked up from plating the last of our arugula.

'Oh, it's starting,' he said, and I turned my attention to the portly man who had stepped up onto the small stage set up across from the booths a little ways down from ours.

The announcer tapped on his microphone several times, then held it up to his mouth. 'Tasting, tasting,' he said, prompting chuckles from the crowd, who now quieted down. After a few introductory remarks and thank-yous, the man unfolded a piece of paper and held it up for all to see. 'And now for the fun part – the prizes! First, the Judges' Awards, which are based on a combination of flavor, presentation, difficulty of preparation, and originality. Third place goes to . . .'

I watched as the third place winner, the head chef at a French restaurant out in Aptos Village, and the second place winner, a young woman who'd recently opened a pop-up Greek place downtown, accepted their prizes. I knew my father had to be going nuts right about now: he'd either been skunked entirely in this category or had won the whole shebang.

The announcer cleared his throat. 'Okay. And first prize for the Judges' Award goes to . . .' A dramatic pause. 'Mario Solari, for his delectable take on a creamy artichoke soup!'

Dad climbed onto the stage, his grin as wide as the hazelnut *mezzaluna* cookies he baked for Easter each year. Accepting the award with a firm shake of the hand, he then turned my way and pumped his fist. *Yes!* he mouthed, and I smiled back.

The man now conferred with a woman who had waited for my father to accept his award before coming forward to talk to him. 'Okay, folks,' he said after they'd finished speaking, 'we're going to take a short break while the People's Choice ballots are tallied. In the meantime, feel free to visit your favorite booths for seconds, and I'll be right back.'

Dad jumped down from the stage and came over to show me his prize – an artichoke-shaped plaque with an empty space where the winner's name should be. 'I have to give it back for them to have my name engraved,' he said, noticing my look. 'Kind of like the fake diplomas they give you at high school graduation.'

He glanced at his watch – one of those fancy jobs that's waterproof, has a stopwatch, and tells you what time it is in Genova as well as Santa Cruz. 'Oh, shoot. I gotta get outa here. Abby and I are driving up to the City for dinner, and I told her I'd pick her up by three.'

'But what about your booth?' I asked.

'Emilio's got it covered. I'm giving him tomorrow off in exchange for his packing everything up today and running the kitchen tonight. Bye, hon. Good luck on the People's Choice Awards.' Dad pecked me on the cheek and, plaque tucked under his arm, trotted to where his Chevy pickup was parked in front of Solari's.

Fat chance of that, I thought, then set to work helping Tomás pass out the rest of our salads to the hungry horde.

Ten minutes later, the announcer stepped back onto the stage and took the mic from its stand. 'Okay,' he said. 'The People's

Choice votes have now been tallied and, having tasted most of the entries myself, I can tell you it was quite the competition. There were some delicious dishes to choose from.'

I knew I was a dark horse for any of the three prizes awarded in this category, but nevertheless, I found myself holding my breath as the man raised his paper to read out the winners. The third and second place awards came and went, however, without my name being called.

Oh, well. No way would I win first. Maybe next year I could come up with something truly special . . .

'Neil Lerici!' came the announcement over the PA system. *Ha!* So he'd won again, after all. I turned to watch my neighbor, who would surely pump his fist as my dad had done, then take the stage with a show of bravado.

But he wasn't there. He still hadn't returned.

The gal with the A's ball cap turned to me, eyes wide, and I motioned for her to go up in his stead. Looking nervous and unsure, she walked to the base of the stage, and the announcer knelt to speak with her. Then, standing up, the man raised the mic and announced Neil's name one more time. Nothing.

As the crowd murmured in confusion, the man frowned, then motioned with his hands for us to quiet down. 'Okay, folks,' he said. 'We seem to have a no-show. And since the rules specifically state that the head of each cooking team must be present to accept their award, I'm sorry to say that Mr Lerici will have to be disqualified. So . . .' The announcer raised the paper once more and squinted at the names. 'That means Maria García moves up to second, and Pete Ferrari will take home first prize in the People's Choice Award. And our new third place winner is . . . Sally Solari! Come on up to the stage, all of you, to swap your awards and receive the new ones.'

I was so stunned at hearing my name called out that I almost missed the scream that rang out over the applause.

TWO

There was a moment of uncertainty as we all tried to discern whether the shriek we'd heard was merely that of someone overly excited by the change in awards or something more sinister. But when the same voice then cried out, 'Ohmygod, I think he's *dead!*' we had our answer.

After this second exclamation, I realized the shouting was coming from behind me. Turning to look, I saw a young man in a stained, white smock at the entrance to the dumpster and grease-trap enclosure not too far from my booth. I recognized him as one of the busboys who worked at the Crab Shack next door to Solari's. He dropped the black garbage bag in his hands and pointed to a spot within the gray-and-blue painted walls. 'There!' he exclaimed.

Several people dashed to the busboy's side, while others called 911 and then chattered excitedly among themselves. I knew there was nothing I could do to help – I'd simply be another nosy person in the way – but within seconds, my curiosity got the better of me. I had to see who it was the young man had discovered. For I was pretty certain I knew.

I made my way through the ever-increasing crowd toward the trash enclosure, coming up behind a group who had gathered around the busboy. I'm fairly tall – nearly six feet – so I had no problem seeing over the shoulders of those in front of me. But what I witnessed wasn't pretty.

As I'd feared, the man the busboy had discovered was Neil Lerici. He was lying on his back, arms splayed, next to the grimy, metal grease-trap. A bloody gash was visible on his right temple, and by his side lay his enormous red-handled cleaver. A man was crouched next to the body, his fingers on Neil's wrist, but even from where I stood I could tell it was unlikely he'd find a pulse.

'What's that in his mouth?' someone asked.

The man released Neil's wrist and started to reach for his face, but then someone else shouted, 'No, don't touch anything!'

I squinted to make out what the person was talking about. There was indeed something poking out of his mouth. Dark green, with a conical end . . .

'It's an artichoke,' I said.

The crouching man peered at Neil's face. 'She's right,' he said. 'It *is* an artichoke. Weird.' He stood at the sound of the approaching siren. 'Now why on earth would someone shove an artichoke in his mouth?'

I had no answer for that.

Working the hot line that night did a good job of taking my mind off the grisly end to the Artichoke Cook-Off, in part because of how much more nerve-racking the work was than usual. Although the ingredients and methodology for all our recipes at Gauguin are worked out well in advance of their being placed on the menu, the cooks still have to use their own judgment – i.e., their sense of taste and smell – to ensure the dishes come out right. Neither of which I, of course, possessed that night.

But I wasn't about to admit this to anyone in the kitchen, least of all my head chef and new co-owner, Javier. Don't get me wrong: he and I get along great. Javier had been my Aunt Letta's chef at Gauguin, so I'd known the guy for a long time, and in the year since I'd inherited the restaurant from my aunt, the two of us had developed a close working – as well as social – relationship. Which is why I'd asked him to become an equal partner in the business several months earlier. But no way did I want the chef monitoring me continually throughout the shift tonight, testing everything I prepared before it was sent out to the dining room.

The lack of a taster, however, meant I had to be painstakingly careful about my measurements, especially for certain ingredients such as salt, lemon juice, and sriracha sauce, which could ruin a dish if over- or under-used.

Luckily, I'd made all of our menu items dozens, if not hundreds, of times, so the process was fairly routine. If we'd had any brand new specials that night, I'd have been in serious trouble. This being Sunday, however, we were instead repeating our specials from the previous night – pan-fried sanddabs atop mashed fava beans with a lime citronette, and whole Dungeness crabs with roasted asparagus.

'How'd it go today at the cook-off?' Javier asked as we stood shoulder-to-shoulder at the Wolf range, tossing onions and shrimp in our respective sauté pans.

My immediate impulse was to tell him about Neil's death – murder, most likely, given the scene I'd witnessed. Since Tomás had the night off and the story had yet to hit the news, no one at Gauguin had heard about it.

But something made me hold off. It was just too creepy, how another dead body had managed to show up in my life. Javier and the rest of the restaurant staff would find out soon enough, but for one night at least, I was hoping to keep the comments about my being an 'angel of death' at bay.

'We got third place in the People's Choice Awards,' I replied instead, leaving out the reason *why* I'd ended up on the podium.

'That's awesome!' Javier said. 'For your first time cooking at one of those things? Really, that's great. I mean it. I've done them, and it's totally different from running a restaurant kitchen.'

'Thanks.' I plated up my Shrimp with Tequila-Lime Sauce, called out 'Order up!' and set the dish on the pass. ''Cause it was pretty stressful,' I added. Which was as close as I was going to get to saying anything tonight about Neil.

Javier nodded as he splashed Cognac onto his onions. 'Exactly the reason you didn't see me out there today.'

'Well, maybe next year,' I said, which prompted a snort from the chef. 'Oh, and my dad won first in the Judges' Division,' I added.

'Nice!' said Javier. 'I bet he's pretty excited about that.'

'No kidding he is. He's been trying to win for three years straight. And now he's going to be absolutely insufferable about it for at least a month.'

I was right about my father. The next morning, I stopped by Solari's after my bike ride to ask how his date had gone the night before – and, since I was there anyway, to snag a post-ride cannoli, as well. I found him at the hostess stand in the dining room, talking to his head waitress, Cathy. Hanging directly above them, where all the customers would see it as soon as they entered the restaurant, was the first place Artichoke Cook-Off plaque.

'Didn't take you long to put that up,' I said. 'But I thought you needed to give it back for them to engrave.'

'I'll do that later in the week. For now, I want to savor my victory. Oh, and congrats on your third in the People's Choice, *bambina*. Even if someone did have to kick the bucket for you to get it.' This last comment was punctuated by a jab to my ribs.

'Not funny,' I said, knocking his hand away. 'The guy was actually someone I went to high school with, and I don't think he died of natural causes.'

Dad set down the new menu he'd been discussing with Cathy, his face now serious. 'Really? I assumed when I heard about it this morning that it had been a heart attack or something. How do you know it wasn't?'

'Because I saw him, and he had a bloody gash on his head. As well as a big ol' cleaver lying next to the body.'

'Ugh,' said Cathy, swallowing and pulling out a chair so she could sit down. 'That's awful.'

Dad sat as well and motioned for me to do the same. 'So who was he?' he asked.

'The guy who had the booth next to mine. You know, the ones making those deep-fried artichokes that you commented on. Neil Lerici is his name. I didn't know him that well, but his sister was in the same grade—' I stopped at the sudden intake of Dad's breath. 'What? You know him?'

He frowned, then licked his lips. 'I know his mother, Diana. Or . . . knew her, anyway. Way back when, before I met your mom. We went to school together, too.'

'Really? So how come you never mentioned it back when I was in ninth grade? You know, when Grace used come over to our house all the time.'

'I dunno,' Dad said with an impatient shrug. 'I guess it just never came up.' He ran a hand through his closely-cropped salt-and-pepper hair, then shoved back his chair with a loud scrape, startling both me and Cathy. 'Look, I really gotta get back to the kitchen. But do tell Grace and her parents how sorry I am, okay?'

'Will do.' I watched him retreat through the swinging red door into the back of the house, then turned to Cathy. 'Did you think that was as odd as I did?'

'No, not really. He just seemed kinda shocked, is all. Which makes sense, since he knows the guy's mom.' She stood and walked to the hostess station. 'So sad,' I heard her murmur as she set the menu atop the others on the stand.

Gauguin is closed on Mondays, so ever since I'd inherited the restaurant the previous April, my ex-boyfriend Eric and I had tended to spend that night hanging out together. That may seem strange, but even though we'd broken up several years earlier, Eric and I were still pals. More than pals, actually – he was my BFF, the person I'd spill my guts to when I needed someone to listen.

Until Gayle came along, that is.

Eric claimed he and Gayle weren't 'serious', but it was obvious they'd now reached the 'dating' phase of their relationship. And it was entirely my fault that I'd lost my best pal to another woman. The previous fall, Eric had told me he wanted us to get back together, to give it another try. But I'd pushed him away, worried we'd simply break up once again and then I'd lose him as a friend, as well.

But it was an idea that hadn't been very well thought out. Because now that he'd hooked up with a new girlfriend (big surprise there), Eric was rarely around to be that friend. Sure, we still talked and texted a fair amount, and even hung out once in a while. But it wasn't the same. After all, who wants to engage in a heart-to-heart conversation knowing full well that the other person will go straight to their new girlfriend afterwards and divulge all?

So on this particular Monday night, I was not with Eric (who was no doubt dining at some romantic, candlelit restaurant with *her*). Instead, I was chowing down fish tacos and slurping Pacífico beer with Martin Vargas, aka Detective Vargas of the Santa Cruz Police Department.

Which wasn't the worst thing in the world. In fact, we always had a lot of fun when we got together.

No, Martin and I weren't at the 'dating' stage like Eric and Gayle. (Though Eric had started ribbing me lately about 'seeing' a cop.) But over the past month, we had started to get together at least once a week, sometimes more. Maybe it was 'pre-dating' that we were doing. Whatever. And who cared? The detective made me laugh, and spending time with him certainly helped me not think so much about Eric.

I took a bite of my taco, chewed and swallowed, then set it back down on my plate with a frown.

'What's wrong?' Martin asked. 'Is the snapper bad? 'Cause it's usually really fresh here.'

I didn't correct him about the name of the fish. Although it was called 'red snapper' on the menu, I knew it was actually rockfish, probably caught not three miles from where we sat. This is what comes from growing up in an Italian fishing family. But it wasn't the name – or the freshness – of the fish that was the problem.

I shook my head. 'No, that's not it. Though for all I know, it could be old – putrid, even – and I wouldn't be able to tell.' At his questioning look, I explained. 'The thing is, I lost my sense of smell yesterday and it still hasn't returned.'

'Oh, no!'

This reaction made me smile. It was nice that he got what a big deal it was for me. I recounted my theory about the sinus infection I'd had the previous week damaging my olfactory nerves, and how I'd read online that if this happened, you might regain your sense of smell the next day, the next month . . . or never.

Martin leaned across the table and took my hand. 'I am so sorry. I can only imagine how horrible that must be for you. If I could give you my sense of smell, I would – in a heartbeat.'

'Ohmygod, that might be the sweetest thing anyone has ever said to me.' I held his hand for a few seconds, then released it and reached for the salsa. 'Maybe if I douse the taco with hot sauce I'll at least *feel* something in my mouth.'

It kind of worked. Although I still didn't taste the food, I could detect a slight tingling of the lips and tongue. But the process of eating now lacked ninety-nine point nine percent of the pleasure it had for me before this malady had struck.

Oh, well. Maybe at least I'll lose a few pounds off my waistline and thighs.

'So,' I said after taking a swig of beer, 'any chance you're willing to talk about Neil Lerici? I guess you probably know I was there when they found him.'

'Yeah, I saw your statement in the report.' A wry – or perhaps exasperated – smile flashed across his face and then was gone. We were both acutely aware of how bizarre it was that dead bodies kept turning up in my proximity. But at least the detective didn't hold it against me like some. There'd been several instances recently of people staring and whispering when I walked down the street, and one of my *nonna*'s elderly friends from her parish church had taken to crossing herself each time we met.

The detective dipped a tortilla chip into the salsa, popped it in his mouth, and finally nodded. 'Okay, sure,' he said once he'd swallowed. 'What do you want to know?'

'Well, the first thing that comes to mind is that artichoke that was in his mouth. I mean, how weird is that? Was it a cause of his death – you know, by choking?' And then I let out a giggle. 'Oh, God, I'm sorry,' I said in response to his frown. 'It's terrible, I know, but all of a sudden I flashed on how it puts a whole new spin on the word arti-*choke*.'

Martin shook his head, but I could tell from his eyes that the disapproval was at least partially feigned. 'No,' he said. 'It was the blow to the head that killed him. According to the coroner, the artichoke was most likely stuffed into his mouth after he died, based on the lack of bleeding from the puncture wounds the thorns caused.'

'So it was more like some kind of creepy message,' I said, now serious once more. I lifted my bottle of Pacífico, then set it back down. 'Wait, you said "blow" to the head. Wouldn't you call it more of a "gash" or "slash"? I saw the wound – and also the cleaver lying by his side.'

'Yeah, but whoever did it didn't use the blade. He was hit by the blunt side of the knife. But the blow was enough to kill him, striking him on the temple like it did.'

'Almost as if the person wasn't really trying to kill him,' I said, and Vargas shrugged. 'But for someone to stuff an arti-choke in his mouth afterwards?' I went on. 'That sure suggests some kind of serious animosity.'

I sipped from my beer and thought back to the grim scene behind the dumpsters out on the wharf. 'It was one of those baby artichokes in his mouth,' I said. 'The kind Neil was using at the cook-off. But that doesn't really get us all that far, since a fair amount of contestants were using those. The big ones tend to be tougher and take longer to cook.'

Vargas took a bite of taco, taking care not to let the juice drip onto his yellow Oxford-cloth shirt.

'What about his phone?' I asked. 'Was there anything on it to say why he left his booth?'

'No such luck. And nothing to suggest any arguments or enemies he might have had, either.'

I spooned more salsa onto my plate. 'And I don't suppose you were able to get any prints off the knife. That would be way too easy.'

'Nope,' he said. 'But then again, all the contestants were required to wear those vinyl gloves during the competition.'

'So you think it was one of the contestants?'

'Maybe. That woman helping him at his booth, Amy is her name, clearly had the opportunity. As did pretty much anyone there that day, really.'

'Well, I certainly hope you've ruled me out of your investiga-tion.' I chuckled as I said it but at the same time was a tiny bit nervous that maybe I *was* on his list. I did have a connection to the guy, after all, though I wasn't sure if the detective was aware of it. But I'd also been working the booth right next to Neil's.

Vargas smiled and shook his head. 'I think you're safe for the time being,' he said. 'I'm actually more focused on his family right now than I am the other contestants. I interviewed the parents and the brother and sister today and got the distinct impression there's been some in-fighting going on. Though none of them, of course, came out and said so. But they seemed kind of, I don't know, nervous or at least a little on edge when I asked about their relationships with each other – especially the two siblings.'

'I actually know the family,' I said.

He arched an eyebrow. 'Really?'

'Well, it's been quite a while, but I hung out with Grace, Neil's sister, during high school. We hadn't seen each other since graduation, but ended up reconnecting yesterday when she came to the cook-off, and we talked about getting together sometime soon.'

'Huh. That's interesting . . .'

'*And* it turns out my father knows the mother, as well. He told me this morning that he went to school with her, and I'm guessing they must have been pretty good friends, from the way he reacted this morning when he found out it was Neil who'd been killed.'

Martin thought a moment, then shoved aside his plate and leaned forward, his beefy forearms on the table. 'Okay, this may seem a little, well, unorthodox, but would you be willing to do me a favor?'

'Uh, I guess it depends on what exactly that favor is . . .'

'Nothing unethical. Or dangerous,' he added quickly. 'I was just wondering if maybe – you know, if you're going to be hanging out with the sister anyway – you could keep your eyes and ears open? And then tell me if you learn anything you think might be relevant in any way to the death.'

Vargas drummed a finger on the polished wood table several times, then fixed his eyes on mine. ''Cause I just can't help thinking there's something fishy going on with that family.'

THREE

The next morning, I took Buster – the dog I'd inherited from my Aunt Letta along with her restaurant – for a walk along West Cliff Drive. As the two of us made our slow way down the path that hugs the coastline, I thought about what to write to Grace. It hadn't taken much convincing for me to say yes to Martin's request. Not only would it be an easy favor to perform, but the idea of acting as a covert spy for the SCPD held a certain appeal. Plus, I had to admit that the detective's obvious pleasure at my agreeing to do so gave an unexpected pleasure to me, as well.

Buster's leash went taut as he halted at a gopher mound, and while the dog investigated the enticing hole, his nose twitching in excitement, I gazed out at a small fishing boat making its way across the steel-blue Monterey Bay. A noisy pair of seagulls overhead fought over a scrap of bread, then were swept up the coast by a gust of wind.

Best start by sending a sympathy message, I decided. *But something that'll make her want to write back.*

I pulled out my phone, found Grace on Facebook, and typed a private message to her:

> I can't tell you how sorry I am about Neil. It's so horrible. But it almost seems like fate that we reconnected that same day. Is there anything I can do?

After re-reading the message several times to make sure I'd captured the right tone, I clicked on the 'send' icon, then shoved the phone back into my jeans pocket. It was good, I thought. Short, sweet, and to the point. *Now let's see if she responds.*

Having satisfied himself there was no furry critter lurking within the hole he'd discovered, Buster was now staring intently at me, anxious to get a move on. 'Okay, okay, I'm ready,' I said to the big brown dog, and we continued along the asphalt path until we reached the bronze statue of the young longboard surfer standing guard over the famed surf spot, Steamer Lane. Squinting into the sun across the inlet toward the municipal wharf and the Santa Cruz Beach Boardwalk beyond, I could just make out my father's skiff, a blue-and-white Boston Whaler, sitting behind the Solari's restaurant near the end of the hundred-year-old wharf.

At a buzzing in my pants pocket, I reached for my phone: a message from Grace. *Call me*, it said, and gave her number.

She picked up after one ring. 'Hey, Sally. I just got out of my yoga class and saw you'd written.'

'Hi Grace. Thanks for getting back to me so quickly. Like I said in my message, I just wanted to say how sorry I am about Neil and let you know that if you need anything, I'm here for you. I can't even imagine what you must be going through.'

'Yeah, it's been pretty awful . . .' She trailed off.

'Well, I can imagine a little yoga is probably a good thing for you right about now.'

'Uh, huh. I'm not actually all that into yoga, but the gal down here at the Prana Studio where I take my class has been amazing, helping me deal with all that's happened.' Grace paused, then cleared her throat. 'But you know, more than anything, I think I could use a friend right now. Any chance you'd like to come riding with me up at the farm sometime?'

'Sure, I'd love that.'

After settling on the coming Thursday morning, I shoved the phone back in my pocket and, with a smile, continued with Buster down the coast.

Perfect.

I'd been hoping my sense of smell would return within a day or two, but when Tuesday evening arrived with no change whatsoever, I started to become truly worried – and depressed. Then, seeing Eric come into Gauguin that same night with Gayle and take their usual seats at the bar, my mood plummeted to depths I hadn't experienced since studying for the wretched and grueling rite of passage they call the California Bar Exam. (The misery of that experience was the sole reason I'd kept up my status as an 'inactive' member of the bar, even after leaving my law firm to work for my dad and then later, take over Gauguin. No way would I ever want to go through *that* again, should I ever decide to reenter the practice of law.)

I tried to pay no attention as the couple ordered Martinis and studied the menu, then leaned in close to each other to laugh about some private joke.

Okay, so maybe I wasn't all that successful at not paying attention.

Pulling the next ticket off the rail, I studied the orders – two sanddab specials and one Duck à la Lilikoi. I grabbed a duck breast from the cooler, its thick layer of creamy fat already sliced through in a cross-hatch pattern by Tomás, and laid it skin-side down in a sauté pan.

It would take several minutes for the fat to render and become crispy and golden-brown, so rather than firing the two fish orders just yet, I reached for another ticket. As I did so, I couldn't help glancing once more toward the bar area, where the romantic twosome sat.

And then I looked again – more closely. Were they bickering? Gone was the happy couple of minutes earlier, having now been replaced by a pair whose body language suggested very much the opposite. Eric was hunched over the bar, staring straight ahead, while Gayle had swiveled in her barstool to face him. She leaned toward Eric and spoke a few words, to which he responded with a wave of the hand. Gayle then said something else, and when he didn't reply, she stood and headed for the ladies' room.

Whoa. That was definitely a lovers' spat, if I'd ever seen one. As I watched Eric shake his head and sip from his Martini, a confused mixture of emotions swept over me: curiosity as to what the spat was about, shame at having watched the little scene, defensiveness on behalf of Eric . . . and hope.

It was this last one that made me snap out of my daze. *Get over it, Sal*, I chided myself, and picked up a pair of tongs to inspect my duck breast, now sizzling in a pool of melted fat. *You made your decision, so live with it.* Besides, these kinds of arguments always tended to blow over, and Eric and Gayle would likely engage in some steamy making-up tonight after dinner.

Forcing myself to ignore the goings-on over at the bar area, I returned to my hot line duties. I had plenty of other more pressing things to worry about than my ex's love life. Including what I was going to do when I saw Grace on Thursday. Martin Vargas had merely asked that I keep my ears and eyes out for relevant information. But did I want to engage in more affirmative action as well?

Once the sanddabs and duck had been plated and sent out to the dining room, I set to work on an order of Seared Pork Chops with Apricot Brandy Sauce. After frying the chops and sautéing a handful of sliced onions and brandy-soaked dried apricots, I deglazed the pan with more brandy and some chicken stock, then finished the dish with a healthy dollop of butter.

'Order up!' I called out as Javier set the order of spot prawns for the same table next to my pork.

Brandon trotted over to fetch the dishes from the pass. In his right hand the server held one of our large white dinner plates. 'Hey, Sal,' he said, nodding toward the partially eaten order of sanddabs. 'There was a complaint at table six.'

'About what?' I asked, a feeling of dread creeping over me. Table six had been my ticket.

'They say it's too salty.'

'Here, give it to me,' Javier said, and Brandon handed the plate to him over the pass, then hurried away with the new orders.

Javier dipped his pinkie in the sauce that had pooled up next to the pan-fried fish, tasted it, then shook his head. 'They're right,' he said. 'It is too salty. Here, you try it.' He held the plate out toward me but I just stared at the offending dish.

'I can't,' I said.

'It's okay; we're not going to send this one out again, so you can touch it.'

'No, it's not that. I can't . . . taste.'

Javier smiled, as if I were simply making a joke. But when he saw the tears that now filled my eyes, he lowered the plate and frowned. 'What do you mean?'

'It happened Sunday morning. When I woke up, I realized I had no sense of smell – which means I can't taste anything, either. I think it must be from that cold and sinus infection I had last week.'

'So you can't taste *anything*?' The way Javier's voice rose at the end of the sentence, along with the wide eyes that had replaced the frown, made clear the panic my head chef was feeling. 'How are you going to be able to cook?'

'I know,' I said, letting out a long breath. 'And I'm sorry I didn't tell you before, but I thought it would only last a day or two.' A tear slid down my cheek and I wiped it away.

'Oh, God, Sally.' Javier stepped forward and put a hand on my shoulder. '*I'm* sorry. Here I am all worried about the restaurant when I should be worrying about you. That must be awful, losing your sense of smell.'

I nodded, doing my best to hold it all in. Much as I needed a good cry right about now, the Gauguin kitchen during a busy dinner rush was not the time or place for it.

'So, how long . . .' Javier trailed off, anxious to know the answer to the question yet uncomfortable asking it.

'I have no idea. I called this morning to make an appointment to see a doctor, but the first date the ENT had wasn't for three weeks. Not that it much matters, since I read online that there's not really anything they can do in cases like this. You just have to wait for the nerves to regenerate on their own. It could take days, weeks, or even longer.'

Or never. For I'd also read that the damage was sometimes so severe that the sense of smell was permanently lost. But I didn't want to admit this to the chef. Or to myself.

Javier dropped his hand with a sigh and set about preparing an order of sanddabs to replace the returned dish. 'So what are we gonna do in the meantime?' he asked, ladling a dipper of clarified butter into a sauté pan.

'I can still cook. I've made our dishes so many times I could prepare them in my sleep, and we can have whoever's on the line with me just taste my stuff as well as theirs.'

'I guess so.' He dusted the translucent fish with flour, set it into the bubbling butter, and sprinkled the fillet with sea salt and cracked black pepper. 'I mean, it's not as if we have much choice.'

Javier was right about that. Gauguin did fine for a high-end restaurant: we stayed consistently in the black and didn't have many outstanding loans. But we weren't rolling in cash, either. So hiring a temporary line cook to replace me was not really an option.

I wiped my eyes again and reached for the next ticket. It was a relief that my secret was now out in the open, but that didn't help allay the gloom that had settled over me at the prospect of forever living in a world with neither taste nor smell.

And then I made the mistake of peering through the pass once more toward the bar. Eric and Gayle had moved their stools close together and were talking and laughing again, as if the previous quarrel had never occurred.

Just like I predicted. I should have turned away at that point – focused on the order of *coq au vin* printed on the ticket in my hand. But I didn't have it in me. And as I spied on the couple from behind the hot line, Gayle leaned over to whisper something into Eric's ear, ruffling the back of his blond head as she spoke. He turned to her in response with a boyish smile.

And then they kissed.

Wednesday came and went with no change in my nasal passages, and when I awoke on Thursday still unable to detect even the faintest aroma of my brewing coffee, I allowed myself an indulgent little cry, there in the privacy of my kitchen. Buster emerged from under the kitchen table to lick my hand, which gave me some comfort. And then I remembered my date that morning to go horseback riding with Grace.

Good. The exercise and fresh air would help take my mind off my plight. Maybe I could even offer to muck out her stable – since I certainly wouldn't have to worry about the nasty smell – which would ingratiate myself to my old friend for months to come.

Since we were meeting at her parents' place at ten, I didn't have a whole lot of time for dawdling. It had been well past midnight when I'd finally made it home from work the night before, and I'd only awakened when I did – a little after eight o'clock – because of Buster's rough, insistent tongue on my face, telling me it was time to start the day. So, after downing my tasteless-but-caffeine-providing coffee and then taking the dog for his morning walk, I settled into the bucket seat of my 1957 Thunderbird convertible and headed off.

The Lerici Farm was about seven miles up Highway 1, nestled in a grassy basin within the Santa Cruz Mudstone that makes up the geology of our coast north of town. I turned down the familiar asphalt drive, cruised past rows of arti-chokes, their fat, spiky globes now at the height of maturity, and pulled up in front of the old farmhouse. The Victorian-era building had seen better days, and its white clapboard siding looked like it could use a fresh coat of paint, but the place was still a gem.

The front door opened as I shut off the T-Bird and yanked up the emergency brake, and a dog came bounding and barking down the steps towards the car, followed by Grace. It was a black-and-white bull terrier – one of those Spuds Mackenzie dogs, with an egg-shaped head and compact, muscular body.

'Bondo, hush!' Grace shouted to no avail. But I could tell the dog was friendly from the vigorous tail-wagging that accompanied the barks. Nevertheless, I allowed him to smell the back of my hand before emerging from the car. You never know about strange dogs, so it's always best to be cautious. He responded with a slobbery kiss, after which he tried to jump up onto the seat with me.

Grace hurried over and grabbed him by the collar. 'No, Bondo, sit!' she said. The dog obediently complied, his pink tongue panting in excitement. 'He loves to go for rides in the car. Anyone's car. And I gotta say, girl, he's showing great taste in this instance. Where the hell did you get *this* beauty?'

'I inherited it from my Aunt Letta,' I said, climbing out of the T-Bird and patting its creamy yellow hood. 'I don't know if you were back in town yet when she was killed last year, but . . .'

'I wasn't, but I heard all about what happened from my mom. I'm really sorry.'

'Yeah, as am I about Neil.' I stepped forward, arms out, and we embraced each other in a tight hug. 'So, how you holding up?' I asked.

She released me with a sigh. 'As okay as I could be, I guess. It's just a lot to take in all at once.'

I nodded. 'I can imagine.'

Grace bit her lip, then forced a smile. 'You want something to drink? Coffee, a soda?'

'No thanks. I'm good.'

'C'mon down to the stable, then, and I'll introduce you to Ralph.'

'Ralph?' I said, following after her toward a small brown building behind the farmhouse. 'That's the name of your horse?'

'Well, his real name is Rafael, but Jack – that's my husband – started calling him Ralph as a joke and it stuck.'

Grace unlatched the door to the stable and led me to one of the two stalls within. An enormous brown head popped out, its dark eyes calmly taking me in. I reached out to tickle the soft pink skin under the horse's lower lip, and he flared his nostrils and nickered.

'He's a sweetie, this one,' Grace said. 'Super calm and gentle. Jack's not much of a rider, so when I heard about this twelve-year-old quarter horse gelding for sale out in Salinas last summer, I thought he'd be perfect for him.' She scratched Ralph behind the ear, then headed for the next stall. 'And this is Amira. It means "princess" in Arabic, which is perfect because she definitely thinks of herself as royalty.'

Inside stood a dappled gray horse, much smaller and more delicate than the big-boned Ralph, eating hay from a rack. She looked up at our approach, arched her neck several times, and snorted.

'An Arab,' I said. 'Wow, she's gorgeous. I've heard they can be a handful, though.'

'That she can be, but we have an understanding, don't we, girl.' Amira responded with another snort, then returned to her hay. Grace laughed as she walked to a door at the far end of the stable. 'Okay, let's go get the tack.'

Fifteen minutes later I was astride Ralph, my left leg stretched before me on the tooled-leather saddle while Grace tightened the girth. 'He likes to blow up his stomach so it's not so tight,' she said, 'but I've learned his little tricks.' She kneed the horse in the belly, causing him to let out a stream of air, then yanked on the cinch and buckled it down snugly. 'Told ya,' she said, climbing aboard the gray Arab mare. 'Ready to go?'

'Giddyap, cowgirl,' I responded, and we set off.

I hadn't been horseback riding in years. Other than one occasion on a beach outside of Puerto Vallarta with Eric ten years earlier, when my mount had been so jaded and bored that I could barely urge him into a slow trot, the last time I'd been on a horse had been back in high school with Grace. And although I'd ridden her aged Pinto around and around that ring, imagining myself some kind of Annie Oakley or Calamity Jane, I'd never become what you'd call an expert horsewoman.

So, needless to say, I was glad she'd given me Ralph to ride rather than the nervous Amira, who almost danced out from under Grace as soon as she'd gotten settled in the saddle.

We started up a trail behind the house, skirting the artichoke fields and heading toward the redwood-covered hills to the east. 'I didn't even know these trails existed,' I said as we turned off the first path onto another one leading to the right.

'That's 'cause Mom didn't allow me to ride on them alone back when I had Patches. And since we only had the one horse, my only option was to ride in the ring.'

We walked the horses single-file along the narrow path for a few minutes, after which the terrain opened up from cultivated farmland to sprawling fields, and the trail became wider. 'So tell me about growing up on a farm,' I said, coming up alongside Grace. 'I never talked to you about it back in high school, but I'm curious now. Did you feel lonely living so far outside of town?'

'Not as a kid, though when I got older I sure did. But thankfully Ryan had a car his last year at school, so he'd sometimes drive me places I needed to go.'

'Right. I remember riding in your brother's car – that black Plymouth Valiant with the red interior. I thought it was so cool cruising around town with this senior when we were just these little freshmen. Even if he did pretty much ignore me. What's he do now?'

'He and his wife are real estate agents. Like just about every other person you meet these days in Santa Cruz.'

I chuckled. 'Totally. My dad's new girlfriend sells real estate, too.'

Ralph had stopped to munch on a succulent patch of grass, and Grace swiveled around in her saddle to watch me yank on both reins, trying in vain to pull his strong neck back up. 'Try using just one rein,' she said. 'It puts him off balance.'

The big head popped immediately up. 'Ha! Good trick, that.' I kicked the horse lightly with my heels and clucked a few times to get him moving again. 'So you and Ryan never considered staying on and working the farm after you finished school?' I asked once I'd caught up to Grace again.

She let out a short laugh. 'Ryan went all the way to Portland for college just to get away, and I split for Chico State as soon as I graduated high school. That way there was no possibility Mom and Dad would try to convince me to work at the farm.'

'But Neil ended up staying . . .' I prompted.

'Yeah, he always loved it here. He did do a couple semesters at Cabrillo, but never even moved out of the house. And once he quit college he started working at the farm full time.'

'It seems like a pretty big operation,' I said, gesturing back toward the rows upon rows of cropland behind us. 'Did the three of them run the place all by themselves?'

'Well, Mom and Dad have always hired seasonal workers to help out at harvest time. And recently they've had another full time person, as well. You actually probably met her,' Grace said with a glance my way. 'Amy, that gal who was helping Neil at the cook-off.'

'Really? She works at the farm?'

'Uh-huh. She's interested in learning the ropes of farming so she can maybe buy her own place sometime, so she offered to be a . . . I guess you'd call it like an apprentice. Dad's health hasn't been what it used to be – nor his mind, for that matter,' Grace added with a shake of the head. 'Anyway, it was a pretty good deal and the timing was right, so Mom and Dad took Amy up on it.'

'So why was she helping out at the wharf last Sunday?' I asked. 'Is Amy a cook, also?'

'No, I don't think so. Though I've only spoken to her a few times, so I don't really know anything about her life – other than her working here at the farm. But Neil was totally into that cook-off thing. He thought it was a great way to advertise the farm – you know, get the Lerici name out there to the public. And then after he'd done it a couple times and won, he got *super* competitive.' Grace shook her head derisively, but then her whole upper body slumped and she shook her head again, this time slowly and sadly.

'Anyway,' she went on after a bit, 'since Amy and him had become pretty good friends working together, I guess she just offered to help out at the cook-off this year as a favor.'

I pulled Ralph to a stop. Now, *this* was interesting information. 'Do you think they might have been involved?'

'He never said so, but who knows?' And then Grace reined in Amira, too, and turned to me with a frown. 'Wait. Are you saying maybe Amy was the one . . .'

'No, no, I'm not suggesting anything like that,' I said quickly. Even if I were thinking that, I didn't want her to know I was. 'I was just wondering if he'd been seeing anyone, is all.'

But it did strike me as odd that Grace's thoughts would immediately jump to that as a possibility regarding Amy. Did she know something I didn't? Or was she merely on high alert because she knew she was with someone who'd been involved in several murder investigations over the past year? Could her mother have told her about that, as well as my Aunt Letta's death?

We rode on for a while in silence, gazing out at the Pacific Ocean, which had come into view now that we'd gained some elevation. Red-winged blackbirds, their crimson shoulder patches flashing as they flitted from bush to bush, cried out nasally to one another, announcing the advent of spring. It was a glorious day. But one marred by the memory of Neil, whom someone had seen fit to bash in the head with the backside of a cleaving knife.

Could *it have been Amy?* I wondered. I didn't see any obvious motive at this point, but if she and Neil were in fact involved and the relationship had gone bad, that would certainly provide one. And she certainly did have the opportunity, as Vargas had noted, working that day as she had with Neil.

'By the way,' Grace said, startling me out of my musings.

'Neil's memorial is this Saturday. There's going to be a private burial first, but then a reception here at the farm afterwards at noon – you know, a "celebration of life" – which you're welcome to come to if you want.'

'Would you like me to come?' I asked.

'I would,' she said. 'That would be nice.'

'Okay, then, I will.'

And it would be nice for me, as well, to have a good reason to talk to the rest of the family.

FOUR

When my phone chirped Friday morning, the last person I expected the text to be from was Eric. But there it was: *This one of your Fridays off?*

Yes, I wrote back. Javier and I now traded Fridays working at the restaurant, as an attempt to at least pretend we had some kind of normal social life. And tonight was indeed my free night.

Seconds later my phone pinged again: *Great! Can I take U to dinner, my treat? Cuz I need to ask your advice about something.*

No way was I going to refuse the offer of a free meal. *Sounds good. Genki Desu at 6?* Might as well go for sushi, as long as he was paying. And who knew? Maybe if I ordered something super strong like pickled mackerel, with its potent vinegar and fatty fish, I'd actually be able to taste something.

But what the hell did Eric want to ask me? Could it possibly be about Gayle?

Even though I wasn't working dinner tonight, I did have to go in to Gauguin that afternoon. Inventory and ordering called, and Javier and I had a meeting at two with a new meat purveyor who claimed to have grass-finished beef, pastured pork, and free-range chicken for a much better price than we were now paying.

Then, at three fifteen, our line cook Kris called to say she'd be late because she had to pick her kid up from soccer practice instead of her husband. As a result, I ended up staying to do all her prep work, getting the *mise en place* items cleaned, chopped, blanched, soaking in brandy, and set in their stainless steel pans, ready for the line.

As soon as Kris finally showed up right before six, I rushed the three blocks to Genki Desu and ended up arriving several minutes late – but still beating Eric there. I took one of the empty stools at the sushi bar, wincing as I sat down. Although

I was used to long hours in the saddle of my Specialized Roubaix bicycle, the same could not be said for the western saddle I'd been atop the day before.

Eric slid onto the stool next to me two minutes later wearing a hangdog look. 'I waited for you to order drinks,' I said. Which was technically true.

He nodded, then absently picked up the menu and set it down again.

'*Maido!*' Ichirou called out from behind the glass case bearing chunks of glistening tuna, salmon, yellowtail, scallops, and other delicacies. The sushi chef wiped his razor-sharp filleting knife on a damp side towel, then came to stand before us. 'Something to drink?'

'An Asahi, please. Large,' Eric said, and Ichirou looked to me.

'Make that two.'

I waited till our bottles had been served and we'd poured the golden beer into our chilled glasses before turning to Eric. 'Okay, so what gives? Why the long face?'

'It's work,' he said.

'Oh?' I managed to respond, hoping my disappointment didn't show. I'd been so sure he was going to say it was Gayle.

'Yeah. I got passed over as lead counsel for this big case we've got – a fraud action involving a local tech mogul that's gonna get a ton of press when it goes to trial.' Eric took an angry gulp of beer and shook his head. 'I've been working on that file for almost a year, and then Tom Scofield gets appointed lead counsel?'

'That sucks,' I offered, and Eric snorted.

'No kidding. But Scofield's been totally brown-nosing the new DA ever since he got elected last year, so I shouldn't be at all surprised.' He poured more beer into his glass and drank half of it down. 'But I *so* deserved that case,' he added in almost a growl.

Ichirou finished arranging an order of sashimi on a sheet of bamboo, then came to stand before us once more. 'Are you ready to order?' he asked.

'Sure, why not.' Eric perused the specials scrawled on the board behind the sushi bar. 'I guess I'll go for the *toro, unagi,* and smoked *sake nigiri*. Oh, and the *umeshiso* hand roll, as well.'

'Not feeling all that hungry tonight, are you?' I can pull my weight with the best of them when it comes to food, but this was a lot to eat, even for Eric. 'And I'd like two orders of the *saba nigiri* and one of the *iwashi*. And go heavy on the wasabi, would you?'

I could feel Eric's eyes boring into me as Ichirou left to start on our meal. 'What?' I said.

'Mackerel and sardine? Really? You trying to become super Japanese all of a sudden? Maybe we should order you some *uni*, as well.'

'No thanks, I've never been a big fan of sea urchin gonads.' But then I decided I might as well come clean, and told Eric about my lost sense of smell and what I'd read online about my prognosis. 'And so, anyway,' I concluded, 'I just thought maybe if I ordered some of the more stinky items on the menu I might have a chance of triggering my nerve endings, get them to regenerate and come back into service.'

'Ouch,' he said. 'I am so sorry. That sucks way more than my being passed over as lead counsel. I know how important food is in your life.'

Ichirou set down our first plate of sushi and we busied ourselves with unwrapping our chopsticks and mixing soy sauce into our dishes of green horseradish paste.

'Oh, hey, speaking of food,' Eric said, 'I heard at work today that you were there when they found that body at the Artichoke Cook-Off last weekend. Is that true?'

I selected one of the thin slices of sardine from the plate and dipped it in my soy sauce. 'Unfortunately, yes, it's true. He had the booth next to mine, actually, and I knew the guy – sort of. I was friends with his sister back in high school. You know anything about the case?'

'Huh-uh. As far as I know, we haven't gotten any info yet about it from the cops. But everyone's been talking about the death, 'cause it looks an awful lot like a homicide.'

'Looked like that to me, as well,' I said, the memory of Neil's bloody forehead and the enormous cleaver lying by his side flashing before me like a slide from a PowerPoint presentation. 'Do you at least know if they have any suspects yet?'

'If I did, I sure wouldn't tell you. That would *certainly* preclude me from being appointed lead counsel on the case if I started spilling information about it to our local Miss Marple.'

'Which means you don't know if they do or not.'

He chuckled. 'True, dat.'

I bit off half my sushi and chewed the tender sardine, trying to detect any hint of its oily, fishy flavor. But other than a slight burning from the massive amount of wasabi I'd mixed into my soy sauce, there was nothing. *Damn.* I took a drink of beer, which – although it had no taste, either – at least offered the benefits of being an intoxicant.

'So, getting back to what you told me about your job, you thinking of doing anything about it? You know, like complaining?'

He shook his head. 'That would only make it worse. All I can do is be a good little boy and hope I get assigned the next big case. But here's the deal.' Eric set down his chopsticks and looked at me, his eyes serious again. 'That's not the only thing that's been bugging me at work. I've started to have a really bad attitude about the job in general. I mean, I used to get all amped up about legal research and finding that perfect case law to nail whatever slimy dude I was prosecuting, but now, I don't know . . .'

'You sound like me, my last couple years at my law firm.'

'Exactly.' The sound of Eric's hand slapping the bar top made me jump. 'Which is why I wanted to talk to you tonight. I wanted to find out how you did it – how you got through all those days when you totally hated your job.'

'You just answered your own question,' I said. 'By simply "getting through" the days, one by one, is how I did it.'

His face fell.

'What? You thought I could give you some kind of magic feather to help you love your job? Not. The only thing that alleviated my misery was quitting and going to work for my father at Solari's. Not that that turned out to be a whole lot better.'

Eric leaned back and drank down the rest of his Asahi. 'Yeah, you're right.'

'Have you asked Gayle what she thinks? She still works as a lawyer, after all – unlike me.'

He didn't answer right away, instead motioning for Ichirou to bring him another bottle of beer. 'Yeah, I talked to her,' he finally said, not wanting to meet my eye. 'But she wasn't very sympathetic. All she did was laugh and say, "Well, that's what you get for working for the evil empire".'

'Ah. Not terribly sympathetic, that.' Gayle was a public defender, and thus not a huge fan of the work done by the prosecutor's office.

Eric responded with a grim smile.

'Was that what you two were arguing about the other night at Gauguin?' I asked.

'We weren't *arguing*,' he said through clenched teeth, then drew a slow breath and let it out. I'd clearly hit on a touchy subject. 'We were just having a little difference of opinion, is all.'

Uh-huh. Right.

Neil's parents had intended for the reception after their son's burial to be held outdoors, but the rainy weather that arrived the Friday night before put the kibosh on that plan. I was glad, however, to have the excuse to spend some time inside the old farmhouse – and maybe even do a little snooping around while I was there.

A large oak table in the dining room had been pushed up against the wall and was rapidly being covered with the plates of sandwiches, casseroles, bowls of pasta, cakes, pies, and cookies brought by the guests. *Let's hope the Lericis have a lot of room in their freezer*, I thought, gazing at the bounty before me. Because no way were the folks attending the celebration of life going to make much of a dent in all that food.

I moved several dishes closer together to make room for the tray of blondies I'd baked that morning, then turned and surveyed the room. Dozens of flower vases were scattered about, bearing blue-and-yellow irises, delicate white lilies, pale pink roses, and towering rust-red gladiolas, all no doubt transported here from the burial service.

An older woman, perhaps in her late-sixties, was sitting in the corner on a folding chair, surrounded by several other women about the same age. The one seated was dabbing her eyes, which I now saw were red, her face streaked with tears. *Neil's mother.* She had the same oval eyes and broad nose as Grace, though her hair had grayed since I'd last seen her. One of the standing women bent to embrace her, then pulled up a second chair to sit by her side.

Some two dozen other people were milling about, including a pair of young children chasing each other around the living room, where additional folding chairs had been set up. A man I thought I recognized was leaning against the wall on the far side of the table laden with food, a scowl marring what otherwise would have been a handsome face: square jaw, full nose, and dark, brooding eyes. *Right.* That was Ryan, the older brother. But why was he frowning?

I turned to follow his gaze and saw that he appeared to be watching his mother. *Odd.* Wouldn't you have an expression of sadness or concern if you saw your mother weeping over your dead brother like that?

A blonde-haired woman stood next to Ryan, and she too looked as if she'd been crying. As she blew her nose on a tissue, Ryan turned and said something to her, to which she responded by glaring at him, and then strode off. His hard eyes followed her to the living room, then returned to his mother.

That must be Ryan's wife, I surmised from their interaction. I'd have to ask Grace about her. But the eldest brother certainly seemed to have a chip on his shoulder. Or perhaps he was just a surly sort of guy. He hadn't been terribly friendly to me during high school, after all.

I looked around to see who else might be in attendance, but the only other person I knew was Martin Vargas, who had just arrived. The detective glanced my way but gave no sign of recognition other than the slight flicker of a smile. He'd asked permission of Ryan to come to the reception today, and we'd decided in advance that it would be best to act as if we didn't know each other.

Vargas crossed the room to Ryan, who smiled stiffly as he greeted the detective and shook his hand. Spotting Grace descend the stairs behind them into the front hall, I called out her name.

'Sally!' she said with a smile, coming forward to give me a hug. 'I'm so glad you could make it. Have you been here long?'

'I only just arrived.' I stepped back and took in her face. Behind the smile, her eyes were tired and her brow drawn. 'I take it it was hard, the burial?' I asked, and she nodded. 'Yeah, your mom and brother don't look like they're doing so great,' I said, glancing back into the dining room. 'And Ryan's wife seems like she's taking it pretty hard, too.'

'Cynthia, right. It was hard for all of us. That's why I was upstairs just now, so I could wash my face and fix my make-up, which got smeared from all my crying. But I'm glad you're here.' She took my hand. 'C'mon, let's go see Mom. She totally remembers you, and wanted me to bring you over as soon as you arrived.'

We waited till a man paying his respects to Grace's mother had given her a kiss on the cheek and then made his way to the refreshment table, and then walked up to where she sat.

'Mom, here's Sally Solari,' Grace said, and the woman looked up with a smile.

'Hello, Mrs Lerici, it's so nice to see you again after all these years. Though I'm so sorry it had to be because of this sad occasion.'

'Please, call me Diana,' she said, patting the now-empty chair next to her. 'Sit. I'd love to hear about what you've been doing since high school.'

As I complied, Ryan's wife Cynthia came up to our group, followed by the younger of the two children I'd seen earlier. From the way the boy hugged close to her, I figured she must be his mom. 'Someone just brought in a pot of soup,' Cynthia said to her mother-in-law, 'and I was wondering which bowls you'd like us to put out.'

'I'll deal with it, Mom,' Grace said, and the three of them retreated to the kitchen.

Diana turned to me and took me by the hand. 'I knew your father back when we were in high school, you know. How is he doing?'

'He's fine,' I answered, wondering why neither of them had ever mentioned their friendship back when Grace and I had hung out together. 'Busy at the restaurant, of course, but he seems really happy these days. He's got a girlfriend, now, which helps. You heard my mom passed away several years ago from cancer, I imagine?'

'Yes, I did hear. I'm so sorry,' she said, giving my hand a squeeze. 'That must have been hard for both of you.'

'And I'm so sorry about Neil. It's just awful.'

Diana bit her lip and blinked several times. We sat a moment in silence, and then she dabbed at her eyes again with her free hand and turned to face me. 'So tell me what you're doing now, my dear. Grace said something about you being in the restaurant business like your father.'

I told her about inheriting Gauguin from my Aunt Letta the previous April, and how my head chef, Javier, had recently become half-owner of the place. 'If you ever want to come in for dinner sometime, I'll make sure that you're well taken care of,' I said.

She smiled. 'That's very sweet, but Ernie and I don't go out much anymore. Didn't you go to law school, though? That's certainly a big change, from lawyer to restaurant owner.'

'Well, I never much liked the law,' I said. 'So when my mom died, it didn't take much to make me quit my firm to go help Dad with Solari's. And then after Aunt Letta left me her place, well . . .'

Diana's eyes had grown sad again. 'So many deaths,' she murmured, followed by something I wasn't sure I understood – 'And then there was one,' it sounded like.

'Pardon?'

'I'm sorry.' She relinquished my hand to pluck at a loose thread sticking out from her black wool slacks. 'Talking about the law made me think about something that's rather . . . difficult, is all.'

'Something that I could help with?'

Now, I wasn't technically permitted to assist others with legal issues, being an 'inactive' attorney, but I couldn't resist the opportunity to perhaps learn something important about the Lerici family – and maybe even about Neil's death. Plus, I did truly like Mrs Lerici, so if I could in fact help her with anything, I was willing to risk the wrath of the State Bar.

'I doubt it.' Diana tried breaking off the black thread at its base, which only resulted in a pucker in her pants at that spot. 'It's just that Neil was the only one who supported me with regard to the property division.'

'Property division?'

'Yes. Ernie got it in his head last year that he wanted to subdivide the farm to give each of the three kids a parcel. His health and memory has been declining, and he thinks it would be better to do it now rather than wait till we're too old to run the place anymore.'

'Wow,' I said. 'I had no idea. Grace didn't mention anything about that when we went riding the other day.'

'Probably because she's slightly embarrassed about it.' Diana let go the thread and set about smoothing out the fabric. 'You see, she and Ryan would like to sell to a developer who's interested in the property, but Neil and I were both opposed to that and wanted to keep it all as farmland. I don't want to move, and I certainly don't want to see the place become a hotel or block of condos. Neil was the only one of the three kids who truly understood my love of the farm, because he shared it as well. But now that he's gone, there's no one to support me in my wishes.'

'I am so sorry.' I took Diana's hand once more and held it as we gazed out at the people milling about her dining room and talking in low voices about the child who, it appeared, had likely been her favorite.

And now I had finally uncovered a motive for that son's death. But if that were the case, it meant his siblings were the two primary suspects.

FIVE

My grim thoughts were interrupted by the arrival of a couple in matching green rain jackets who rushed toward us from the front door. Their clothes were only slightly wet, so the steady rain we'd been having all morning must have let up some.

'Oh, Diana,' the woman said, leaning over to embrace Mrs Lerici, and the man followed suit.

I relinquished my chair and stood. 'Here, I'll let you three have some alone time.' Leaving them to talk, I wandered over to where Neil's father was standing in the living room. If I could steer the conversation around to the subject, perhaps I could find out more about the property division his wife had mentioned.

He was alone, staring at the polished walnut sideboard upon which pictures and mementos from Neil's life had been arranged. Dominating the display was a large framed photograph of Neil wearing a crew-neck sweater and a crooked smile. The fuzziness of the picture suggested it had been blown up specifically for today's memorial from a relatively small file – perhaps something taken off his Facebook page.

I came to stand by Mr Lerici's side and studied the photos along with him: Neil as an impish Cub Scout, proudly clutching a fishing pole and the tiny trout he'd just caught; standing on the beach in a black-and-yellow wetsuit with a surfboard under his arm; waving from a tractor in the middle of an artichoke field; and a recent one of him sandwiched between his two parents, posing on the front steps of the old white farmhouse in which I now stood.

As I gazed at the photos, I took the opportunity to study the father, as well. Although he'd aged considerably in the twenty-plus years since I'd last seen him, Ernie still had the sinewy build that comes with the arduous work of the farmer. He'd never been a tall man, and with the stoop that his advanced age had brought – I figured him to now be in his early seventies – I towered over the man.

After a moment, he sighed and turned to face me. 'Hello, Mr Lerici,' I said, extending my palm to shake. 'I'm Sally Solari, Grace's friend from high school.'

He took my hand in a grip that belied his frail appearance and looked me in the eye. 'Sure, I remember you,' he said. The gravelly tone of his voice made me want to clear my throat. 'Your folks own that restaurant out on the wharf.'

I didn't correct him with regard to the plural he'd employed. 'I'm so sorry about Neil,' I said instead. 'I didn't know him well, but I did used to talk to him here at the farm sometimes when I'd come over after school with Grace.'

Ernie nodded, his attention now returned to the large framed photo atop the antique sideboard.

'I love the one of him on the tractor,' I said. 'When was that taken?'

'A number of years ago. You can see the old greenhouse is still there.' He picked up the photo and studied it, running his thumb over the glass in the frame. 'But you can also tell from the size of the plants that it was well after we switched over to the artichokes.'

'What made you decide to grow them?' I asked.

He set the photo back on the sideboard and turned toward me, his face coming to life for the first time. 'They're the perfect crop for this area,' he said. 'They fetch good prices with consistent yields, and suffer few problems with disease. It's 'cause of our climate, being so moderate year-round.'

'Uh-huh.' I knew that our coastal 'marine layer' – which I so detested for the chilly fog it brought to Santa Cruz County during much of the spring and summer – was a boon to local farmers who grew such crops as artichokes, Brussels sprouts, and lettuce.

'They're Italian, artichokes, aren't they? Like us?'

Mr Lerici smiled. 'Well, they did originally come from the Mediterranean region, but they go back to a time well before Italians even existed as a culture. The name, though – or so I've heard, anyway – comes from a Ligurian word: *cocali*, for pine cone, which ended up as *articolcos*. So the original Sixty

Families – you know, who came to Santa Cruz from Liguria way back when – they do have a special relationship to the plant. And it was also an Italian who first brought the crop to this area. Did you know that a hundred percent of all the artichokes commercially grown in the United States come from California?' The pride in his voice was evident, but I could also tell this was a spiel he'd given many times before.

I touched the photo of Neil driving the tractor with my index finger, wanting to move the conversation back to the family. 'How old was Neil when he first took an interest in the farm?'

The smile remained, but now turned sad. 'He was helping out in the fields by the time he was ten,' Ernie said. 'Just like me.'

'Oh, so you grew up on a farm, too?'

He nodded toward the photo. 'I grew up on *this* farm,' he said. 'It was planted with sugar beets when I was a kid, and then Brussels sprouts, until I switched to artichokes back in the eighties after I inherited it from my dad.'

'Wow. I didn't realize it had been in the family that long. So why would you want to subdivide and sell the land now?'

Mr Lerici frowned, and I thought perhaps I'd gone too far with my direct question. He shoved his hands into his tan slacks, and I could see the pockets rise and fall along with the clenching and unclenching of his fists.

'I'm sorry,' I said. 'It's just that I'd heard you were thinking of dividing the farm up between the kids, but I guess this wasn't an appropriate time to—'

His right hand swept up to cut me off. 'It's fine.'

But the distant look in his eyes suggested otherwise. After blinking a few times, he began to speak – so softly that, with all the other conversations going on in the room, it was difficult to hear what he was saying. Something about a puppy named Bruno and harvesting sugar beets, then marrying Diana and how she didn't speak English when they met.

But that couldn't be right. She'd grown up in Santa Cruz, hadn't she?

Ernie's speech had taken on an almost ranting tone now, and he was making less and less sense. 'They didn't want me to go to the hospital, but I did anyway. Too many people . . . And that *hamburger*.' He licked his lips, as if tasting anew some long-ago eaten meal, then locked his eyes on mine. There were tears in them, and he reached out to touch my arm. '*Papà* wouldn't have wanted this,' he said, his voice now hoarse. 'It was his life. But I had no choice. And now . . . He's *not* my son . . .'

'Wait . . . what do you mean?' I asked. But Ernie simply shook his head, then turned and walked away.

How weird was that? I thought as he crossed the room to the entranceway and then headed out the front door. *And what on earth could he mean by 'he's not my son'?* Was Ernie so angry with one of his boys, or so horrified at something one of them had done, that he would feel as if they were no longer his kin? And if so, could he have gone so far as to actually *disown* them?

But then another possibility occurred to me. *Or maybe the statement had been literal.*

I picked up the photo of Neil on the tractor once more and studied the young man's features. He did have a different build than his parents, who were both shorter and more sinewy than their tall and buff youngest son. But a lot of that could be simply chalked up to his generation. Many people I knew were bigger and more robust than their parents.

But then, setting the photo back down with a shake of the head, I smiled inwardly. I was clearly letting my imagination run away with me, caught up in my role as secret sleuth for Martin Vargas. Both Grace and Diana had mentioned that Ernie's mental facilities were in decline, so the obvious answer was that I'd simply been witness to the rantings of a senile old man. His strange behavior just now certainly supported that conclusion.

Martin Vargas wandered into my line of vision and glanced my way. Waggling my eyebrows back at him, I tilted my head in the direction Mr Lerici had gone, and he nodded back, which I took to mean he'd witnessed our interaction. The detective continued on past without speaking, heading for the kitchen where I could see Amy, the gal who'd helped Neil at the cook-off, standing with Ryan.

I was about to turn away from the photos on the sideboard when my eyes fell on a high school yearbook lying next to the tractor photo. It was from Neil's senior year, two years after I'd graduated from the same school. Flipping to his senior portrait, I found a young man looking decidedly uncomfortable in the black tux and bow tie that all the twelfth grade boys had been made to wear for their photos. His dark hair bore streaks of blond, and I wondered if he'd bleached it purposefully or if it was the result of hours spent out in the sun surfing.

I paged through the yearbook, contemplating all the smiling, sneering, and earnest faces looking back at me and remembering how I'd felt as a high school senior about to embark on my new life. And then one of the photos made me stop. The face had been rubbed out with a pencil eraser and the boy's eyes replaced with large Xs. Whoever had defaced the picture had also added a pair of horns sprouting from the head.

I read the name below the photo. Pete Ferrari: the guy who ended up winning the People's Choice Award at the Artichoke Cook-Off because of Neil's death.

I knew Pete – not super well, but enough to chat with when we ran into each other, since he now ran the Crab Shack his parents had started, which was out on the Santa Cruz Municipal Wharf next door to Solari's. But I hadn't realized he and Neil had been high school classmates.

There was nothing on the page to suggest who had defaced the photo – or why – but clearly somebody didn't like the guy. *Could it have been Neil, or did one of his friends do it while signing his yearbook?*

I was inspecting the inside covers of the book to see if someone had written among all the 'Good luck at college!' and 'See you over the summer, dude!' notes anything which might suggest a dislike for Pete, when I was joined at the sideboard by Grace.

'How're you doing?' I asked, closing the yearbook.

She shrugged and ran a finger across its red-and-white cloth cover. 'It's just such a strange combination – having a social gathering dedicated solely to grief.'

'But it's not supposed to be that,' I said. 'A wake is meant to celebrate the person, to tell stories and remember all the things you loved about them. I mean, sure you're supposed to cry, but you're supposed to laugh, too.'

'I guess.' She flipped idly through the pages of the yearbook without really looking at them, then closed it again. 'C'mon, you wanna go get some food? I hear it's good for what ails ya.'

'No complaints on this end,' I said, and we headed for the buffet table. Grace took a delicate china plate from the stack and handed it to me. It was decorated with pink roses with a border of tendrils of entwined green foliage – similar to the set of china my *nonna* had inherited from her mother.

Selecting a second plate for herself, Grace speared a slice of ham with a fork, then dabbed mustard on top. 'I saw you talking to my dad,' she said, spooning a small serving of macaroni salad next to the meat. 'How's he holding up?'

'He seemed pretty good, actually. Or at least as good as you'd imagine, anyway. Talking about the farm and about artichokes . . .'

'Oh, lord, he does love to go on and on about his precious artichokes,' she said with a laugh. But then her expression changed. 'And he passed his obsession on to Neil, as well,' she added softly.

'Right. I could see that at the cook-off. It was almost like Neil was proselytizing the Gospel, the way he clearly revered the Lerici artichokes. But getting back to your dad: when he and I were talking, all of a sudden he just switched super abruptly and started acting really strange. Confused, like.'

'Yeah, that's been happening more and more often these days, especially when he's feeling stressed or upset. His mind just kind of goes . . . astray.'

'So it makes total sense, then, that it would happen today,' I said.

Now that Grace was in my sights as a potential suspect, I didn't want to tell her – at least not yet – that I knew about the land division idea. I'd instead let her think it was the strain of Neil's burial and celebration of life that had set her dad off. But I did want to ask her about what Ernie had said about his son.

'He was talking about being at a hospital,' I went on. 'I think maybe at the birth of one of you kids? And he mentioned what he ate, and then he said something really strange: "He's not my son". You have any idea why he would have said that?'

Grace frowned and shook her head, and if she was faking her reaction, she did a brilliant job of it. 'Weird,' she said, confusion in her eyes. 'I have no idea what he might have meant by that, unless maybe he was mad at Ryan or Neil about something. But I do think it's been getting worse of late, the dementia. Dad definitely has good and bad days, and he can get pretty angry and irrational on the bad ones. At least he's not acting belligerent today. Huh, Ryan?'

The oldest son, who'd come up to the table while Grace and I were talking, nodded and helped himself to one of my blondies. 'And thank goodness for that. Wow,' he added, mouth full of the brown sugar-and-butter laden treat. 'These are great. Here, try one.' He held the platter out toward Grace and me.

'No thanks,' I said. 'I'm the one who made them, so I know how fattening they are. And since I seem to have completely lost my sense of smell from a damn sinus infection, the calories would be utterly wasted on me.'

'Bummer,' said Ryan 'Aren't you a cook?'

'I am indeed. And it is indeed a colossal bummer, especially since it could very well be permanent. But I do still have to eat, so I guess I'll go for texture rather than flavor.' I scanned the offerings, then reached for what looked to be a crispy jalapeño popper. Even if I couldn't taste the creamy melted cheese, at least I'd get the benefit of the mouth-feel imparted by all that grease and the spicy hot pepper.

As we ate, Amy passed by the buffet table to grab half a turkey sandwich, then made for where Ernie Lerici stood just inside the front door. Neil's dad smiled as she approached and the two stood for a moment in conversation. I figured Martin had already talked to the farmhand, but I wanted to chat her up, as well.

I waited till she leaned over to give Ernie a light kiss on the cheek and turned to go, then excused myself from Grace and Ryan and followed after her out the front door. The sun was now out, and the raindrops clinging to the flowers and trees in the front yard glistened like a thousand tiny snow globes.

Amy was striding across the grass toward the long, winding

driveway where folks had parked their cars, and I shouted after her. Hearing her name, she turned and waited by her black SUV for me to catch up. 'Yes?'

'Hi, I just wanted to talk to you a sec before you left.'

She gave me a second look. 'Oh, right, I remember you. You're the one who had the booth next to us at the Artichoke Cook-Off.'

'Right. I'm Sally Solari. And I wanted to say how sorry I am about Neil. It must have been such a shock for you . . .' I trailed off. What was I going to say? How your cooking and farming partner was found bludgeoned to death behind a garbage dumpster?

'Yeah, it's been a pretty tough week,' she said, staring down at her scuffed Doc Martens boots. The absence of the Oakland A's baseball cap allowed me to see the blaze of blue across her spiked platinum-blonde hair.

'I can imagine. Grace said you and Neil had gotten pretty close, so it must all be pretty hard.'

Amy, who continued to focus on her oxblood-colored boots, nodded. She chewed her lip for a moment, then looked up, and I saw that she too had obviously been crying – the whites of her baby blue eyes were tinged with red.

Neil's burial had apparently been hard on pretty much everyone in attendance. *With the possible exception of Ryan*, I thought, *who seemed more angry than sad*. But maybe that was simply his way of grieving.

'That's why I'm leaving early,' Amy finally said, wiping her eyes. 'I'm not much good at this kind of thing.'

'Well, I don't think anyone's "good" at this kind of thing. But I totally understand what you mean.'

She smiled and opened her car door. 'And I'll be back again on Monday to work, so I can talk to Diana and Ernie more then, when there's less people around.' She climbed into the SUV and tossed her bag next to a pile of envelopes and junk mail, the topmost of which looked to be a real estate agent's hit-up, with its obligatory photos of a fancy home and blond hunk in a suit with gleaming white teeth. Poking out from underneath the stack of papers was a familiar-looking plaque.

'Wait,' I said. 'Is that an award from the cook-off?'

'Uh-huh. A woman came and delivered it here yesterday. I guess they decided to go ahead and give us the prize after all, since it wasn't Neil's fault he wasn't there to accept it. We're sharing first place with the other guy, the one who owns the Crab Shack. I tried to give it to Ernie, but he didn't want it. He said I should keep it.'

She glanced toward the plaque with a frown, then looked away, and I imagined she wouldn't be in any hurry to hang it up in her house, either. Not the sort of reminder you wanted staring down at you from your living room wall.

After Amy drove off, I pulled out my phone to send a text: *We need to talk. Wanna meet for coffee?*

Martin's reply came before I'd even made it back inside the farmhouse: *Cruzin' Coffee in 30.*

I smiled as I shoved the phone back in my pocket. You gotta love a man who bothers with apostrophes in his texts.

SIX

Santa Cruz must be home to at least a hundred different coffee houses, from old-school Denny's diners and doughnut shops to hipster hangouts heavy on the sharp angles and chrome, with everything in between. Cruzin' Coffee falls closer to the modern style favored by the early-twenties, Gen Z crowd, so I was a little surprised at Martin's choice of the place. He struck me as more of a round-wooden-tables-with-Oasis-playing-over-the-sound-system kind of guy.

But when I got inside I realized why he'd picked it. I'd forgotten that the room had a row of booths separated from each other by tall backs, which made it the perfect spot to talk without being overheard.

Five minutes after I arrived, the detective slid onto the bench across from me. He exhaled as he set his phone on the table. 'God, I hate doing that,' he said. 'Barging in on a family's day of grieving to eavesdrop on their private conversations and pepper them with intrusive questions.' He picked up the card-stock menu, frowning as he examined the offerings, then let it drop back onto the polished metal tabletop.

I was pondering whether the fact that I didn't mind eavesdropping on private conversations – that I, in fact, actually enjoyed it – made me a bad person, when a guy with shoulder-length dreadlocks and a bodybuilder's frame sauntered toward us. 'Howdy. Get ya something?'

In answer, Martin studied the menu once again, so I took the lead. 'An Americano for me, thanks.'

'And I'll have a double espresso,' Vargas said. 'I can use the caffeine.' Once the buff server had departed, he shoved the menu aside. 'Okay, you go first.'

'All right. So the main thing I learned is that the dad, Ernie, decided last year he wants to divide the farm up between the kids. The mom told me that she and Neil were both opposed to it, 'cause they wanted to keep the place as farmland, but that Ryan and Grace want to sell to a developer.'

Martin sat back and shook his head. 'None of them mentioned that to me when I interviewed them last Monday,' he said. 'Even after I specifically asked about their relationship with each other.'

'Nor did Grace say anything about it when we went riding the other day. Even though I specifically asked her about Neil and she told me how much he loved the farm, yet failed to mention anything about its potential sale to a developer. Suspicious, don't you think?'

'Indeed.' The detective gazed across the room at the barista operating an espresso maker that, with all its elaborate copper tubing and shiny knobs, had the look of some fantastic steam-punk machine enveloping him in a cloud of smoke.

'And get this,' I went on. 'It was obvious that the mom and Grace – and Amy, too – had all been crying, but Ryan, no. Which by itself isn't that strange, since guys tend to try to hold that kind of thing in. It didn't look like the dad had been crying, either. But what was odd was that not only did Ryan not seem sad or upset; he seemed angry about something. And I got this feeling, from the way he was looking at her, that it might be his mom he was mad at.'

'What do you mean?' Martin asked.

'Okay, so the mom's sitting there and sobbing, with all these friends gathered around trying to comfort her, and across the room I see Ryan glaring at her – at his *mother*, crying over the death of her son. Doesn't that seem weird? Oh, and Ryan seemed pretty annoyed with his wife, too, who'd also been crying. And then I saw him say something to her which must have pissed her off, 'cause she walked off in a huff as soon as he said it.'

Our server approached with our drinks and set them down. Reaching for the cream pitcher, I added a healthy glug to my mug while Martin busied himself with unwrapping the sugar cubes that had come with his espresso. 'Maybe he was jealous,' he said, stirring the sugar into his white ceramic cup.

'Of his dead brother?'

'I'm not saying it's a good thing, but it is possible.'

I considered this as I sipped my coffee. 'You know,' I said, setting down my mug, 'it did kind of seem like Neil was the mom's favorite, which makes sense given how he was the one who stayed on and who loved the farm so much.'

'Yuck!' said Martin.

'What? I'm not suggesting—'

'No.' He reached for my cup, examined the contents, then held it out for me to see. '*This* is what's "yuck".'

A clump of white had risen to the top, along with several smaller dots which I could only describe as curds. The detective picked up the small pitcher of cream, took a whiff, and grimaced.

'It's bad?' I asked, and he nodded.

'Smells like rotten eggs left out in the sun for about a week. I can't believe you didn't notice . . . Oh, right. Sorry.' He ducked his head in apology.

'It's okay,' I said with a forced smile. 'But I am clearly going to have to pay more attention to what my food and drink looks like for the time being, since I sure can't rely on my other senses.'

I stood and carried the curdled cream and ruined coffee to the bar, then returned with a fresh pitcher and another black coffee. 'Anyway, as I was saying, so what if the mom *did* like Neil best, and had made it obvious to the other siblings over the years? That would certainly have given Ryan reason to be annoyed at her crying her eyes out at his memorial.'

'Possibly,' Vargas replied. 'But then why wouldn't the sister have acted the same way?'

'Because she didn't care as much? Ryan's the oldest, so maybe he felt like he wasn't given his "firstborn due". Oh, that reminds me of something else.' Vargas waited as I added cream to my new coffee, stirred, and examined it with a critical eye. 'Okay,' I went on after taking a quick sip, 'so when I was talking to the dad, he seemed totally normal at first, but then started going off on this kind of rant, talking about growing up on the same farm they have now, and about his puppy and harvesting beets and stuff.'

I described what Ernie had said about Diana not speaking English when they married, and about the hospital, and how his father wouldn't have wanted 'this'. 'Whatever "this" means,'

I said, making air quotes with my fingers. 'And right after that, he goes, "He's not my son". He walked off before I could get him to explain what he meant, but it seems like it might be important.'

Martin thought a moment. 'Well, I gather from what the family told me that Ernie's been suffering from bouts of senility of late, so I think we need to take anything he says with a hefty grain of salt.' He tapped his index finger on the tabletop. 'But it could be relevant. If he was angry enough at Neil to say that about him, then maybe we need to take a hard look at the dad as a suspect.'

'So you think Ernie was referring to Neil when he said it?'

Vargas shrugged. 'Who knows. From what you just told me, it sounds like the oldest son has some issues too, so maybe he's mad at Ryan for some reason.'

'Maybe.' I took another sip of my coffee, pondering Ernie's strange behavior. 'There's another alternative,' I said. 'Though I admit it's a little on the soap opera end of the spectrum. But what if one of the Lerici boys truly *isn't* his son?'

'I guess we do need to consider that as a possibility,' Martin said, his arched eyebrows suggesting otherwise. 'Though if so, we don't know which son he would have been referring to.'

'Or it could be a person we don't even know about,' I said. 'The son of someone *he* had an affair with, who claims their kid is Ernie's. But if he was talking about an actual illegitimate son, then my money's on it being Neil.'

Martin's eyebrows grew even more tall.

'C'mon, think about it: Neil's the only one who looked different from the rest of the family, taller and more stocky than his parents. And it would make sense – if she'd really cared for the father – for Diana to have special feelings for her love child, different than for the other kids.'

'I guess that would explain why Ernie didn't seem as upset today as Diana,' Martin said. 'Which I noticed, as well. And it could also explain why he brought it up today, Neil not being his.'

One point, team Sally. I allowed myself the tiniest of a gloating smile as I took another sip of tasteless coffee.

'Okay, so speaking of what you noticed,' I said, 'I've spilled my news. What did you find out at Neil's celebration of life?'

'Not a whole lot.' He drained his cup and set it back onto the saucer. I observed that he took care not to meet my eye. 'Just basically some of the same things you already told me. You know, who seemed upset, who didn't. I was pretty much limited in what I could find out to watching everyone else interact. People don't talk to a cop like they will a family friend. Which is why I was so glad you were there.' The detective grinned and picked up his phone to check the time. 'I should really get going,' he said.

'Me too. I have to be at Gauguin at three, and Buster needs a walk beforehand.'

Martin pulled out his wallet and waved off my attempt to do the same. 'I got this. Consider it payment for your services this afternoon to the City of Santa Cruz.'

'Thanks.'

Once outside, he gave me a hug and a light kiss on the cheek. I watched him climb into his unmarked – but obviously law enforcement-related – SUV and drive off.

So why had he been so cagey? Did he really not learn anything today, or had he simply been unwilling to share any new knowledge with me?

Sunday dinner the next day at Nonna's house was a small affair. Dad's new real estate agent flame, Abby, had an open house to conduct, my cousin Evie was spending the weekend in San Francisco with her housemates, and Eric – who loved the fuss my grandmother always made over him as much as he did her Sunday gravy – had begged off with other plans. A date with Gayle, most likely, but I wasn't going to think about that.

So it was just Nonna, my father, and me that afternoon. Dad was helping me tear up iceberg lettuce for the salad while we listened to Nonna grouse.

'I can't believe you chose to cancel last Sunday's meal for some silly game,' she said, dumping a box of penne into the large pot of water she had boiling on the stove.

'It wasn't just a game, Ma,' my dad said. 'It was an

important competition, one that could bring new customers to our restaurants, especially since we both won awards.'

If Dad was expecting to impress his mother with this fact, he was sorely mistaken. She gave the pasta a swift stir, then set the long wooden spoon on the counter. 'Well, I say it's silly. Food shouldn't be about competing. It should be about eating and enjoying.'

I had to agree with my *nonna* on this, but I wasn't going to say as much in front of my father. I'd learned long ago it was best not to take sides when the two of them got going. Neutrality was the far safer course to steer.

A ringing from the hallway put an end to the discussion, as Nonna left the kitchen to pick up the handset of her black, 1960s-era telephone. I could hear her start to jabber in a mixture of English and Italian, so it was likely a friend from church. *Good.* I hadn't wanted to talk around her about Neil's death, but since my grandmother loved nothing better than gossiping with her fellow parishoners, I figured I had a few minutes before she got back to the kitchen.

'So I went to the celebration of life they had for Neil at the farm yesterday after the burial,' I said, selecting a tomato from the basket on the counter.

'Oh?' Dad looked up from the cucumber he was now cutting into chunks.

'Yeah, and I found out from Diana that Ernie, the dad, had decided to subdivide the farm between the kids, and that Neil and her were opposed to the other two kids' proposal to sell the place to a developer.'

My father set down his knife. 'And?'

'And so Detective Vargas and I both think that could be relevant to his death. Especially since neither Ryan nor Grace mentioned that fact when the police interviewed them and specifically asked about the farm and also how their relationship was with the rest of the family. Plus, it also appears that Ryan might have been jealous of Neil and—'

'Hold it right there,' Dad said, his voice taking on the tone he'd used when I would misbehave as a child. 'I don't even want to hear it. There's no possible way you could suspect them.'

'Why not?'

'Because no one would do that – kill their own brother.'

'It happens a lot, Dad. Cain and Abel, Romulus and Remus, Goneril and Regan?'

'Who?' he said to this last pair, then waved his hand before I could add that they were actually sisters, not brothers. 'Never mind. I just don't think it's remotely possible in this case. So you need to prove it wasn't them; you're good at that.'

I gaped at my father. Why did he care so much about the Lerici kids? Was it all about his past friendship with Diana?

But what was also odd was that in the past he'd always been unhappy with – no, dead set against – my getting involved in murder investigations. *This one must truly mean a lot for him to actually ask me to get involved.*

'And how do you propose I do that?' I said. 'Prove it wasn't them.'

'I don't know.' Dad picked the knife back up and sliced viciously at the cucumber, as if his anger or frustration or whatever it was he was experiencing could fly away through its sharp blade. 'Who else would have had something to gain by Neil's death?'

'Well, there is Pete Ferrari, the guy who ended up sharing first prize only because of it.' I told Dad about the defaced photo of Pete I'd seen in Neil's yearbook. 'So any animosity the two had could have gone all the way back to high school.'

Dad used the knife to scrape his chunks of cucumber into the bowl of iceberg lettuce, then gave the cooking pasta a stir. 'There ya go,' he said. 'I know Pete, and he's a real blowhard. I could see how the two of them might have been like oil and water. Plus, I heard Pete talking big the week before the cook-off to some of the old-timers out on the wharf about how he was gonna kick Neil's butt this time around.'

'But would that be enough motive to want to *kill* him?' I asked. 'I mean, I hate to sound like Nonna, but it is after all just a food competition.'

'Who says it had to be intentional? They could-a just been arguing out by the dumpsters, and then Pete lost his temper and walloped him, like. You know, un-premeditated, as they say on TV.'

'Maybe. But then why would whoever did it have shoved an artichoke into his mouth after he was killed?'

'Huh?'

I described what I'd seen behind the dumpster that day, including the red-handled cleaving knife by the body and the artichoke poking out of Neil's mouth. 'So given that, it seems pretty intentional, if you ask me.' I thought a moment as I cut the tomato into wedges and added them to the salad. 'And there's also that woman Amy,' I said, 'who was helping Neil out that day at the cook-off. You know, the one with the A's baseball cap who was getting the deep fryer ready?'

Dad nodded. 'Sure, I remember her.'

'Well, Grace told me she'd been working as a kind of apprentice at the farm for the past year or so and that Neil and her had become good friends. But what if they were more than that, and then he'd jilted her?'

'I like it,' he said with a grin. 'See? There's lots of better suspects than the Lerici kids.'

Nonna came back into the kitchen at this point, and we turned to other topics. But as we gorged ourselves on my grandmother's melt-in-your-mouth-tender braised pork and beef swimming in savory red sauce, I thought about what my father had said.

Why *was* he so interested in this case and so set against it being anyone in the family who had killed Neil? Just how close had he *been* to Diana in high school?

And then I had a thought that almost made me choke on my Sunday gravy. *Ohmygod. Could* my *dad be Neil's father?* That would explain how upset he'd been when I'd told him who it was who'd been killed at the cook-off. And it would also explain why neither Diana nor him had ever mentioned their friendship to Grace or me.

But Neil was far too young to have been conceived when my dad and Diana were in high school. Which would mean, if he was the father, that they'd continued – or rekindled – their relationship after he'd married my mother.

I stared at my dad as he joked with Nonna about her new hairstyle and tried to calm the thoughts that were racing through my brain. *Could Dad have been cheating on my mom?* The possibility made me slightly sick to my stomach. Moreover, if my dad *were* Neil's father, that meant I had a half-brother – a brother who was now dead, without my ever getting the chance to know him in any real way.

So if my fears were true, then my father had not only cheated on my mother, but he'd cheated me out of a brother.

Dad glanced my way, then frowned. 'You okay, hon?'

'Yeah, I'm fine,' I said. 'I just thought of something I have to do at work, is all.'

Dad returned his attention to Nonna, which allowed me to study his features to see if I could discern any resemblance between him and Neil. They did share the same stocky build. *Had Neil's eyes been blue like my father's?* I couldn't remember. But the other Lerici kids, I knew from seeing them the day before, had the same dark eyes as their parents.

With an internal shake of the head, I speared a fat chunk of pork. *It couldn't be true. Dad would have told me if I'd had a half-brother.* I was simply letting the drama of the Lerici family's sad circumstances get to me. And yet . . .?

The first thing I did when I got home from Nonna's house was grab my box of high school papers and mementos from the top shelf in the closet and pull out my senior yearbook. There, in the sophomore class, was Neil's picture. I squinted at the small photo, trying to make out the color of his eyes. Brown, I finally decided, though it was hard to tell for sure. But that didn't prove anything, since blue is a recessive gene for eye color.

I turned to my class's section to look for Grace. Her brown, oval eyes were obvious in the picture, which was much larger than Neil's, being her senior portrait.

And then I noticed a photo on the opposite page, which had been rubbed out and defaced, similar to the one of Pete in Neil's yearbook. Pre-Facebook, old-school 'unfriending', I thought with a wry smile.

I read the name: Winthrop Lamb, a kid who'd been mercilessly taunted throughout childhood both because of his name and his bad case of adenoids. I remembered at the time being super annoyed with the guy who'd drawn the fake glasses and buck teeth on Winthrop's photo in my yearbook – a jerk by the name of Brad Johnson who still lived at home and worked for his dad's life insurance company.

So maybe it hadn't been Neil who'd drawn those horns and Xs on Pete's photo. It could have been someone else who had a thing against Pete and decided to mess with Neil's yearbook – like Brad had done in mine. Curious, I searched for Neil and Pete in the book's index. Turning to a page that listed both their names, I saw a spread featuring boys' aquatics teams: swim, water polo, and diving.

I read the small print below the various photos until I found their names, then studied the picture of the swim team. A gaggle of skinny guys in tight swim trunks posed awkwardly at the edge of the pool and there, in the front row, were Neil and Pete, arms about each other, beaming at the camera.

Huh. So they'd obviously been friends during sophomore year. Which meant that if it *had* been Neil who'd rubbed out Pete's picture two years later in his yearbook, they must have had some sort of falling out. But if so, what could have been its cause?

SEVEN

Grace texted me early Monday morning to see if I wanted to come horseback riding again up at the farm that day. *Sure*, I wrote back.

My butt and leg muscles had finally recovered from last Thursday's ride, and it would give me an opportunity to ask about the property division. Upon further consideration – not to mention both Vargas and my dad's reactions to the news – I'd decided to simply come out with it and see what she had to say. There was a good chance Diana had told her daughter that she'd told me, in any case, so what could it hurt?

I arrived at the farm at ten fifteen and pulled up between the black SUV I recognized as Amy's, and a brand new red Nissan Leaf. The farmhand was standing near the front porch, talking with Diana. Amy was wearing tan canvas pants and a blue flannel shirt, and had on sturdy black rubber boots. From the wet mud on both pants and boots, it was obvious she'd already been working that morning.

Bondo once more came running up to the car as I got out, but this time the dog remembered me and immediately jumped up on my legs. I gave him a scratch behind the ears, and he followed me up the pathway toward the farmhouse. As I approached, I could hear Diana and Amy discussing the harvest of the current artichoke crop.

'Oh, hello, Sally,' Diana said, turning at my approach. 'I didn't know you were coming by today.'

'Grace invited me riding this morning. It's good to see you again, Mrs Lerici.' I smiled as I said this, but was in fact having severely mixed feelings about the woman I now suspected might have been in competition with my mother.

'Diana, please,' she said, giving me a warm hug.

'Right, Diana. Sorry.' I offered my palm to Amy. 'Hi, how you doing today?'

'Better, thanks.' She shook hands, then turned back to her boss, and I waited while they finished their discussion about the timing of the harvest. Once Amy had left, heading toward the toolshed down by the horse barn, Diana touched me on the arm.

'I was wondering if you could do something for me, Sally,' she said.

'Sure, whatever you need.'

'It's a legal issue. I was wondering if you could look at the trust Ernie and I had drawn up a few years ago and give me your opinion about it.'

'Uh, I'm not technically allowed to give legal opinions these days,' I said. 'I went inactive with the California Bar when I quit my law firm to go work for my dad at Solari's, and once you do that you're not allowed to "engage in the practice of law", as they say, which includes giving any advice.'

'Oh.' She pursed her lips. 'Well, could you at least take a look at it to tell me whether you think I ought to speak with a lawyer – one who's allowed to talk to me? I'm just concerned about making sure it's all squared away now, what with Ernie becoming more and more . . .' She didn't finish her thought.

'Sure. I could do that, I suppose.' I was curious as to what the trust said, and if all I did was tell her whether or not she should consult someone else, I figured that wouldn't run afoul of the Bar rules – or at least not much. 'Though you should know that I'm no expert on trust law or anything,' I added, 'so you'd probably want to talk to a trusts and estates attorney in any case.'

Diana smiled. 'I really appreciate it. I have to get going now, but would tomorrow work?'

'Not really. I'm going fishing in the morning with my father, and then I have some errands to run before getting to Gauguin by four, but how about Wednesday? I could come back up here at say, ten o'clock or eleven?'

She thought a moment and then, with a glance toward the house, shook her head. 'No, I'd actually rather meet someplace where we can be alone, if you understand.'

I nodded. 'Okay.'

'I'm going to be in town anyway on Wednesday to meet a friend for lunch. Any chance we could meet someplace afterwards?'

'Sure. How 'bout at Gauguin? I'll be there all afternoon doing some paperwork, so you could just stop by whenever you're done with your meal. Come around to the side door into the kitchen, which will be unlocked.'

Diana smiled and gave me another hug. 'Thank you so much. It means a lot to me. I'll see you Wednesday, then. Oh, and Grace is already here, so you can just go on into the house and find her.'

Grace was in the kitchen talking on the phone, so I made myself comfortable on the living room couch and flipped through the magazines on the coffee table while I waited for her to finish her call: *Time*, *National Geographic*, and *The Progressive Farmer*. I was admiring some photos of shiny new tractors in this last one when something Grace said from the other room caught my attention.

'Well, all I can say is he's a *moron* for not getting the grapes picked before the rains came.' There was a pause as she listened to the person on the other end of the call, and then her voice came back, quieter now – as if she was afraid of being overheard – but far more intense.

I set down the magazine and crept toward the doorway.

'. . . but who knows how long it'll be before I get that money,' she hissed, 'so you need to fix this *now*.'

The other person spoke again, and I heard Grace say, 'Fine,' then swear under her breath. *Uh-oh, she must have ended the call.*

I'd only just made it to the front door when she emerged from the kitchen. 'Sally. I didn't realize you were here.' Her expression struck me as a combination of surprise and anger and perhaps . . . fear? Or was I simply reading that last one into it, based on my hunch that she wouldn't be happy to know I'd overheard her conversation.

'Yeah, I just arrived. I was talking to your mom out on the porch and she said you were inside.' I followed Grace back into the kitchen, where a coffee maker sat puffing steam on the counter. 'Ah, coffee,' I said.

'Uh, yeah. Would you like a cup?'

I'd merely been trying to distract her from fretting about what I might have overheard, but now that I thought about it, the idea of a second cup of coffee seemed pretty good. 'Sure, that would be great. Unless you're in a hurry to get out on the trail.'

'No, that's fine.' She reached for a pair of mugs from the cupboard, poured us each a cup, and gestured toward the fridge. 'Help yourself to milk, if you want. Sugar's on the counter.'

We sat at the rustic wood table in the center of the kitchen, and I asked how she was doing. 'I know from experience that it's good having the closure of the burial,' I said, 'but it's also hard afterwards, the finality of it all.'

'Uh-huh.' Grace stared at a ceramic bowl on the table containing four enormous artichokes that must have weighed over a pound each.

I reached for one of the fat globes and hefted it. 'Are these from the farm? They're gorgeous.'

'I know, aren't they? They're doing the first harvest this week, you know, of the big ones at the top of each plant. Great timing,' she added with a shake of the head.

I set the artichoke back in the blue-and-white glazed bowl. 'So what's going to happen to the farm, now that Neil's not here to help your parents?'

'I have no idea,' she said.

'I only ask because your mom mentioned something about it being subdivided . . .'

Grace frowned as she took a sip of coffee, and I couldn't help thinking perhaps she was buying time to decide how to react. Setting down the cup, she let out a long breath. 'Yeah, my dad had told us a while back that he thought it might be a good time to divide the property up among us kids. I was in favor of it, since Mom and Dad aren't getting any younger – which is why Dad suggested it to begin with – but Mom and Neil were dead set against the idea.'

'Uh-huh,' I said by way of encouragement.

'And while Neil was here to work it, I guess it made some kind of sense to keep the place going as a farm, but now?' She turned her cup around in circles on the wood tabletop, then sighed once more and looked up. 'Anyway, so I gave my parents some literature a ways back from this developer who's interested in the place, but Mom refuses to even look at it.'

'And how does Ryan feel about all this?'

'He agrees with me and wants to sell. It was Ryan who found the developer last year, someone he's worked with at his real estate brokerage, I think. But now I'm not sure what to do. Mom won't listen to reason, and with Dad getting more and more forgetful, well . . .'

'That's a tough one, all right,' I said. 'Because at a certain point, he won't be competent to make the decision whether to divide the property or not.'

'Yup.' Grace finished her coffee and stood. 'C'mon, let's go riding.'

'Good plan. But I need to hit the bathroom first. Meet you down at the barn?'

'Sure thing. I'll start getting the horses saddled.'

As soon as she was gone, I looked around me. Where would I be if I were a developer's advertising pamphlet someone had brought to the house? The only reading materials I could spot anywhere in the living room were the magazines on the coffee table, and there was no desk in the room. *I suppose it could be in the study, if there is one – and if Diana didn't simply throw the pamphlet in the garbage as soon as Grace gave it to her.*

But I'd try the kitchen first, which was where I tended to stash stuff like that. Pulling open drawers, I found placemats and napkins; flatwear; kitchen gadgets; the ubiquitous junk drawer full of tape, string, rubber bands, scissors, pliers, glue, and a light timer; and then, finally, one full of printed material. I pawed quickly through the stack of utility bills, pizza menus, grocery coupons, and sheets of return address labels with pictures of cutesy animals on them, until I came across a glossy pamphlet from Francis A. Sumner & Assoc., Builders. *Yes!*

A glamorous photo of a stately home surrounded by soaring palm trees and hot-pink bougainvillea graced the first page, along with several glowing blurbs from happy customers.

Inside was a picture of Francis Sumner in a business suit and orange hardhat standing proudly in front of a wood-frame structure that looked to be a future apartment building. The handsome face looked vaguely familiar, but I couldn't place where I might have known him from. *Probably a Gauguin customer*, I figured.

Pulling out my phone, I took photos of all four pages of the pamphlet and shoved it back in the drawer. I then headed for the bathroom, since it did seem like a good idea after having just consumed a large cup of coffee.

As I came back into the living room, I spied someone in the kitchen. It was Ryan, and he was leaning against the counter in front of the same drawer where I'd found the developer's pamphlet. *Did he see me riffling through the papers earlier?* I hadn't heard anyone come inside, but he could have already been in the house without my knowing.

'Hello, Sally,' he said. 'Fancy meeting you here.'

'Oh, hi, Ryan. Just had to hit the restroom before going riding with Grace. What brings you by the farm today? Gonna help out with the harvest?'

'Right,' he said with a snort, then pushed off from the counter and crossed to the fridge. Taking a Diet Coke from the top shelf, he popped its top and took a long drink. 'I just stopped by to drop off a couple copies of Neil's death certificate.' Ryan nodded toward some sheets of paper on the counter. 'You can tell Grace to tell Mom when she gets back,' he said, then strode from the kitchen.

I stared after him as he went out the front door. His mood had certainly not improved since Saturday. Maybe he was simply always a sourpuss.

Out of curiosity, I examined one of the death certificates Ryan had left on the counter. The cause of death was listed as 'intracranial pressure/herniation' and 'diffuse axonal brain injury', which I took to mean that he'd died from being bashed on the head with a blunt instrument.

I was about to set the paper back down when I noticed the line for 'Name of Father/Parent'. Earnest Lerici was typed in the space provided.

Interesting, I mused as I made my way down the path to the barn. *So either Neil was indeed his son, or the fact that he wasn't was not in the official record.*

Grace had both horses bridled and was saddling Ralph when I finally walked into the barn.

'What took so long?' she asked. 'Or maybe that's a rude question.'

'Ha, ha,' I said. 'No, I'm fine. I was just talking to Ryan, is all. He brought by some copies of Neil's death certificate and wanted me to let you know.'

'Ah, I thought I heard a car come and go.' Grace kneed Ralph in the stomach as she'd done before, and once he'd let out the air he'd been holding, she tugged the cinch tight and buckled it down. Next, she hefted the cavalry-style saddle at her feet – a sort of combination of an English and western design – onto Amira's back and fastened it snugly.

We mounted and clucked our horses into a walk along the side of the barn, then out toward the artichoke fields. As we made our way past the rows of spiky, gray-green plants, I saw Amy and several other people out between the rows. They all had large basket-like things on their backs, and as I watched, they bent over, tossed an artichoke into their basket, then moved on and repeated the process.

It looked like hard, labor-intensive work. No wonder the pricey vegetables cost what they did.

Riding down the narrow path alongside the fields, I was in the lead, telling Grace about Javier and how the chef had recently become half-owner of Gauguin, when I realized she'd stopped. I reined Ralph in and swiveled around in my saddle to see what had happened. Grace had dismounted and was tightening her cinch, but quickly climbed back aboard and caught up with me.

'I guess Ralph must have taught Amira the trick of blowing out his stomach,' she said with a chuckle, and we continued on.

Once past the cropland, we headed up the same path as before, gaining altitude until we reached a point where you could see all the way south to the Monterey Peninsula and Santa Lucia mountain range beyond. It was breezy but clear, and at least a dozen tiny fishing and sail boats were scattered across the bay.

I was dying to ask about that phone call I'd overheard earlier, and what connection Grace might have with a winery – for that was the sort of grapes I guessed she'd been talking about. But because of what she'd said afterwards about her 'getting that money', I held off. *Had she been talking about her share of the sale of the farm?* If so, it certainly suggested a motive for Neil's death, and was therefore something I was loath to question her about.

Instead, I turned the discussion to Ryan. 'Is he always this grouchy, or is it just me,' I asked as we picked our way across a grassy meadow dotted with gnarled live oak trees.

Grace shook her head, sending her auburn hair flying in the breeze. 'Well, as you know, he was never Mr Congeniality. But he does seem to have gotten worse of late.'

'Like how late?' I asked. 'The past few weeks or the past few months?'

'More like months.'

I urged Ralph into a slow jog to come up next to Grace. 'Did his increased grouchiness by any chance coincide with your dad deciding to subdivide the farm, or maybe shortly thereafter?'

'Why would . . .?' She trailed off and then turned to look at me. 'Wait, you think it might have to do with Mom and Neil's being opposed to the sale?'

'Well, it wouldn't be the first time someone was pissed off at a family member for being the holdout on a property sale.'

Grace frowned, then tugged firmly on her left rein to prevent Amira from munching on a patch of tall, spring grass.

'Any chance Ryan's in need of some ready money right about now?' I pressed on. 'Because if so, that could explain his crankiness, as well as his being annoyed with your mom – which he sure seems to be, if you ask me.'

Was I being too pushy? Eric liked to accuse me of being a 'Miss Marple' when I got too involved in other people's business, and right now would be a prime example of the kind of nosiness he meant.

Grace, however, didn't appear to think so. At least she didn't say anything to suggest she did. If anything, she seemed to like the idea. 'Ryan doesn't share those kinds of details with me,' she said, the hint of a smile playing across her lips, 'but it *would* explain a lot . . .'

She gazed uphill toward where the meadowland met the beginning of the redwood forest, not speaking. Had I just given her a reason to take the heat off herself for Neil's death? Was that why she seemed so pleased with the notion that her brother was the one in need of quick cash?

I was pondering these questions when a sudden movement startled me. Grace had spun the nimble Amira around to face me, and the subtle smile on her face had become a broad grin. 'C'mon,' she said, 'I'll race you back to the farm.' And with a kick to the Arab's gray flanks, she was off downhill, back the way we'd come.

It didn't take any coaxing on my part for Ralph to follow suit. Before I even had a chance to get a firm grip on the reins, he was tearing after his stablemate at a dead run.

Now, unless you've ever ridden a horse along the beach or on a track, you've likely never experienced what it is to be aboard one at a full-on gallop. I never had before that moment.

Ralph had started off at a trot, but broke almost immediately into a canter – which is a bit like being on a rocking horse, with your body swinging forward and back along with the movements of the horse. Within seconds, however, his gait ramped up another notch, and it was as if I were atop a rocket flying down that hill – eerily smooth, but with the speed of a Kentucky Derby thoroughbred.

It would have been okay if not for the numerous ruts in the path and all the rocks and branches scattered everywhere from the winter rains. But as it was, I clutched tightly to the saddle horn, praying the horse wouldn't stumble on the uneven trail. After several useless attempts to rein in the racing horse – who I was sure had taken the bit between his teeth so he wouldn't feel my frantic yanks – I merely did my best to keep my balance and stay aboard.

Once down the hill, where the trail levels out and skirts the artichoke fields, Ralph finally slowed to a trot, and I allowed my hands to loosen their grip on the leather horn. *Thank God . . .*

But I'd let down my guard too soon. At that moment, a flash of white flew out from the side, causing the horse to shy and then rear up, his front legs pawing the air in fear. My right foot slipped from its stirrup, and I grasped frantically for the saddle horn once more. Before I could locate the stirrup, however, Ralph took off again, then shied at something else. This time there was no way I could hang on; the quick swerve was too sudden and severe.

As if in slow motion, I felt my hands lose their grip, and I was thrown from the saddle and through the air.

EIGHT

I hit the ground hard and lay there, the wind knocked out of me, for at least a minute. Then, once my breathing had returned to normal, I tried to figure out if I'd broken anything. Thankfully, I'd landed on my upper arm and not my head. But the sharp pain in that region suggested I might have dislocated the shoulder. Slowly and gingerly, I rolled onto my back, then stretched out my arms.

Okay, so far so good.

The sound of an approaching horse made me flinch. *Ow.* But the involuntary movement, though painful, told me I had neither broken nor dislocated the arm.

'Ohmygod, are you okay?' Grace gazed down at me from above, eyes wide. 'I just saw Ralph go racing by without you and wondered what the hell happened.'

Sitting up, I rubbed my shoulder. 'I think I'm fine. He just got spooked by something, is all. A plastic bag caught in the bushes, it looked like.'

'Oh, no.' She dismounted and crouched next to me. 'You sure you're all right? I could call nine-one-one.'

'Not necessary,' I said, pushing myself to my feet to prove to her – and myself – that this was true. I did feel slightly dizzy, but no way did I want an ambulance coming for me. 'I'll likely have a bruise to show from it, but that seems like all.'

Grace stood back up and touched me on the arm. 'I'm so sorry. That was stupid of me to race you back down like that, since you're not that experienced a rider. I guess I just got carried away, but that's no excuse. And then to have that bag be there. I mean, I knew Ralph was afraid of bags – pretty much all horses are – but I didn't expect any out here. Which I guess is pretty dumb, given how you see them by the side of the road all the time. And with this wind we've been having . . .'

'It's all right,' I said. 'I didn't break any bones or anything, and I get that horseback riding can be dangerous. "Assumption of the risk" and all that, as we lawyers like to say.' But privately, I did agree her actions had been pretty reckless – another popular term in the legal community – though I wasn't going to say as much to her. 'So, is Ralph okay?'

'He ran straight into the barn, which is where I'm sure he still is, hoping for his lunch. But c'mon, let's go make sure.'

We walked the short distance back to the farm, me slightly stiff but happy to have come away from the incident relatively unscathed. It could have been far worse – if I'd landed on my head, or if my foot hadn't come out of the other stirrup and I'd been dragged by the terrified horse. *Ugh.*

Shaking off these thoughts, I glanced over to where Amy and her cohorts were still at their harvest, several rows away. The farmhand had stopped for the moment and was standing still, gazing in our direction. But as soon as she saw me looking her way, she got back to work, bending to slice off another fat artichoke.

Ralph was indeed in the barn, awaiting our return. We got the horses unsaddled and rubbed down, then into their stalls, and Grace tossed them each a pitchfork-full of hay. After we'd stowed away all the tack, she checked her phone.

'I'm afraid I have to go,' she said. 'I'm trying to get all the tax stuff finished for the business this week, and it's turning into kind of a nightmare.'

'I hear ya. We're sweating the Gauguin taxes right now, too.'

Grace stuffed the phone into the back pocket of her jeans and started toward her car – the red Nissan Leaf I'd noticed earlier. 'I'd ask if you want to go riding again sometime – you know, get back on the horse an' all that – but maybe you want to wait a while?'

'Maybe,' I said with a laugh. 'At least until my bruises heal. But we could do lunch sometime.'

'Sounds great.' She gave me a hug, then got into the car and started the engine, waving as she drove down the driveway toward the road.

Once she was out of view, I turned toward my T-Bird, then stopped. With a glance at the farmhouse to make sure no one was watching, I changed direction and headed up the path alongside the artichokes, back the way we'd come on the horses. Amy and her crew were now on the opposite side of the field, far enough away that I doubted they'd notice me snooping around.

After about five minutes, I came to where I thought I remembered Ralph being spooked. That oak tree looked familiar . . . Continuing down the trail, I searched along the edge of the path for something white.

And then, there it was. As I'd suspected, it was a white plastic grocery bag, flapping about in the wind. I knelt to get a closer look. *Could someone have tied it there on purpose?*

But no, I could discern no knot. The bag looked to have simply snagged on the bush all of its own. Shaking my head at my imagined bugaboo, I walked back down the path to my car. I clearly needed to take a chill pill.

At seven o'clock that night, I was standing in Martin Vargas's kitchen, watching him pour bourbon and sweet vermouth into a shaker full of ice. I'd called to tell him about my morning at the farm, and the detective had responded by asking me to dinner.

Since it was a Monday – the day Gauguin is closed, which he no doubt knew – I gladly accepted. It was the first time he'd invited me over, and I was eager to see his place. You can learn a lot about a guy from seeing how he lives.

But I was also pleased that he'd offered to make me dinner. It's not often I get invited over for meals, as folks tend to worry about cooking for someone who does it for a living. Of course what they don't realize is that cooks love food – *all* food. And we also get really sick of cooking. So you can make pretty much anything, from a fancy mushroom and chèvre soufflé to a simple bean and cheese burrito, and I'll think it's delicious and will be wildly appreciative that you took the time to prepare it for me.

Though with my sense of smell having gone AWOL, it wasn't likely I'd find anything I ate tonight 'delicious'. But then again, neither would it be a problem if he were to make something I disliked, such as kidneys or liver and onions.

Martin strained our Manhattans into a pair of chilled Martini glasses, dropped a neon-red maraschino cherry into each, and handed me mine.

I raised my glass in a toast. '*Cin cin!*'

'Okay,' he said once we'd clinked glasses, 'let's sit and enjoy our cocktails for a while before I finish making dinner, and you can tell me all about your morning.' I'd been eager to launch immediately into my account as soon as I'd arrived, but he'd insisted I hold off until he made our drinks.

I followed him into the living room and checked out the décor while I got settled on the couch. The room was cozy without being cute or fussy. Comfy furniture, books and magazines strewn about, and a large-but-not-gargantuan TV on a wall where it didn't dominate, leaving the fireplace and mantel as the focus of the space.

'So you went riding again with Grace this morning, right?' Martin prompted me.

'Uh-huh. Though riding and falling, is more like it.'

'Oh?' He looked up with concern.

'No, it's okay,' I said with a wave of the hand. 'I escaped the incident with mere bruises. But I'll get to that in a minute.'

I sipped from my stemmed glass, set it on the teak coffee table, and recounted my story in chronological order – starting with Diana asking me to take a look at the family trust, then moving on to overhearing Grace's phone conversation. 'So I'm thinking that, one, she must be involved with a winery in some way, and two, she's in need of cash right now.'

Vargas got up and walked to the kitchen, returning with a pad of paper and a pen. 'You don't mind if I take some notes, do you?' I shook my head, and he scribbled a few lines onto the paper. 'Go on,' he said, looking up.

'Okay . . . Well, so then I asked her about the property subdivision, and—'

'You asked about it right after that phone conversation?' he interrupted me.

'No,' I answered, a little annoyed that he'd think I was so inexpert an investigator as to do that. 'I got her talking about the farm first, and then acted like I'd just remembered her mom telling me about the division. And she affirmed what Diana had said, that she – the mom – and Neil were opposed to it but that

Grace and Ryan were in favor. She also told me she'd given her mom some information about this developer Ryan knows who's interested in the property, but she wouldn't even look at it.'

Vargas took a few more notes, then sipped from his Manhattan. 'You know the developer's name?' he asked.

'I do indeed. It's Francis A. Sumner, which is easy to remember, since it's so much like Francis Albert Sinatra.'

His blank look told me he was not a big fan of old-school jazz vocals.

'Okay, maybe not so easy for some,' I said with a laugh. 'But I can do better than a name.' I pulled out my phone to show him the pictures I'd taken of the company's advertising pamphlet. 'I found it in the kitchen when I was at the farm. Here, I'll text the photos to you.'

'Great. I can contact him to see if he knows anything.'

Next I told Martin about my horse shying and bucking me off during our ride.

'Are you suggesting someone did it on purpose?' he asked.

'Well, even though Grace seemed super worried and apologetic about what happened, I have to say that was my immediate thought.'

'So what, you think she put the bag there before you went riding?'

'No, I don't. I mean, I initially worried she might have, 'cause she did stop and get off her horse at one point early on in the ride, and I didn't see exactly what she was doing. And then she raced me back to the barn, knowing the horse I was on would take off like a Kentucky Derby winner, which was pretty reckless – as well as obnoxious. But then, after Grace had left the farm, I went back to the spot where it happened and it looked like the bag had just snagged there all on its own. It wasn't tied with a knot or anything. I guess I was just a little paranoid because of, well . . .'

'Okay, Sally. Why would anyone have possibly wanted to hurt you?' Martin fixed me with a stern look, then shook his head. 'Never mind. I think I can guess why. So tell me, what exactly *have* you been doing over there at the farm?'

'Nothing,' I said, my defensiveness causing my voice to rise in pitch. He continued to eyeball me. 'Okay . . . so maybe I did snoop around a little to find that pamphlet.'

'Uh-huh . . .'

'And maybe Ryan could have seen me doing the snooping . . .'

He let out an exaggerated sigh. 'I should have known I was creating a monster when I asked you to keep your ears open – which is *all* I asked you to do.' Drinking down the last of his cocktail, Martin started to stand.

'Wait, there's one more thing,' I said, and he plopped back down. 'There's a picture in my high school yearbook of Neil and Pete – you know, the guy who owns the Crab Shack and who ended up winning first prize in the cook-off because of Neil's death – when the two of them were sophomores. They were on the same swim team, and in the group photo they're standing with their arms around each other and huge smiles on their faces.'

'What, you think they were involved?'

'No, no, I'm not saying that. A lot of the guys on the team had their arms around each other. It's the fact that they were obviously friends back at that time. But then, two years later in their senior year, the photo of Pete has been rubbed out in Neil's yearbook, and someone's drawn Xs over his eyes and given him devil's horns. Did you see the yearbook at the reception? It was sitting there on the table with all the photos of Neil.'

Martin shook his head. 'No, I didn't look at it. Sounds like it's probably just high school stuff, but I'll keep it in mind. Thanks.' He stood once more. 'Hungry?'

'Always,' I said.

'I know you probably won't be able to taste it, but I figure you gotta eat, and who knows? Maybe tonight is the night, and your smell will return in response to my marvelous cooking.'

I appreciated his optimism – about both himself and me. Maybe it would rub off, and I'd start believing my smell would indeed return sometime soon.

He turned on the fire under a cast iron skillet sitting atop the stove, waited for it to heat, then added a drizzle of olive oil and a chunk of butter. While this was melting, he cracked black pepper onto a pair of plump tenderloin steaks lying on a plate. 'I'm making Steak Diane,' he said. 'My mom used to serve it back in the seventies when I was a little kid and I always loved it. And it's something I figured wouldn't be too difficult to prepare, so I wouldn't mess it up.'

'Yum,' I replied. But what I was thinking was: *Steak Diane – that's a serious 'date' dinner.* Was this getting more serious? Did I *want* it to get more serious?

Once he'd pan-fried the steaks (me instructing when to flip them and when to pull them out so they were still a juicy medium-rare), I watched as he consulted his cookbook and added more butter and some chopped shallots to the pan, sautéed these a while, then carefully measured and added brandy, Dijon mustard, Worcestershire sauce, and heavy cream.

I could tell Martin was slightly nervous having me watch, but also proud at the same time. And I got the feeling that, although he liked to cook, he was still relatively new at it. Had he been involved with someone before who'd done the cooking, and now he was learning it himself, being single once again? He hadn't talked about an ex, but then again, I hadn't talked to him much about Eric.

Once he'd plated up our dinners – roasted baby potatoes sprinkled with parsley, a tossed spinach salad, and the filet mignon steaks with the creamy sauce spooned over them – we sat down to eat.

'And how is it?' Martin asked after I'd taken a few bites. 'Can you taste anything?' The eagerness in his eyes was apparent. He so wanted it to be his cooking that triggered my return to a normal sensory life.

'I think maybe I can,' I lied. 'At least the tang of the mustard and the lemon you finished the sauce with, anyway.' And although I didn't in fact taste a thing, I could feel the marbled fat of the meat and the creaminess of the sauce on the roof of my mouth, and I thought I might even sense a slight prick of acid on the sides of my tongue. So maybe my sense of smell *was* returning. I could always hope.

After dinner, we sat again in the living room and watched an episode of *The Good Fight*. This time, Martin sat next to me on the couch and, after a few minutes, draped his arm over my shoulder. When I didn't move or object, he scooted closer and we snuggled together until the end of the show.

I liked it, but I did also feel a bit like a high schooler on a first date.

And then when I told him I should be heading home, we stood at the front door for a long while, me griping about how unrealistic lawyer shows always seem to be.

'Not that they do much better with cops,' Martin said. 'But really, who wants to watch a TV show about the real working life of a litigator or a detective. Boring.'

'True,' I agreed, then pulled out my phone to check the time. 'Look, I really do have to get going,' I said. 'I have to get up at six tomorrow to go fishing with my dad.'

'All right.' He smiled awkwardly. 'Um, is it okay if I kiss you goodnight?'

'Uh, sure.'

Totally like high school.

He leaned over and kissed me gently on the lips. It was lingering but not long. And really nice.

His smile now more confident, he stepped back and nodded. 'Whew. Glad we finally got that out of the way.'

'Yeah, me too,' I said with a laugh. 'So, see you soon, I hope?'

'Definitely.'

Martin closed the door and I walked out to my car, grinning like a sixteen-year-old.

NINE

After laying awake much of the night, however, worrying whether or not Martin and I were moving too fast – or whether we should even be 'moving' at all – my mood had changed. Gone was the giddy teenager, having been replaced by the over-thinking, over-anxious grown-up.

It was still dark at six thirty the next morning when I arrived at Solari's, but by the time Dad and I had filled his Boston Whaler with all our gear, dragged the small boat on a dolly over to the davit and lowered it into the water, the low sun was casting its pale yellow light across the inky-dark waters of the bay.

Do I really have doubts about getting involved with Martin? I wondered as I zipped my fleece-lined jacket up against the chill of the early-spring morning, then pulled on a life vest. *Or is this more about Eric, and what he told me the other day about Gayle and him having problems?*

The two of us got settled, Dad on the bench where he could man the steering wheel, me perched atop the tiny seat on the prow, facing backwards. He yanked on the outboard's string to power up the motor, then swung the skiff around, cast off, and sped along the side of the wharf till reaching its end. We then turned due south, toward Monterey, heading for one of the two submarine ridges that occur about a mile offshore from Santa Cruz.

Although the fishing season had opened only a few days earlier on April first, there weren't many boats out on the water besides us, this being a weekday. But Solari's is closed on Tuesdays, and – since I didn't have to be at Gauguin till the afternoon – I'd agreed to tag along with my dad. And who knew, maybe we'd snag a nice-sized lingcod I could use tonight at the restaurant.

It was too loud to talk, what with the motor going and the wind, so for the twenty minutes it took to reach the rocky shelf where the rockfish and lingcod like to hang out, I continued to ponder what had happened last night.

I did truly enjoy Martin's company. He was smart, funny, and relatively easy-going – for a detective, at least – and he seemed to truly care about me.

Tasting the saltwater spray on my lips, I thought back to the kiss we'd shared on his doorstep. If he'd been a lousy kisser, that would have been a dealbreaker, for sure. And part of me had wanted that to be the case. It would have made things so much easier. But then he had to go and prove he actually had a fair amount of talent in that department. *Damn.*

I pulled the blanket from the bottom of the boat and wrapped it around my legs, gazing back at the cliffs and Boardwalk receding into the distance. Sitting as I was at the prow of the tiny boat, the ride was bumpy as we cruised through the choppy water. But having been out on Dad's skiff countless times since childhood, I knew how to keep my seat on my small perch and wasn't too worried about getting seasick. (Though, to be on the safe side, I had forsaken any breakfast that morning.)

I was wondering just how bad a spat Eric and Gayle had had last week at Gauguin, and whether they'd fully made up yet, when Dad startled me from my thoughts by shutting off the motor. We glided to a stop. 'This is good,' he said and reached for his tackle box.

The quiet after the roar of the gasoline-powered motor was a relief and, before setting up my own rig, I allowed myself to listen to the sounds of the ocean: the water slapping against the sides of the boat; the call of a seagull soaring overhead.

We were using fresh squid as bait, with two hooks weighted down by eight-ounce bullet sinkers. Since the rockfish and lingcod we were after liked to hang out at the rocky shelf beneath us, the idea was that you'd cast down-drift from the boat and then jig the line up and down constantly, both to draw the interest of the fish but also to keep from getting caught up on the rocks and losing your line.

For some folks, talking is frowned upon while fishing. But not with my dad. 'Since I'm the one who took you all the way out here,' he likes to say, 'it's your job to keep me entertained. The fish sure aren't gonna hear us through all that water.'

So as soon as Dad had his hooks baited and weights attached, he tossed the line out from the boat, then turned to me and asked, 'What's going on with your investigation?'

'*My* investigation. Right.' It was still bizarre having not only Vargas, but also my father encouraging me to stick my nose into a murder case. I dropped my line into the steel-blue water and watched as the weights sank rapidly and disappeared.

'It's going okay,' I said, buying time to decide what exactly to tell him. I didn't want to talk about my suspicions regarding Ryan and Grace, that was for sure.

'I found out the name of this developer, Francis Sumner, who's hot to buy the farm,' I said instead. 'Detective Vargas thinks he might be a suspect, since I gather Neil was opposed to the sale, so he's going to talk to the guy.'

This was treading on dangerous territory, for if my father followed the train of thought to its logical conclusion, he'd realize that this would make the other siblings suspects as well. But simply hearing another name was enough to keep Dad from going down that path.

'That's great, hon,' he said, smiling as he reeled in his line, checked that the squid was still attached, then cast once again.

'And also, there's still that farmhand, Amy. The one who was helping Neil at his booth that day at the cook-off. I need to find out if they were more than just friends, 'cause if so, that for sure puts her in the running.'

My father nodded. 'Love gone awry can only lead to bad results,' he said, gazing out to where the twin smoke stacks of the Moss Landing power plant marked the halfway point between Santa Cruz and Monterey.

'Uh-huh.' *Could he be referring to himself and Diana?* I cleared my throat. 'And then of course there's Pete Ferrari, too.' I told him about the photos I'd seen in the two yearbooks, and my theory that Neil and Pete had been good friends but later had some kind of falling-out.

'Maybe we should go there for lunch,' Dad said, a devious glint in his eye. 'To the Crab Shack. We could do a little father-daughter sleuthing together.'

'Sounds good to me. I'll be ready for a big lunch after all this.'

'And I was thinking I could invite Abby to join us, if that'd be okay with you.'

'Sure, that would be fun. I really like Abby, and would like to get to know—' I was interrupted by a hard jerk on my line.

'I think you got a big one!' Dad jumped up and reached for the gaff as I let the spinner go, allowing the fish to take the bait and run with it, lest it break the line. I let it go for a while, then started to reel it in.

'He's getting tired,' I said as the line went taut again, but less so than before.

Soon, an enormous gray fish emerged, splashing about in the water. Dad secured its large, ugly head with the steel hook and dropped it into the boat. It was a lingcod and – notwithstanding the bulging eyes and gaping, Mick Jagger mouth – would make for some delicious specials tonight at Gauguin, with its tender, flaky flesh. Javier would be thrilled.

I unhooked the beast and held it up against the measuring tape affixed to the inside of the Boston Whaler to ensure it met the twenty-two inch requirement. 'Twenty-seven,' I said with a grin and laid it on the ice in our cooler. 'Now I need to get one for you.' The bag limit for lingcod is one each, so if there were no more than two discovered in our boat by Fish and Game, we'd be fine, even if I were the one to catch the second fish as well.

'I can catch my own, thank you very much,' he responded, checking his bait once again.

We fished in silence for a while, Dad now seriously in the competition, his jaw set and brow furrowed. It was clear he did not want to get skunked in front of his daughter on his first day fishing this season.

After about ten minutes he finally got a bite. 'All right!' I said as he pulled out a bright orange rockfish. 'A canary!'

'Yeah.' He extricated the hook from its mouth and dropped the fish on top of my much larger lingcod.

After Dad had caught two more rockfish and I nothing more, his mood improved. 'Okay, you're supposed to be entertaining me,' he said, 'so what're we gonna talk about?'

'Tell me about you and Diana.'

I hadn't intended to bring her up, but since it's what I had been thinking about right when he spoke, it just came out.

Dad opened his mouth as if to speak, then shut it again, reminding me of one of the fish sitting in our cooler. He jigged his line several times, then turned to me with a frown. 'What do you mean?'

'It's just that it seems a little strange, how you never told me about being friends with her back when I used to hang out with Grace all the time. And now you're acting weird whenever her name comes up. So, what gives? Were you two involved or something?'

He let out a laugh, but it wasn't terribly convincing.

'C'mon, you can tell me. I don't care what you did before you met Mom.'

'There's nothing to talk about,' he said, not bothering to keep the impatience from his voice. 'Let's move on to something else. How's it working out having Javier as co-owner of Gauguin?'

And that was it. No admission, no denial, and – most important to me – no clarification that whatever *might* have happened between Diana and him had occurred before he got involved with my mom.

An hour and a half later, we were back on the wharf, seated at the corner table of Pete's Crab Shack and perusing the offerings on their plastic-coated menus.

'I'm gonna try their crab sandwich,' Dad said, leaning back in his chair. He stared at a spot on the wall behind me, then laughed. 'Ha! See that?'

'What?' I swiveled around to look where he was pointing and observed that Pete had hung his first-place Artichoke Cook-Off plaque on the wall for all to admire. 'No different than you,' I said, turning back around. 'Though I see Pete waited to get his name engraved on it. He's sharing first place with Neil and Amy, you know.'

'Yeah, I heard.' Dad looked up with a smile and waved to Abby, who stood at the restaurant door.

'Hi, guys.' She crossed to our table, kissed my father lightly on the lips and gave me a hug and a peck on the cheek, then pulled out the chair next to Dad. 'Thanks for inviting me. It smells heavenly in here. What are you all having?'

'I'm going for the crab sandwich, to see how it compares to mine,' Dad said.

'That sounds good to me, too,' I said.

Abby picked up a menu and studied it for a moment. 'I think I'll have the Shrimp Louie. So how was fishing?'

'Sally got a lingcod and a rockfish and I got four rockfish.'

'So you beat out your daughter, then.' She flashed me a grin which I took to mean: I get that it's the *kind* of fish more than the numbers that truly counts.

'Right,' was all Dad said in response.

A deep voice made us all look up. 'I thought that was you, Mario. What brings you over here to the competition?'

Pete was wearing bright red chef's pants and a long-sleeved T-shirt bearing the logo of some rock band I didn't recognize, over which he'd tied a white apron, now spattered with grease. He turned toward me. 'Hullo, Sally. How's it going?'

'Sally and me just got back from fishing, and thought we'd treat ourselves to some of your award-winning food.' Dad nodded toward the plaque on the wall and chuckled.

Pete returned his smile. 'You can laugh all you want, but I say it's better to win the People's Choice than the Judges' Award, since it's "the people" who patronize my restaurant. And by the way, you'll be interested to hear that my covers have been up *big time* ever since that article in the paper about the winners last week.'

After he'd taken our orders and headed across the room to another table, Dad turned to me. 'See?' he said in a stage whisper. 'There's a motive for you. Financial gain.'

I just shrugged. 'Maybe.'

'Are you talking about that man who was killed at the cook-off?' Abby asked, then clapped a hand over her mouth. 'Oops. I guess I shouldn't say that so loud.'

Dad nodded. 'Yeah,' he said, still keeping his voice low. 'And Sally and I think Pete here is a likely suspect, since he ended up getting first place only because of Neil's death.'

'Whoa.' Abby's eyes grew large as she watched the lanky Crab Shack owner head back to the kitchen. 'I actually know

Neil's sister-in-law,' she said, leaning forward. 'Ryan's wife, Cynthia.'

'Really?' Dad and I said in unison.

'Uh-huh. She's an agent with the same realtor that I work for. She's been there like ten years and has been super helpful to me since I moved up here to Santa Cruz last summer.'

Interesting, I thought. And potentially quite useful.

Once our plates arrived, we set about applying mayonnaise, salad dressing, and Louisiana hot sauce to our lunches. Dad examined his crab sandwich with an expert's eye before taking a bite.

'How is it?' I asked.

He chewed slowly, then grunted. 'It's okay. Not as good as mine, though. It could use a little more lemon and cayenne pepper. And the bread – which is obviously store-bought – seems a little stale.'

I tried mine, and as he watched intently to see my reaction, I realized I'd never told my dad about the loss of my sense of smell. 'Uh, you're right about the bread,' I said. 'But as for the lemon and cayenne, I'm not too sure. That sinus infection I had a while back did a number on me and I can't smell – or taste – a thing.'

'Oh, no. That's awful, hon. I hope it gets back to normal soon.'

You and me both.

'Well, this salad is just yummy,' Abby said, spearing a plump shrimp and dipping it in her ramekin of Louie dressing. Pete, who'd come back out to deliver a plate of deep-fried clams to the next table over, looked up with a grin at Abby's comment.

I waited until Dad excused himself to go to the restroom outside in the passageway a few minutes later, then leaned across the table once more. 'I was wondering if maybe you could help me with something,' I said to Abby.

'Sure. Whatever you want. Does it have anything to do with . . .?' She nodded her head in the direction of the kitchen. 'You know.'

'Kind of,' I said. 'But you have to promise not to tell my dad, 'cause he doesn't want me to get too involved in all of this.'

This wasn't an out-and-out lie, since it was technically true that Dad wouldn't want me to get *too* involved in the case. But I admit that it was a bit of a fudge.

Abby nodded vigorously. 'Absolutely. I promise.'

'Okay, here's the thing. I think there's something weird going on with the Lerici family, and have this feeling it might be connected to Neil's death.'

She sucked in her breath. 'You think one of them killed him?'

'No, I'm not saying that, but I do think it could be relevant. Like, for instance, Ryan has been acting really . . .' I searched for the right word. 'Well, like a total jerk, lately. I mean, I've known the guy since high school and he was never super warm or anything, but in the past few months, he's gotten a lot worse.'

Abby was nodding again. 'That's exactly what Cynthia says. In fact, she's been bitching to me about him even more than usual lately. She seems really pissed off at the guy, but I don't know exactly why.' She frowned and gazed out the window toward Lighthouse Point across the inlet from the wharf. 'Oh, hey,' she said, turning back and touching me on the wrist. 'There's this real estate business mixer this Friday that Cynthia will for sure be at. You could come with me and I could introduce you, if you wanted.'

'Really? That would be terrific. But won't Ryan be there, too, since he's also a realtor?'

'I doubt it. He almost never attends those things. And if he is, we'll just get Cynthia alone while he schmoozes with all the guys. Oops, here comes Mario.' Abby flashed me a conspiratorial grin. 'I'll text you later,' she mouthed as my dad sat back down.

'What are you gals up to?' he asked.

'Oh, nothing. Just talking about *you*, is all,' Abby said, reaching out to squeeze him on the shoulder.

'Well, in that case, maybe I should leave again. As long as it's good, that is.'

She graced him with a flirtatious grin. 'What else could it be?'

I watched the romantic couple with amusement, happy that my father was so happy. But my mind was mostly elsewhere: *Now, how can I convince Javier to trade nights with me this Friday?*

TEN

The next afternoon, I was up in the Gauguin office going over some paperwork for our bookkeeper, Shanti, to pass along to the guy who does our taxes. I would have preferred to have had all the Gauguin tax forms already filed by now, but because of the change in ownership of the restaurant from sole proprietor to partnership the previous December, the process had ended up being slightly different – as well as more complicated – this year. As a result, several of the documents we'd provided to the accountant had been incorrectly filled out, which errors he'd only caught a few days earlier. To save money, I'd agreed to slog through the paperwork myself to correct the mistakes, rather than pay him to do it.

I was sorting through a stack of forms, ensuring that each one correctly stated the name of our new partnership rather than merely my name, when Tomás stuck his head through the office door. 'There's a woman here to see you,' the prep cook said. 'She says you're expecting her?'

'Oh, right. That'll be Diana. Thanks.'

I'd forgotten about her coming over today. Nothing like scintillating tax work to keep one's mind off the more mundane issues of life.

I found her in the *garde manger*, staring at the containers of food lining the shelves above the stainless steel countertop. 'What do you use the pickled mango for?' she asked when I came into the small room used for our cold food and appetizer prep.

'We serve it with a cold noodle salad that has a sort of Hawaiian-Japanese bent.'

'Oooo. Sounds delicious.'

'It is. You should come in sometime when we're open and try it.' I gestured toward the front of the house. 'How about we go sit where we can talk?'

Diana followed me through the kitchen and wait station into

the Gauguin dining room, where we took a seat at one of the tables near the bar that hadn't yet been set for dinner.

'You're probably pretty busy so I suppose we should get straight to it,' she said, digging into the canvas bag she held. She pulled out a manila envelope and handed it to me.

'Lerici Family Trust' was written on the front. I extracted the sheaf of papers, found a table of contents on page two, and flipped to the section entitled 'Distribution of Property'.

'"Upon death of Settlor",' I read aloud, '"or of last surviving Settlor, if more than one" – you and Ernie are the settlors, so that means you get everything if Ernie dies first, and vice versa – "the Trust assets shall be distributed in equal proportion or allocable amounts to the Beneficiaries". Yada yada . . . Here, lemme see who's listed as the beneficiaries.'

Turning back several pages, I read that paragraph over to myself. 'Okay, it specifies your three children by name as the beneficiaries, but that if any of them are deceased at the time of the distribution, then their children will take their place.' I set the trust down on the table. 'So, in other words, since Neil has no kids . . . right?'

'Not as far as I know,' Diana said.

'Then all the trust property will be divided between Ryan and Grace, if you and Ernie both predecease them.' I tapped a finger on the document. 'As I said, I'm no trusts and estates expert, but I don't see anything obviously wrong with this one. Here . . .' I turned to the last page to make sure the document had been signed, dated, and notarized. 'Yeah, it looks valid to me. And I actually know this guy who drew it up, and he's a perfectly competent lawyer, so I'm guessing it's probably fine. Though, as I said before, you really should have an expert take a look at it to be sure.'

Diana picked up the trust and stared at the first page. 'So that means – assuming you're right that it is valid – that Ernie can't divide the farm up now without my permission? That it won't be . . . distributed until we're both dead, right?'

'No, not necessarily.'

Her face fell.

'Look, there's no list of what comprises the trust corpus attached to this. You know, what property has been put into the trust. But I'm guessing it consists of your community property, whatever you and Ernie own in common.'

'Right . . .'

'But from what he told me that day after Neil's burial, Ernie inherited the farm before you two married, which would make it his own *separate* property. Unless he ever converted it to community property.'

She was shaking her head. 'If so, he never told me. But I never even thought about it. He always referred to it as "our" farm.'

'Well, that would be the first thing to find out, then,' I said. 'Because if the farm *is* separate property that isn't part of the trust, then he can do whatever he wants with it, irrespective of what this says.'

Diana sank deeper into her chair and stared at the woodblock print of a sugar cane plant on the wall. 'So now with Neil gone,' she said, 'they'll just sell to that developer and it'll all be gone.'

'But couldn't they have done that anyway, even if he were alive? Sell their two-thirds share to the developer?'

She shook her head and sat back up. 'No. It's apparently all or nothing. The guy doesn't want just part of the land. So as long as Neil was alive, he was able to keep the sale from happening.' A tear was sliding down Diana's cheek and she wiped it off impatiently.

Neither of us spoke. She was likely digesting the bad news I'd borne her, but I was musing how this information made it all the more likely that either Ryan, Grace, or the developer had been the one who killed Neil. *Or maybe more than one of them had been in it together.*

'So where will you live if it does happen?' I asked after a bit. 'Has Ernie even thought about that?'

'Oh, don't worry. He's not so far gone that he's going to make us live out of our truck or anything,' she said with a harsh laugh. 'We own an investment property here in town, a three-bedroom house out near Natural Bridges. And I know that *it's* community property, since we bought it together about twenty years ago. His idea is that we'll give notice to the tenants and move there, closer to the stores and such, to make our lives easier.'

She gathered up the trust, slid it back into its envelope, and stood to go. 'I do thank you for your time, and for being so kind to me. I know you're a busy woman.'

'Well, it's the least I could do for Grace's mom. And for such a good friend of my father's,' I added, searching her face for any reaction.

Her only response was a sad smile, however, as she followed me back through the kitchen and the *garde manger* to the restaurant's side door. 'Thank you again,' she said, and gave me a tight hug.

I watched her walk slowly across the parking lot to her car. *What on earth could have gone on between her and my father to make them both so damn taciturn about whatever it was?*

I hadn't heard from Grace since being bucked off Ralph three days earlier, but on Thursday morning I got a text from her asking if she could take me to lunch that day. *It's the least I can do to try to make it up to you*, she wrote.

I'm never one to pass up a free meal! I responded and, after a few back-and-forths, we decided to drive up to Davenport for the meal, in the hopes of spotting some whales along the way.

I'd just set my phone down and was fetching a second cup of coffee when it rang out with the strains of Puccini's '*Recondita armonia*' from *Tosca*. I grabbed the phone and swiped right.

'Hi, Dad.'

My father had been named after Mario, the tenor who sings this aria, by his opera-loving father, Salvatore (after whom I'd been named), so I thought it an appropriate ringtone. But it's also a gorgeous melody, and therefore had made being awakened by my father early in the morning back when I still worked at Solari's a little more palatable.

'What's up?' I asked, pouring half-and-half into my mug.

'I thought you might like to hear about who I saw last night. And with *whom*.'

'Oh, yeah? Do tell,' I said.

'So Abby and I went out last night, and—'

'Wait. Didn't you have to work?'

'If you'd just let me finish,' Dad said, sounding like the exasperated father who'd been interrupted countless times by his daughter that he was, 'I'll tell you. We closed pretty early last night since it was so slow, so I called her to see if she wanted to go out for a drink.'

This was not the Dad I knew. He never went out after work. Chefs may be known for their late hours and decadent lifestyle, but not my father. He liked to go home as soon as possible, watch a little late-night TV, then hit the sack.

His new love life was certainly having an effect on what had been, up till now, his normal patterns.

'Where'd you go?' I asked, curious about which watering hole my father would pick for late-night drinks.

'That place on Cedar Street, down from Gauguin,' he said. 'Abby says it's one of the only places she likes that stays open past eleven. Anyway, that's not the point. The point is, I saw that woman Amy who works at the Lerici farm there. And she was with a *guy*.'

'Oh, yeah?'

'Yeah. And from the way they were cuddling and smooching right there in front of the whole wide world, it didn't look like they were just friends, either.' The distaste in his voice was apparent.

I knew my father loathed PDAs – public displays of affection – and I couldn't say I was thrilled with them either. But in this case I didn't mind. I hadn't had to watch it, for one thing. But also, it likely provided an answer to the question I'd had as to whether Amy and Neil had been involved.

Dad was continuing with his story. 'They were talking real loud, too, which was also annoying. Except it did make it easy to eavesdrop. And I heard the guy say something about a trip they'd taken together to Baja. Sounded like it was maybe last summer, from the way he was talking about how hot and muggy it was.'

Make that *probably* provided the answer to my question. If you're making out in a bar late at night and talking about a trip you took together to Mexico last year, it's a good bet you're romantically involved, and have been for a while.

'Well, that puts a big damper on my theory that she bashed Neil in the head out of anger that he'd broken up with her, unless she's been carrying on two separate relationships. What's this guy she was with look like, anyway?'

'I dunno . . .' Dad said. 'He had light-colored hair, with this short, trendy-looking cut. Normal looking face, average build. They were sitting down, so I don't know how tall he was. There wasn't really anything to make him stand out in a crowd.'

'Was he good looking?'

'I guess you could say so. I mean, he didn't have six chins or drool or anything like that. But that's not really my thing, checking out other men to see if they're handsome or not.'

I laughed. 'You're never going to amount to much of a sleuth, Dad, if you don't pay more attention to the people you're spying on – even if they are men.' I sipped from my coffee as I thought a moment. 'But you are sure that it was Amy you saw, the same woman who was working at the booth next to mine at the Artichoke Cook-Off?'

'Totally sure. I *did* get a good look at her. And she was even wearing that same A's cap she had on that day at the cook-off.'

I rolled my eyes, though Dad couldn't see my reaction over the phone. Of course he'd checked *her* out. Guys were so damn predictable.

'Okay, well thanks for calling and letting me know. Even if it isn't that great for our case, it's still good to have the intel.'

A little before noon, I pulled into the Lerici property for my lunch date with Grace. Her car wasn't there yet, but Amy's black SUV was parked in front of the farmhouse. Leaving the two cars, I walked down to the barn in the hopes of locating the farmhand. Not finding her there, I walked out toward the artichoke fields, where I spied her on the dirt track next to the field, talking in Spanish to a skinny young man in faded jeans, a black sweatshirt, and a red baseball cap.

I waited till they'd finished speaking and the man had climbed aboard the tractor parked next to them and driven off, then approached Amy.

'Hi,' she said. 'You looking for Diana?'

'No, I'm meeting Grace here and we're gonna drive up to Davenport together for lunch.'

'Ah. Well, I haven't seen her all morning, so I can't help you there.'

She turned to go, but stopped when I spoke again. 'So I saw

you at the bar last night.' A little white lie wouldn't hurt anyone, now would it?

'Oh?' Her eyes conveyed both suspicion and displeasure.

'Uh-huh. But I didn't want to interrupt to say hi, since it looked like you two were having a lot of fun.' I waggled my eyebrows, hoping to make this seem like 'girl talk', but the move probably came across as more of a Groucho Marx-style facial tic.

It seemed to work, however, as her expression softened and her body seemed to relax. Encouraged, I went on. 'Not bad looking, the guy.'

Amy smiled, and though it was hard to be sure in the bright sunlight, it looked as if she might be blushing. 'Yeah, he is,' she said, then held out her left hand. A ring with a large stone – a diamond, I guessed, though what I don't know about precious stones could fill a legal treatise-sized tome – glinted in the sunlight. 'We got engaged just last night.'

'Congratulations!' I said. 'When's the wedding?'

'Not till this September. Which is a good thing, because I know how complicated it can be, planning an event like that.'

'Yeah, you're so right. I helped my dad throw a big dinner last fall, and it was a huge deal. Where are you thinking of having it?'

She nodded toward the farmhouse. 'Well, we haven't yet decided for sure, but I'm actually hoping to have it here. That grassy area in front of the house would be perfect for the ceremony, with the view of the hills behind. And there's plenty of parking, and a nice kitchen to use for the prep work and cooking.'

'Uh, yeah,' I said. 'That would be great.'

But as she headed out to the field to join the other workers, I wondered if she was aware that the farm might not even belong to the Lerici family come September.

More importantly, however, I also wondered how this might change my feelings about Amy as a suspect. From what my dad had reported to me this morning, I'd already known she'd had a beau for some time. But now I knew how very serious that relationship was. Did this new information go to prove her innocence, or – if she *had* been involved in an affair with Neil – did it do exactly the opposite?

ELEVEN

Two hours later, Grace and I were standing on the cliff at Davenport, gazing out at the Pacific Ocean in search of whales. We'd stuffed ourselves on humongous burgers accompanied by mounds of French fries at the local bakery/bar & grill and I, for one, was feeling like I could really use a nap.

'Is that one?' Grace shielded her eyes from the sun and pointed out to sea.

'Where?'

'There,' she said, 'about a hundred yards off shore.'

I squinted at the area where she was pointing, and then we both shrieked as a massive body erupted from the water, executed a mid-air twist, and landed on its back with a spectacular splash.

'Ohmygod, it's a humpback!' I shouted. 'How cool is that?'

Davenport was founded as a whaling community in the late 1800s by an enterprising ship captain of the same name, and the tiny town is now, not surprisingly, one of the premier whale-watching spots in Northern California. From January through May, adult gray whales and their calves migrate north from Mexico to Alaska, but the humpback whales don't appear in these parts until April, when they come to feed on the schools of anchovies, sardines, and krill that populate the Monterey Bay. Which meant we were seeing one of the earliest arrivals this season of the acrobatic humpback contingent of the migratory marine mammals.

After ten minutes we'd spotted no further sign of whales, so we turned away from the cliff and headed for my T-Bird, parked across the street at the restaurant, to drive back down to Santa Cruz. Grace had begged to ride up to Davenport in the car, and I'd been happy to show off the classic convertible, cruising up the coast with the top down and KPIG radio blaring Lucinda Williams, Tom Petty, and the Cowboy Junkies from its tinny speakers.

During the drive up the coast on the way to our lunch, I had taken the opportunity to ask Grace about Pete Ferrari. 'My dad and I ate at the Crab Shack the other day,' I told her, 'and it got me thinking about him and Neil being in the same grade in school. Were they friends, do you know?'

'They were for a while,' she said. 'They were both really into swimming, on the school team an' all, and Pete used to come over to the farm all the time. Kind of like you and me, except they did guy stuff instead of ride horses. You know, play video games and ride their BMX bikes around the property.'

'But then they had some kind of falling out?'

Grace turned to face me, her head tilted. 'Yeah. But how do you know that?'

'I was looking through Neil's yearbook at his celebration of life, and Pete's senior portrait had been rubbed out and replaced with devil's horns and Xs for his eyes. I figured that for Neil to have done that, he must have been pretty pissed at Pete for something.'

'Huh. I didn't see that.' She chewed a nail as she stared out at a herd of cows grazing on the now-green but soon-to-turn-brown grass alongside the highway. 'But it doesn't surprise me. Neil seemed pretty mad at Pete for a long time. And I'm not sure if they ever resolved whatever it was, before . . .'

She didn't finish, but then again she didn't need to.

I pulled into the restaurant parking lot and yanked on the brake. 'So you have no idea what the falling-out was over?'

She shook her head. 'Not really. Though I think it might have had something to do with a girl. But Neil never talked to me about his love life. He was always super private about stuff like that.' With another shake of the head – but this time more from impatience, I'd say – she climbed out of the car. 'C'mon, let's go eat. I'm hungry, and I don't want to spoil our meal by getting all morose about this stuff.'

As a result, I hadn't asked further about Neil or his death during lunch. Grace was likely already suspicious enough of me anyway, and I figured there wasn't much more informa-tion I could get out of her regarding that, in any case. But I was itching to find out about the meaning of the phone conver-sation I'd overheard, when she'd talked about 'the grapes' not being picked before the rains came and 'getting that money'.

So I'd asked about her life in general, instead. 'Okay,' I said once we'd been seated and had our menus. 'Tell me what do you do when you're not riding horses or doing bookkeeping for Jack's business.'

Most folks love nothing better than to talk about themselves, and I was hoping she might launch into a story about how she'd gotten involved with a vineyard or winery or something. But no such luck. She merely shrugged and told me about a time-traveling cop show she and her husband had been streaming of late.

I tried another tack. Picking up the menu, I scanned the wine list. 'I might have a glass of red with lunch,' I said. 'You know anything about the ones listed here?'

She studied the offerings, then shook her head. 'Huh-uh. I don't know much about wine, really. I'm more of a beer and tequila kind of gal. Maybe you should ask the waitress for a recommendation.'

Dang.

I set down the menu. 'Yeah, well, I wouldn't be able to taste it, anyway, so what would be the point? And I do have to work later this afternoon, so it's probably best if I don't have anything to drink.'

But then, midway through our mammoth burgers, Grace's cell had buzzed. After checking the caller ID, she pushed back her chair and stood. 'Sorry, I gotta take this,' she said, walking away from the table. I watched as she leaned against the wall just around the corner from the restrooms, her frown growing more obvious the longer the conversation continued.

I have to hear this, I thought, and stood up myself. Walking past Grace, I pointed to the restroom and mouthed, 'Be right back.' With a nod of acknowledgment, she turned to face the wall as she listened to whoever was on the other end of the call.

But instead of proceeding into the ladies' room as I'd said, I stopped outside the door and stood there, pretending to study the framed newspaper reviews on the wall. If Grace popped her head around the corner, I'd just tell her the restroom was occupied.

She didn't speak again for a while, but when she did, her voice was low and full of exasperation. 'No!' she hissed. 'That won't work.' Silence. Then: 'Dammit, I can see I'm gonna have to come up there myself and talk to him. I'm at lunch with someone right now, but tell him I'll be there in an hour or two, and he better have an answer for me.' Another pause, and then: 'Okay, see you later.'

Time to get out of there. I darted across the hall to the ladies' room door and waited a minute before reemerging. Shaking water off my hands in an exaggerated manner as I crossed the room, I sat back down. Grace was staring at her screen, the frown still present.

'Everything okay?' I asked.

'It's fine,' she said with a sigh, setting the phone on the table. 'It's just that dealing with morons is never easy.'

'Oooh, do tell. It's always great fun hearing about other people's morons.'

But Grace merely shook her head derisively, then took a bite of her half-eaten burger. She clearly didn't want to talk about it.

I was tempted to follow her after lunch to see where she went, but there was no way I could get away with it in the bright yellow T-Bird. She'd spot me tailing her a mile away.

But an idea was forming in my head. It continued to percolate all through our meal and then, afterwards, as we stood on the cliff searching for whales, I considered how I could put the concept into action. By the time we headed back down Highway 1 toward Santa Cruz, my plan had gelled.

Now to see if I could pull it off.

When we arrived back at the farmhouse, I pulled up next to Grace's Nissan Leaf. 'Nice wheels,' I said, shutting off the engine. 'My dad's thinking of getting an electric car.' This, of course, was complete and utter fabrication. My V-8 Chevy-loving father would sooner ride a dairy cow around town than ever be seen in an electric car.

I extricated my tall frame from the T-Bird's bucket seat and walked over to the Nissan. 'So, how do you like it?' I asked, laying a hand on its shiny red hood.

'Oh, I love it!' she said. 'I get over two hundred miles on a charge, and it's got all sorts of cool gizmos for music and navigation and stuff.'

While Grace went on about the car's Bluetooth, GPS, and temperature controls, I pulled out my phone, pretending to read a text I'd just received. But what I did instead was open my cycling tracker app, punch the 'record activity' button, and hit 'start'.

'Here, you should check it out for yourself,' Grace said, opening the door and motioning for me to get into the car.

Which was exactly what I'd hoped she'd say.

I did as directed and, as I was oohing and ahing over all the futuristic doodads on the console, I leaned forward, dropped my hand down in front of me, and slid my phone under the seat.

I waited three hours, then called Grace from the Gauguin landline. 'Yes?' she said, 'Who is this?'

Right. It would be an unknown caller, since I doubted Gauguin's number was in her contacts. I was lucky she'd picked up.

'It's Sally, calling from the restaurant.'

'Oh, hi. What's up?'

'I lost my phone,' I said. 'Which is why I'm calling from this number. I've looked everywhere and finally decided it must have slipped out of my back pocket while I was sitting in your car. Any chance you could check for me?'

'Yeah, sure. Hold on. I have to go outside to look.' I heard a *clunk* as she set her phone down, and then nothing for at least three minutes. I was starting to worry that maybe the phone had fallen down some weird electric vehicle crevice that didn't exist in regular cars and had somehow disappeared, when she got back on the line. 'Found it,' she said. 'It had slid all the way onto the floor of the back seat.'

'Oh, thank God. Look, I'll be at work till probably midnight at least, so maybe I could come by your place tomorrow and pick it up?'

'I can do better than that,' Grace said. 'Jack and I are coming into town tonight to go to the movies, so I'll just swing by the restaurant beforehand and bring it to you. I certainly wouldn't want to go that long without my phone.'

'That's awesome, Grace. You're a saint.'

I returned to the *garde manger*, where I'd been helping Tomás pick the meat from the Dungeness crabs we were using for tonight's Crab, Avocado, and Wasabi Shooter appetizer.

That laborious task complete, I sent the prep cook off to clean and carve up the White Seabass we'd gotten in that day (which is neither white nor a member of the seabass family; it's actually a species of Croaker). Javier and I had come up with a special for the meaty but mild fish that I was anxious to try myself that night – coating the steaks with a dry rub of crushed lemongrass, red pepper, and ginger, then searing them on the charbroiler and finishing it all with a drizzle of sweet and spicy green curry sauce.

Maybe, just maybe, I was hoping, *the zip and zing of the dish will trigger something in my nerve endings, and tonight will be the night I regain my sense of smell.*

Hope springs eternal in a young gal's mouth.

Javier and I were working the hot line together that night, and at five o'clock we gave the okay for Gloria to open the doors to the first diners of the evening. About fifteen minutes later, the hostess poked her head through the pass window and called out my name.

'A woman just came in and told me to give you this,' she said, holding out my cell phone.

'Oh, great.' I took the phone from her. 'Is she still here?'

'Yeah, she and the guy she's with said they were gonna stay for a drink.'

I peered through the pass and saw Grace and Jack sitting at the bar, chatting with the Gauguin bartender.

'Well, tell Sid to comp their drinks, okay?'

'Sure thing, Sal.' I watched as Gloria crossed the room to speak with the bartender, after which Grace swiveled around on her stool to smile, wave, and blow me a kiss.

I smiled back, then clicked the phone's home button. Nothing. It was dead, which was no surprise, given how much juice the cycling app requires. But that was fine, as it meant Grace couldn't possibly know the app had been running most of the afternoon, tracking her every move – not to mention her speed, elevation gain, and (had she been on a bicycle, rather than driving a car) calories burned.

'Be right back,' I said to Javier, who nodded acknowledgment as he reached for the lone ticket on the rail.

I retreated to the upstairs office, plugged the phone into the wall socket, then pressed my thumb on the home button to bring the device to life. Once I'd logged in I brought up the cycling app, which showed that, although the activity had stopped recording when the battery had died, it had recorded all the progress made until that time. *Good.*

Taking a seat at the desk, I studied the profile of Grace's 'afternoon ride'. From the Lerici farmhouse, she'd headed north on Highway 1, turned right at Bonny Doon Road, then left onto Pine Flat Road, and then left again onto a tiny street called Mill Creek Lane, where the app showed she'd stopped for twenty-four minutes before resuming her activity. (She'd completed the Bonny Doon Road segment of the ride, a climb of 1,484 feet, in eight minutes and twelve seconds, the app said – a 'personal best'. Yeah, and a time neither I, nor any other cyclist, would ever come close to again.)

From there, she'd continued up to Empire Grade and all the way back down to UCSC, then out the freeway to Soquel Village, where I knew she and Jack lived. After another two hours at the same location, the activity abruptly ended when the phone had run out of power.

I scrolled back to the location where Grace had paused for twenty-four minutes on Mill Creek Lane, then, using my thumb and index finger, enlarged the map until the names of commercial establishments popped up on the screen. There it was: Sempervirens Vineyards.

I'd been right.

Pulling up my phone's browser, I typed the name into the Google search bar. The winery's website informed me that Sempervirens Vineyards, named after the towering Coast Redwood trees on the hills above the rows of vines, produced Pinot Noir (clone Pommard), Chardonnay, and Zinfandel (clone Primitivo) grapes, which they sold to a variety of wineries throughout California.

I set the phone down and stared out the window at the

neighbor's back yard, now bursting with pink and white apple blossoms, purple wisteria, and the first roses of the season. The setting sun cast pale yellow rays through the branches of a Japanese maple, and the familiar calico cat was taking advantage of the last of the filtered light, stretched out full atop a low brick wall.

Now that I had proof that Grace was in fact likely involved somehow with a winery, the next question was: had she invested, and then lost money, in the venture? And if so, could it have anything to do with Neil's death?

And then the gravity of what I was doing hit me, causing a wave of heat to sweep over my body like a Santa Ana wind. Or perhaps it was merely a hot flash. But one certainly triggered by feelings of . . . what? Guilt? Fear of uncovering something unthinkable? Undoing the top buttons of my chef's jacket, I sank into the chair behind the desk and took several deep breaths.

I'd started out this adventure – eavesdropping and snooping around the Lerici family on behalf of Vargas – as a bit of a lark and as a way to make the detective happy. But now that I'd actually uncovered information that could end up implicating Grace in her brother's murder, the whole thing seemed far less fun.

I simply couldn't believe my childhood friend capable of such a horrible deed. Nor did I want to be the one to prove it true.

TWELVE

*I*f a ruse works once, why not try it again? Such was my thought driving up Empire Grade through the dense redwood forest the next morning to Sempervirens Vineyards. After a long, wakeful night wrestling with my conscience, I'd finally decided that I had to go through with my plan, no matter what unwelcome evidence it might turn up.

And hey, I'd told myself, *maybe I can prove that Grace had no involvement whatsoever with Neil's death. Maybe I'm actually doing her a favor by digging into her private life.*

So went my lame justification, in any case.

I was counting on someone being at the business, even though early April isn't a particularly active time for grape growers. The vines would have been pruned by now and just starting to bud out, and thinning wouldn't be necessary for another month or two. But since there'd clearly been people there yesterday afternoon when Grace had paid a visit to the place, it seemed likely the same would be true today.

This being merely a vineyard – as opposed to a winery open to the public for tastings – the sign marking the establishment was small, and I almost missed the turnoff. I drove down the narrow lane, tires crunching on the gravel surface, until I came to a large warehouse-type building. Stacks of oak barrels and several stainless steel crushing machines stood along one side of the structure.

I parked and climbed out of the T-Bird, heading for the large open door, through which I could see an ancient red tractor and another newer one that looked as if it had been squashed by a trash compactor, making it both taller and far more narrow than normal. *Right, a vineyard tractor*, I remembered from having taken a tour up in the Napa Wine Country some years back with Eric.

Poking my head inside the warehouse, I spied a glassed-in office to my right, where a man sat at a desk, peering at a boxy computer monitor. It didn't have a black screen with green text, but the machine looked to be at least twenty years old.

'Hello?' I called out from the doorway.

The man turned at the sound, then waved me inside. 'C'mon in,' he said, swiveling around on an office chair that likely predated the computer by another twenty years. 'You looking for someone?'

'Some*thing*, actually. My friend Grace was up here yesterday and thinks she may have left her phone when she left. Since I was passing by anyway, on my way to a friend's house in Bonny Doon, I said I'd swing by and see if maybe you'd found it.'

'Oh.' He glanced around him – at the desk, the bookshelf, and the credenza along one wall – all the while scratching a spot behind his ear.

'Was she in this office yesterday?' I asked.

'Uh-huh. But I don't remember seeing a phone anywhere. It is kinda messy in here, though . . .'

'Maybe she set it down over here.' Heading for the credenza, I stood with my back to the man, slipped my own phone under a stack of papers, then pretended to shuffle through them. 'Ah-ha! Found it!' I said, turning back around and brandishing the device like a prize. 'Awesome. She'll be super happy. She was kinda frantic when I talked to her this morning.'

'Well, glad it was so easy,' the man said with a smile. 'I like your shirt, by the way.'

'Oh, thanks.' I'd purposely worn my ratty, wine-dyed T-shirt bearing the slogan, 'Friends don't let friends drink White Zinfandel', in the hope that it would spark conversation with whoever was at the vineyard.

And it worked. 'I used to have one of those back in the eighties,' he went on, 'but it ended up as a rag a long time ago.'

'Yeah, well this one's not too far off from that status, either,' I said with a laugh. Picking up a flyer about Sempervirens Vineyards, I pretended to examine it as I tried to figure out how to turn the subject to what happened with Grace, without being too obvious. 'You know,' I said, tapping a finger on the map depicting the different vineyards and listing the varietals they produced, 'we buy a few of the wines that come from your grapes.'

'We?' he said.

'Yeah, I co-own the restaurant Gauguin, and one of our biggest selling reds is the Red-Legged Pinot. They use your grapes, right?'

'They do.'

'I'm Sally, by the way.' I held out a hand, and he stood and took it.

'Mike. Pleased to meet ya. I'm the viticulturist here.'

'Nice. And good job. You obviously know what you're doing, 'cause that wine is amazing.' I paused as I studied the flyer. 'Bummer about last season, though. You know, with those early rains?'

'Oh, God, don't remind me.' He plopped back onto the chair, sending it rolling several feet across the floor.

'Sorry. It's just that Grace was talking about it, and . . .' I shrugged.

'Yeah. That was horrible timing. I thought it was kind of a gamble to wait so long before harvesting, but the vineyard manager wanted the pH to bump up a little more – though the Brix was there. And then that storm just came on outta nowhere, it seemed like.'

'That sucks,' I offered, shaking my head in sympathy.

'And it's hard enough to get pickers these days, but when all the vineyards in the county are scrambling to hire at the exact same time?' He snorted. 'Good luck with that.'

I leaned against the credenza and stared out the window at the rows of grapevines across the parking lot, their squat trunks and gnarled branches reminding me of primeval forest creatures from some ancient folk tale.

'Well, Grace seems pretty stressed out by it all,' I said, turning back to him. 'I don't think she really gets how much risk there is investing in grapes.'

'Probably true,' Mike agreed. 'It seems pretty clear she doesn't know a whole lot about the business. But you need to tell her again how sorry I am. It was just such crappy timing, us losing that big contract right after her brother died when she really needed that money for his funeral an' all . . .'

'Uh-huh,' I said.

But my brain was churning. *Could that really be what*

happened? That Grace had only freaked out *after* Neil died, because she needed the money to pay for his funeral expenses? If so, then it was hard to see any possible connection between her financial straits and his murder.

Yes! That was terrific news.

But then again, I immediately realized, it was equally possible she'd simply lied to Mike about the reason for needing the money.

I'd been scheduled to work that evening at Gauguin, as this was supposed to be Javier's night off and my turn working on Friday. But the bribe of a bottle of Johnnie Walker Black, plus my agreeing to attend the next two Santa Cruz County Restaurant Owners Association meetings – an activity Javier detested more than cleaning out the guts of our Wolf stove – had been enough to convince him to work tonight in my stead.

Abby met me at six o'clock at the entrance to the Mexican restaurant where the real estate mixer was being held. A low roar emanated from the building, and people in business suits were streaming through the doors, ready to start off their weekend with an evening of tequila shots and schmoozing.

We made our way to the bar at the back of the restaurant and waited in line to order. Our drinks finally secured – a Maker's Mark for me, Chardonnay for her – we found a place to stand against the wall and scanned the crowd. A few of the faces were familiar, but only because they were Gauguin regulars. I don't have much reason to hang out with realtors in my day-to-day life.

'Oh, there she is,' Abby said, pointing with her wine glass to a group of people standing by the happy hour food offerings. 'And I don't see Ryan anywhere. Good. Here, I'll introduce you.' Grabbing me by the wrist, she dragged me across the room and came to stop behind a woman in a blue blazer and tan slacks with shoulder-length blonde hair.

Abby touched her on the shoulder. 'Hey, girl. How's it going?'

As soon as she turned around, I recognized Cynthia. Though her expression was far more animated this evening than it had been that day at Neil's celebration of life. In fact, from the way she slopped her Margarita onto Abby's blouse while giving her a hug, I guessed Ryan's wife was already a little tipsy.

Abby introduced us. 'This is Sally Solari, who owns that fabulous restaurant downtown, Gauguin.'

'Hi,' I said, leaning forward to let her peck me on the cheek, hoping to thereby avoid any spills onto my yellow cashmere sweater. 'We've actually sort of met once before.'

'Oh?' She gave me a second look.

'Yeah. Not to be too much of a bummer or anything, but it was at the Lerici farm last week – you know, at the reception for Neil they had after his burial?'

'Ah, right.' Cynthia put on an expression of recollection, but it was obvious she had no memory of me whatsoever.

'You were pretty preoccupied at the time, so I don't expect you to remember. I'm a friend of Grace's from high school, and she and I used to hang out at the farm a lot back then.'

'Well, cheers,' Cynthia said, clinking glasses with Abby and me.

'I knew Ryan, as well,' I went on. 'He was several years ahead of me in school, though, so he always treated me like kind of a punk kid. You know, not what I'd call warm and fuzzy. Of course, I can't say he was all that friendly to me last week, either,' I added with a laugh.

Cynthia took the bait I'd cast her way. 'Join the club,' she said, and drank down the rest of her Margarita. 'He hasn't been super warm and fuzzy to me lately, either.'

'Well, it must have been pretty hard on him, losing his brother so suddenly like that. Maybe the stress . . .'

She shook her head. 'No, it started well before that. It's been months now that he's been such a pill. *She* knows all about it.' Cynthia nodded toward Abby, who nodded in return. 'I mean, it's not like Ryan's ever been perfect. You knew him when he was young, and I don't imagine he's changed all that much. But he was always sweet to me, you know, like bringing flowers home after work, calling me during the day to see how I was doing. And he was always a good dad, too, taking Jason to play soccer and reading to him at bedtime and stuff like that. But the last few months he's been, I dunno . . .'

'A dick is how you described him to me,' Abby said, and Cynthia laughed.

'Yep,' she said, leaning toward me. 'He even had the nerve to accuse me of being interested in his brother, Neil. As *if.*'

'Wow. What do you think happened, you know, to change him like that?'

'Hold on,' Cynthia said, raising her empty glass for us to see. 'Lemme get another drink first, and then I'll tell you my theory.' Abby and I followed her to the bar and waited while she ordered another Margarita. After taking a healthy slug from the glass, she turned to me with a cloak-and-dagger gleam in her eye.

'I personally think it has something to do with the farm,' she said. 'He was super hot to sell once his dad started talking about subdividing it to give to the three kids. He even got in touch with a developer he knows from work and had him out to the place to take a look.'

'Is he here tonight, the developer?' I asked.

She glanced around the room. 'Sumner? I don't think so. I haven't seen him, in any case. But these mixers we put on tend to attract more realtors and real estate agents than contractor types.'

'Anyway, sorry I interrupted. You were saying that Ryan was hot to sell . . .?'

'Right.' Cynthia licked salt from the rim of her glass and took another sip. 'So, then, when he found out that his mom and Neil were opposed to the sale, he got *super* angry – way more than seemed normal. I mean, I get that he wanted to sell his portion, but it's not like we're hurting bad for money or anything. It didn't make any sense just how upset he got. It almost seemed like it was personal or something . . .'

She frowned into her glass, then quickly looked up. 'Wait. I just remembered. You're that person who's been in the paper the past few months about solving all those murders. You don't think that *Ryan* could have had anything to do with Neil's—'

'No, no.' I waved a hand and flashed the friendliest grin I could muster – given that I was in fact lying through those smiling teeth. 'I'm only asking about Ryan 'cause of something weird his dad said. That day I was at the farm, Ernie was talking to me and going off on this kind of rant, and then he said, "He's not my son" and just walked off. So I was thinking he might have been talking about Neil, since it happened during his celebration of life.'

I now had both Cynthia and Abby's full attention. There's little that trumps the possibility of a disinherited – or better yet, illegitimate – child for a gripping scandal. I could only imagine how much more scintillating the gossip would be if I confided to them my fear that my own dad could be Neil's true father. But I wasn't ready to go there, especially since one of the listeners was Dad's new flame.

Cynthia was quiet for a while, seeming to gaze at a boisterous group at the food table, filling their plates with beef *flautas* and mini tacos. 'That's funny you say that,' she said after a bit. 'Because I bought Ryan one of those DNA test kits for Christmas. I totally forgot about it till now, 'cause he never mentioned getting any results back. I wonder if he ever sent it in.'

Whoa. Now this was interesting news. Could Ryan have learned that *he* was illegitimate? Or could he have somehow gotten access to his brother's DNA to use for the test, and then found out that Neil wasn't Ernie's son?

In either case, the timing was such that it seemed possible the test results could well be the reason for Ryan's changed mood. And for the anger he'd been directing at his mom and brother, as well.

Now I just needed to figure out how to get my hands on the results of that test – if they in fact existed.

THIRTEEN

'Oh, I almost forgot to tell you.' Evelyn halted so suddenly that Coco, her chocolate Lab, who'd stopped to sniff a patch of grass and was trotting to catch up to us, almost ran right into her. 'I got my acceptance letter to UCSC yesterday.'

'Ohmygod, Evie, that's great!' I grabbed my cousin in a bear hug and the two of us jumped up and down right there in the middle of the sidewalk like a couple of gals with ants in their pants.

'I know,' she squealed. 'I wasn't sure I had the grade point average, but it turns out they favor third year transfer students from the Cabrillo College. Plus,' she added with a chuckle as she untangled Coco's leash from her legs, 'I think my being blind might have been an advantage, too. You know, 'cause they gotta make their quota of disabled folks.'

I slapped her lightly on the shoulder. 'You *so* got in because of your amazing grades. Not to mention, I'm sure you wowed the interviewers with your stellar and vibrant personality.'

'Right, except that they don't do interviews.' Evie laughed once again, then continued down the sidewalk toward my house. She was using her cane, but knew the street well, having spent a month living with me the previous December right after her mom had died. 'Anyway, I'm super glad I'll get to stay in town to finish college,' she went on. 'Now I won't have to give up my awesome roommates, or have to leave you.'

I let Buster off his leash when we got to my yard, and he rushed up to the front door and stood panting, waiting to go inside. Evie and I had been walking that morning along West Cliff Drive, and both dogs were likely in need of a drink of water.

'You want to come in for a few minutes?' I asked as I unlocked the door.

'Sure. I'd love a cup of tea, actually.'

'That sounds good. I think I'll join you.' I headed through the living room toward the kitchen while Evelyn unhooked Coco from her leash. Taking the kettle from the rangetop, I filled it with water and set it on the burner, and was about to strike a match to light the old-school stove that had belonged to my Aunt Letta, when a cry from the other room caused me to jump.

'Wait!' Evelyn shrieked, running into the kitchen. 'Don't turn on the stove!'

'Huh?' I asked.

'Don't you smell it?'

'Smell what?'

'The *gas*. The entire house *reeks* of it. Here, let's open some windows.'

I dropped the unlit match in horror. 'What the *hell*?' Bending down, I examined the four burners of the stove. I couldn't smell anything, but once close enough, I could hear the soft *hiss* of gas escaping from one of the valves. Sure enough, the knob for the far back right burner had been turned on. I switched it off, then set about helping Evelyn open all the windows and doors to get a cross-draft going.

'C'mon, let's sit outside till it dissipates,' I said, and we headed to the back yard, followed by the two dogs, who'd now had their sloppy fill of water from the bowl on the kitchen floor.

'Thank God you smelled it when you did,' I said, taking a seat at the redwood picnic table. 'If I'd lit that match the whole place could have gone up at once – like the Hindenburg zeppelin.' Although it was warm outdoors, I shivered at the thought, pulling the sides of my sweatshirt about me protectively.

Evelyn nodded. 'I'm amazed you didn't smell it,' she said. 'It was *so* strong.'

Right. She didn't know about my malady. 'It's 'cause I don't have any sense of smell right now. I think that sinus infection I had a couple weeks ago damaged my olfactory nerves or something.'

'Oh, no. That's *awful*, Sally. I'm so sorry.' She frowned, but didn't ask the obvious next question.

'And to answer what you're probably wondering,' I filled in, 'it may or may not come back, depending on whether the nerves manage to regenerate or not.'

'That so sucks. I know how important food is to you.' Evie reached out a hand across the table and I took it. 'I guess you'll have to be more careful about stuff like leaving the gas on,' she said. 'At least till your smell comes back – which I'm *sure* it will.' She graced me with an encouraging smile.

'But that's the thing,' I said. 'I know I *didn't* leave it on. I'm kind of obsessive about the stove, actually, partly because of having grown up in a restaurant family. So I'm really good about checking the knobs to make sure I've turned them off.'

Evie frowned. 'Which means someone else must have done it.'

We sat in silence, contemplating this disturbing possibility. *Could* someone have broken into my house and turned on the gas intentionally, in the hopes that I'd light the stove and be burnt to a crisp in the subsequent explosion? The thought sent me into another fit of shivering.

'So who else knows about it – your loss of smell?' Evie asked after a moment.

I chewed my lip. Because that was indeed the sixty-four-thousand-dollar question. Who *did* know? 'Lots of people,' I answered. 'I mean, I haven't made any secret of it. Well, not once all the Gauguin cooks knew, anyway. If anything, I've been whining about it to the whole wide world, in the hopes of at least getting some sympathy for my sorry state.'

Which, I now realized, had been pretty darn stupid.

'You should let the police know about what happened,' Evelyn said, releasing my hand. 'Maybe they can dust the place for prints or something, like they do on TV.'

'Yeah, I guess you're right.' I pulled out my phone and made the call, then stood. 'You wanna go back in to be my nose and see if it's safe yet to make that cup of tea?'

A half hour later, Detective Vargas knocked at the door. 'Working Saturdays now?' I asked, letting him give me a light kiss before stepping inside.

'Sometimes. And when I heard your call come through,

I thought it'd be best if I were the one to come investigate.' He looked me in the eye. 'You okay?'

'Thanks to Evelyn, I am. She's the one who smelled the gas. If not for her being with me, I would have lit that match . . . and *kaboom*!'

Both Martin and Evie flinched at the intensity of my sound effect.

'Well, thank you, *Evelyn*, then.' Vargas turned to her with a smile and then, remembering she wouldn't be able to see his expression, patted her awkwardly on the shoulder.

'My pleasure,' she responded. 'Seems like it's become my new vocation in life to protect my Cousin Sally from danger.'

Martin chuckled, then cleared his throat. 'Uh, so you wanna show me the stove that was on?' he asked.

I led him to the kitchen and indicated which knob had been the culprit. 'Of course, you're gonna find my prints on it, since I switched it off as soon as I realized the gas had been left on.'

'Well, hopefully we'll find a different set, as well.' The detective unzipped a pouch he was carrying and set on the kitchen table a plastic canister of dark powder, a brush, a roll of tape, a pair of small scissors, and a stack of what looked like blank postcards. Shaking the canister, he unscrewed it and dipped the brush inside its lid. Then, swirling the brush lightly over the knob of the stove, he applied the powder to the surface.

As Martin extracted a point-and-shoot camera from his jacket pocket and adjusted its setting, I peered at the powder-dusted knob and marveled at how the black swirls of a fingerprint had magically appeared on its surface.

Once he'd taken several photos of the knob, the detective unrolled and cut a length of tape and pressed it firmly onto the dusted surface. He then lifted off the tape and pressed it onto one of the cards, noting the date, time, and location the print had been taken.

'Looks like just the one print,' he said, holding out the card for me to inspect. 'Probably yours, so I'd say whoever did it must have wiped it clean or wore gloves.'

'Yeah, you're probably right. Oh, well.'

'You know how they got in?' Vargas asked.

I shook my head. 'The front door was definitely locked when we got back from our walk.'

'How 'bout the back? Most break-ins tend to occur out of sight of nosy neighbors.' He strode over to the door from the kitchen to the back patio and bent to examine its handle. 'Looks like the lock's been jimmied,' he said, standing back up. 'See this piece of wood that's been gouged out? It's pretty darn easy to break in with these old-style locks. I'd get a deadbolt put on here if I were you.'

'Will do. And I should warn you, you're gonna find my prints on that handle, too. Sorry, but Evie and I wanted to get out of the house fast until the gas dissipated, and I wasn't thinking straight.'

He fetched the powder and brush. 'That's okay. I'd probably have done the same in your situation. And I'm guessing if the person wiped the stove knob clean, they would have done the same with the door, in any case.'

'They must have seen me leave with Buster for my walk,' I said, leaning against the counter, 'and figured they had enough time to get in, turn on the gas, and get out, before I returned.'

Martin looked up from his task, the brush held upright lest he spill black powder all over the floor. 'But you said you were walking with Evelyn. It wouldn't make any sense to do it when you were with someone who'd be able to smell the gas.'

'No, I left alone, and we met at the lighthouse for our walk.'

'Ah. So you're probably right, then.'

The handle dusted and any existing prints preserved, Martin and Evelyn sat at the kitchen table while I finally prepared the tea I'd promised Evie – though Martin and I opted for coffee, instead.

'Okay,' Vargas said once he'd stirred sugar into his mug. 'So who exactly knows about your having lost your sense of smell?'

'Evie and I were discussing that before you arrived,' I said, 'and a ton of people do. My dad and his girlfriend, Abby, everyone at Gauguin . . .'

'Let me rephrase. Who among our suspects knows?'

'Right.' I drummed my fingers on the red Formica tabletop as I thought. 'Well, Grace and Ryan both do, because we talked about it at the buffet table at Neil's memorial. So anyone in the Lerici family could also know, if either of those two happened to mention it to them. And, let's see . . . Amy could certainly have overheard, as well, since she was there that day, too.'

'How about that Crab Shack guy?'

'Pete?' I thought back to the lunch I'd had on Tuesday with my dad and Abby. 'Uh, well, I might have said something to my dad about not being able to smell while he was around when Dad and I ate at his place the other day . . .' *Had Pete been in the dining room when I'd told my dad?* I couldn't remember.

'So it could have been pretty much any of them who broke in today and turned on that gas.' Martin let out a frustrated sigh and added more sugar to his coffee.

'Everyone except the developer,' I said. 'Since I've never even met the guy. Although . . .'

'Although what?' Martin looked up from his stirring.

'Well, I did get confirmation last night from Ryan's wife, Cynthia, that Ryan was in fact the one who found Sumner. So I suppose Ryan coulda mentioned it to him. Though I'm not sure why it would come up in the conversation.'

'You never know what people will talk about,' Evelyn observed cryptically, then went back to sipping her Earl Grey tea in silence.

Vargas gazed momentarily at Evelyn, and I thought perhaps he was going to ask her to elaborate, but instead he turned back toward me. 'Speaking of Sumner,' he said, 'I finally got hold of him on the phone yesterday, and he said he hasn't talked to Ryan or Grace since the week before Neil's death – that he hasn't wanted to bother them since then. If they're still interested in selling the farm, he told me, he figures they'll call him.'

'Huh.'

'And then, when he realized I might think he was involved with Neil's death, he offered to have me check his emails and phone to prove he hadn't been in communication with the family since a week before the death, but I told him that wouldn't be necessary at this point.'

'Was there anything that seemed suspicious about the guy?' I asked. 'I mean, did you get a weird hit off him?'

Martin laughed. 'Well, he did seem a little smarmy, but then again, that's not unusual for guys in his business. But no, he didn't set off any alarms in me, if that's what you're asking.'

I had to wonder, though, whether the detective's contacting the developer the day before had anything to do with what had happened this morning.

Then again, maybe Cynthia told Ryan about our conversation at that realtors' mixer last night. In any case, given the timing, it seemed likely that the attempt on my life this morning was not a mere coincidence.

And then I had another thought which made my breath catch: in light of what had just happened, maybe that incident with the plastic bag hadn't been an accident after all. What if someone *had* attempted to hurt me that day out at the Lerici farm, and when that hadn't been successful, they'd tried a different, and potentially far more deadly, tack.

Which, if true, would mean both incidents were likely perpetrated by someone associated with the farm. Could it be Amy, whom I'd seen looking our way from the fields as Grace and I set off on our ride?

Or perhaps Ryan. *Had* he watched me as I riffled through that kitchen drawer?

Or Grace.

I thought once again back to the beginning of our horseback ride – how she'd been behind me and then stopped, and when I looked back, she'd dismounted and was tightening the girth on the saddle. But she could have also fastened the bag to the bush then, before I'd realized she'd stopped.

And now, given how I'd tracked her up to the vineyard yesterday, she had yet one more reason to be spooked about my involvement in the case – if she'd found out about my talk with Mike the viticulturist.

I hated to even consider the possibility, but could Grace be the one who was trying to kill me?

FOURTEEN

We were slammed that night at Gauguin, and Javier and Kris made the executive decision that I would be at the charbroiler, where I wouldn't get into trouble deglazing a pan with too much brandy or under-seasoning a side of smashed potatoes. Since most of the meats we grilled were pre-salted – to allow them to become moist and flavorful inside, with a dry outside surface that would brown nicely – I could safely handle that station with no need of a taster to monitor every plate I sent out to the dining room.

But I was anxious and depressed as I worked. Not only could I still not detect even the most pungent garlic or stinky cheese, but – notwithstanding that I'd had a guy out to put in a deadbolt that afternoon as Vargas had suggested – I'd spent the entire day glancing behind my back to make sure no one was stalking me with a garrote or handgun.

Who could have broken in to my house this morning and turned on that gas? Did it have anything to do with Vargas contacting the developer yesterday, or with my conversation with Cynthia last night, or with my visit to the vineyard yesterday? It had to have been someone who knew of my loss of smell, so who were those people?

I ran through a list of possibilities, assigning each of the orders I had grilling a name to match my suspect – the salmon steaks were Ryan and Grace; the rib-eye, the developer, Sumner; the chicken quarter, Pete Ferrari; and the pork ribs, Amy.

Basting Pete with a glaze of honey, Dijon mustard, and tarragon, I considered whether the Crab Shack owner could have heard me talking about my loss of smell when I was at this restaurant the previous Tuesday. Definitely possible. I remembered him being in the dining room on several occasions – not just when he spoke with us, but also when he took other tables' orders and brought out their food.

Next, I turned my attention to the pair of salmon steaks,

flipping them gently and brushing their caramelized surface with olive oil, lemon, and garlic. The two Lerici siblings were absolutely aware I'd lost my sense of smell. And I distinctly recalled Ryan sympathizing about my plight when we'd discussed the blondies I'd baked for Neil's celebration of life. So if he was the one who'd killed Neil, and if Cynthia had gone home last night and blabbed to him about all the questions I'd asked, it could easily have been Ryan in my house this morning.

But what about his sister? I wondered, plating the two orders of salmon and handed them over to Kris to finish with sides of asparagus and risotto. Just two days earlier, Grace had been with me when I'd bitched and moaned about not being able to taste my hamburger at lunch, so she could be pretty confident that my smell still hadn't returned as of today. And the timing of the gas stove incident – the very morning after I'd tailed her up to the vineyard – was hard to ignore.

'Is something wrong with the fish?' the cook asked.

'What? Oh, no.' I shook my head, realizing I'd been glaring at the two plates accusingly, as if they were the actual suspects I'd been musing about. 'It's fine. I just have something on my mind, is all.'

As I returned to my charbroiler, Brandon popped his head through the pass. 'Sally,' he called out. 'There's a couple at table four who asked me to tell you they were here. An older man and woman.'

I peered out at the table the server had indicated and spotted a pair of gray-haired people leaning over to read the menu. When the man finally raised his head I saw that it was Ernie Lerici. So Diana must have finally convinced him to come down and try us out for dinner.

At the next lull in tickets I went out to the dining room to say hello. They had just started on their appetizers: the green bean salad with cherry tomatoes and a feta-olive oil dressing for Diana, and the Tahitian sea bass with coconut and lime for Ernie. Diana set down her fork and stood to give me a hug.

'I'm so glad you decided to come try us out,' I said. Seeing only water at their table, I asked if they'd like a glass of wine to go with their meal. 'On the house, of course.'

'Oh, that's so sweet.' Diana looked at her husband, who

shook his head. 'Ernie's not much of a drinker,' she said, 'but I'd love a little white wine.'

'You got it.'

I returned a minute later with a glass of the Kim Crawford Sauvignon Blanc from New Zealand – our 'house' white – and set it before her. While Ernie busied himself with cutting one of his rice balls in half, then dipping it into the coconut-lime sauce, I knelt next to Diana. 'I was wondering if we could talk again sometime. Because there's something I'd like to ask you about.'

Diana nodded, her eyes posing the question she didn't speak out loud. 'Of course. I'd be happy to,' was all she said instead. 'Would you like to come up to the farm again sometime?'

'No, I'd actually rather talk someplace else, if that's possible,' I answered with a glance toward Ernie. Though, in reality, I wasn't particularly worried about his being around, since it was clear he wasn't much interested in what we had to say to each other, instead staring across the room at a trio of young women milling about the hostess stand as they waited to be seated.

My concern was Grace and Ryan, either of whom could easily show up at the farm when I was there. In particular, I didn't want to run into Grace. Even if she wasn't the one who'd turned on the gas at my house – and I still believed in my heart it couldn't have been her – I was afraid she'd soon discover, if she hadn't already, that I'd been pretending to look for her lost phone up at that vineyard. I had no desire to face my childhood friend until I had the chance to try to prove her innocent of Neil's murder.

'Well, is there any hurry?' Diana asked. 'Because I was thinking of bringing Bondo into town on Monday for a walk along West Cliff Drive.' She lowered her voice. 'He's been getting a little chubby of late, since Ernie sometimes forgets and gives him a second dinner. So now the dog's learned to sit by his bowl and stare at Ernie hungrily, even if he's already been fed.'

I laughed. 'Buster would eat six dinners if I let him do it. And sure, a walk along West Cliff with the dogs sounds great. What time works for you?'

Once we'd settled on meeting at ten o'clock at the surfer statue,

I headed back to the kitchen and my waiting line of charbroiler tickets. It was true there was no huge hurry for me to talk to Diana again, but I was anxious to do so. For I'd decided to take the plunge into the murky depths of the Lerici family and simply ask her about what Ernie had said to me that day at the farm.

It was almost one a.m. before I finally made it home from work that night. Two large tables had come in a little before ten, when we closed, and had ordered three full courses and then dawdled over their coffee and desserts. Not that I was complaining. The bills had been large, as had been the tips – which had greatly pleased the waitstaff.

But I was dead tired by the time the last ticket had gone out, and spent the entire time we cleaned up fantasizing about the comfort of my soft bed.

Nevertheless, as soon as I came through the front door, I knew I'd never be able to get to sleep without a little downtime first. Although my body was exhausted, my brain was still on overdrive.

Heading to the kitchen, I poured a glass of Maker's Mark on the rocks, then plopped down onto the couch. Buster jumped up next to me, and I scratched the rough fur behind his ears as I pulled out my phone to check my messages.

Uh-oh. There was one from Grace. I clicked on the voicemail and held the device up to my ear.

'What the hell, Sally? I just got off the phone with Mike at Sempervirens Vineyards, and he said you were up there yesterday to pick up my phone. But you know damn well I didn't ask you to do anything like that. And I gotta say, given what happened with *your* phone ending up in *my car* the other day, this whole thing is starting to really freak me out. Seriously, girl, are you *following me*?'

There was a pause in the recording, as Grace took a few deep breaths. Then, in a cold, hard voice: 'I don't know what to say. I thought we were friends, but I guess it's all been just a game on your part. Or something. Wait, I know: the super sleuth of Santa Cruz thinks she can solve Neil's murder by taking advan- tage of her connection to our family and pretending to actually give a damn about his death. Well, I have news for you. It's over. Don't bother coming back up to the farm, 'cause you're not welcome there anymore.'

The message ended, and I stared at the phone, blinking back the tears it had provoked. My immediate impulse was to phone her right back. But awakening Grace at one in the morning hardly seemed like an appropriate way to assuage her anger.

Plus, what would I say if I did call? That I suspected her capable of bashing her brother in the temple with the backside of a cleaver because he refused to sell his share of the farm and she needed the money? And although the timing of her conversation with Mike and of her call to me suggested it hadn't in fact been Grace who'd turned on my gas this morning, I still had no actual proof she hadn't been involved in Neil's death.

No, before I contacted her, I needed to talk to Diana and try to learn the truth about the family.

I only had to hope that Grace didn't get to her mom first, and convince her to cancel her walking date with me on Monday.

Nonna was like her old self during Sunday dinner the next day. Perhaps she was happy at the big crowd – reminiscent of the days back when my mom was still alive – or maybe she'd simply had a good night's sleep. But whatever the cause, my eighty-seven-year-old grandmother was lively and acting the pistol of a *nonna* I'd grown up with.

'That all you gon' eat?' she scolded as I passed the antipasti platter to my father after taking only two slices of prosciutto and one of provolone cheese.

'That's okay, it leaves more for the rest of us,' Dad said, helping himself to a mound of marinated vegetables and four slices of salami.

It was indeed a large gathering that afternoon. In addition to Dad, Nonna, and me, in attendance were Abby, Eric, Evelyn, and Martin Vargas – who'd been asking for several weeks running to be invited to the family's legendary Sunday meal.

Evelyn, Eric, and I had been hanging out in the kitchen, helping Nonna plate up the antipasti and slice the ciabatta bread, when Vargas knocked at the door, and the look on Eric's face when he saw who it was triggered in me feelings of both satisfaction and sadness.

It must be serious, I imagined him thinking, *for her to have invited him to Sunday dinner.* And although I couldn't be sure, I suspected there might be a tinge of jealousy mixed in with the surprise I'd registered in Eric's eyes.

For his part, Martin played the perfect gentleman during the meal. My grandmother has that effect on people – especially potential suitors brought to her home by members of the family. He complimented Nonna on the tastiness of the tender meat simmered in red sauce, laughed at Dad's not-that-funny jokes, and asked Evelyn about her classes and how she was getting along with her new roommates. And, notwithstanding Eric's obvious discomfort at his being at the table, Vargas did his best to put him at ease by talking about an attempted-murder case both of them had recently been involved with.

It worked. Eric perked up, took a sip of the now-near-vinegar Zinfandel made decades ago by my Nonno Salvatore, and proceeded to give the detective his opinion regarding the ethics and feasibility of prosecuting a minor under laws designed for adults.

Nonna, soon bored by the legal discussion, retired to the kitchen to brew coffee to accompany dessert. Martin took this opportunity to head to the restroom, at which point Eric turned to me.

'You busy tomorrow night?' he asked. 'I thought maybe we could go to Kalo's for dinner – you know, like old times.'

'Oh, man, I'm sorry, Eric, but I already have plans.'

My 'plans' were that I'd asked my friend Allison over for dinner at my place on Monday night. She and Eric were friends, too, so I could have invited him to join us. But I didn't. Partly, it was because I wanted to hang out with Allison alone, since we hadn't seen each other since going out for pizza two weeks earlier. But I also simply wasn't up to spending an evening with Eric and listening to him talk about Gayle – even if the talk was about the problems they may be experiencing.

'Oh, okay.' Eric didn't ask what it was I was doing, and it hit me that he probably assumed I was seeing Vargas. Which was fine with me.

I smiled broadly at Martin as he came back into the dining room, pleased to be the one in the position of power for a change. But the detective didn't return my smile. Rather, his jaw was tight and his eyes avoided mine. As he took his seat, I saw he was clutching his cell phone so hard that the veins on the back of his hand were bulging out.

'Did you get some bad news?' I asked in a low voice.

He nodded once, but still refused to meet my gaze.

Nonna burst through the door from the kitchen at this point, bearing a large glass bowl of the Marsala-soaked tiramisu she prepared each week for the Sunday dinner dessert. *Guess I'll have to wait till later to find out what's going on with him.*

Dad, Abby, and Evelyn, none of whom appeared aware of the uncomfortable interaction between Martin and me, jabbered on about a new Marvel action movie at the theater downtown. But I could tell Eric had noticed. Although he'd stood to help Nonna serve up the creamy dessert, his curious eyes kept flashing toward the two of us, then turning quickly away as soon as he saw me looking.

I joined in the small talk, offering my opinion that the best superhero ever was Wonder Woman. 'And not that movie they did a few years back, but the TV version, with Lynda Carter.'

Eric snorted. 'You only like that version because of how camp it is. For me, though, it's the Silver Surfer, hands down. That dude is rad.'

'Like we don't all know why you like *him* best,' I said, yanking on the hood of Eric's sweatshirt, which bore the logo of O'Neill's Surf Shop. I turned toward my cousin. 'So who's your favorite superhero, Evelyn?'

'Well, duh. I think it's obvious it would have to be Daredevil,' she answered with a laugh.

'Who's he?' asked Nonna, brows furrowed.

It took a second, but then I realized my deeply Catholic grandmother must be worried about Evelyn getting involved in some sort of satanic worship rite, based on the 'devil' part of the character's name. 'It's okay, Nonna,' I said. 'It means the guy is super acrobatic, is all. And the reason Evie's laughing is because he's blind.'

'Ah.' She nodded, then flashed a devious grin. 'Well, I like Wolverine best,' she said.

'Wow, Aunt Giovanna,' Evie said. 'I'm surprised you even know who he is. That's totally awesome.'

'It's only because she has a crush on Hugh Jackman. Right, Ma?' Dad waggled his eyebrows at Nonna, causing her to duck her head and hide her reddening cheeks behind her napkin.

Martin had remained silent throughout most of the dessert course, his only contribution being a curt, 'Superman' when asked who his favorite superhero was. And as soon as all the plates had been cleared, he stood to go.

Both Evelyn and I had ridden over with Vargas, but Eric, bless his heart, could tell I needed some alone time with the detective. 'You wanna ride home with me?' he asked Evie. 'I have to go out that way anyway, and I can tell you all about the Silver Surfer and how he travels faster than light across the cosmos on his gnarly surfboard.'

'Cool,' she said. 'I'd love to.' The two of them thanked Nonna and planted *baci* on her cheek, then took their leave.

After asking my grandmother if I could help with the dishes and – as always – being shooed away, I headed out to the front hallway, where Martin was standing with my dad and Abby.

'So you wanna tell me what the hell's going on?' I asked once Dad and his date had retreated to the kitchen to say goodbye to Nonna.

'I got a call from Grace, and she's not happy.' He looked me in the eyes. 'Nor am I.'

Oh, no. I knew what was coming next.

'She called specifically to complain about *you*. Is it true that you've been following her, and that you made up a story about her losing her phone in order to go and ask questions about her at Sempervirens Vineyards?'

'Well, I didn't actually follow her, but I guess the rest is kind of true . . .' I stared down at my red-and-black sneakers, not wanting to see the anger on his face.

'Damn it, Sally. Not only are you putting yourself at risk, but you're potentially screwing up the entire case by letting Grace know she's a suspect.'

'I know . . .' I finally looked up, only to see my father standing behind Martin at the kitchen door. Dad was staring at me, eyes wide and mouth slack, but then swallowed and gave a slow shake of the head.

Abby had now joined him at the door, and the two of them

bid us goodbye, then headed outside. Neither Abby nor Martin would have noticed it, but the fact that Dad had not hugged me goodbye spoke volumes. He was clearly furious to hear that, notwithstanding my pretending otherwise, Grace was in fact being investigated as Neil's possible killer and that I'd been involved in the investigation.

And now I had a supremely uncomfortable ride ahead with someone else who also felt betrayed by me.

Trying to quell the churning in my stomach – all that rich mascarpone and chocolate were not sitting too well right about now – I climbed into the passenger seat of Martin's SUV. The detective fastened his seatbelt, started the engine, and shifted into drive. But instead of pulling away from the curb, he set the car back in park and turned to face me.

I met his gaze, hoping perhaps his anger might have subsided and that he was about to make nice and perhaps even give me a reassuring hug.

But no. If anything, his eyes were even more steely than before.

'I'm truly disappointed in you, Sally. I thought I could trust you, that you understood what it meant to investigate a crime as part of law enforcement. But I guess I had you all wrong.'

With a slow exhalation, he put the car in gear once more and started down the street. I was silent. After all, what could I say to that?

Martin finally spoke again as we neared my house. 'Okay, so here's the deal,' he said, eyes focused on the shiny silver Tesla in front of us. 'I need you to stay away from the Lericis – from all the suspects in this case, in fact. I don't want you phoning them, or following them, or doing anything further that could jeopardize our investigation.'

Pulling into my driveway, he turned to face me, but did not shut off the engine. 'Is that understood?'

I nodded. 'Got it.' When he made no move to hug or kiss me goodbye – or even pat me on the leg – I opened the door and got out. 'See you around . . . I guess.'

'Uh, huh,' was all he said, and then, without so much as a wave in my direction, he pulled back out and accelerated down the street.

FIFTEEN

Although I'd experienced a hot flash several days earlier up in the Gauguin office, it was nothing compared to the doozy of one I suffered that night. At around three in the morning, I awoke from a dream about sitting for the Bar exam having done no studying whatsoever (how's that for your classic nightmare?), and realized my pajamas were soaked in sweat.

Shoving the sleeping Buster off my legs, I threw off my blankets and lay there in the cool air for a few minutes, then got up to change into a dry flannel top. Once back under the covers, I considered my situation, and what had undoubtedly triggered both the hot flash and the bad dream.

It took almost every finger on my right hand to tick off the people currently upset with me, ranging from displeasure (Eric) to anger and disappointment (Dad and Martin) to out-and-out fury (Grace; though I was tempted to place the detective in this last category, as well).

And not only that, but there was apparently someone out there who wanted me dead. Not the best recipe for a good night's rest.

A mug of hot milk spiked with brandy finally helped me fall back asleep, but I was still anxious and on edge once morning arrived.

It was overcast and gloomy outdoors, the perfect match to my mood. A hard bike ride up the hill to the university seemed just the ticket – something to make my calves scream and perhaps help shake loose the melancholy that had descended upon me overnight.

But it didn't work. Pumping up Bay Street, the UCSC employees' cars whizzing past me – some far too close for comfort – all I could think about was Martin's face as he'd dropped me off yesterday afternoon. It wasn't so much his anger that affected me. I got that; he had good reason to be upset.

Nobody wants to receive irate calls from someone regarding their work, especially when the caller is a person who's not supposed to even know they are the object of that work.

Rather, it was the hurt in the detective's eyes that had returned to me during the night, and which I still couldn't shake as I pedaled past the old lime kilns and wooden barns at the base of the university. I'd failed him. And in so doing, I'd failed a part of myself, as well.

And then there was my father. I knew it wasn't my fault that the Lerici kids were still suspects in their brother's murder, but I had led Dad to believe I wouldn't be involved in helping with the investigation into them. So I'd lied to him, at least by omission.

Failure number two, I thought as I got out of the saddle to pump uphill past the athletic fields and toward the top of campus.

With regard to Eric, I felt mixed. On the one hand, it felt good to have *him* be the one wanting to spend more time with me, for a change. But I took little pleasure out of seeing him go through what was obviously a hard time. We may no longer have been a couple, but I did still truly care for the guy.

And as for Grace, it stung to know she thought the only reason I'd rekindled our friendship was in order to keep tabs on her for the cops. But since that was in fact pretty much the truth – even though our relationship had since become much more than that to me – how hurt could I realistically be?

Finally reaching the end of the long climb, I sat back in the saddle and exhaled deeply several times, ridding myself of the excess CO_2 that had built up in my bloodstream. A cluster of students with bulging daypacks stood at the bus stop, their eyes glued to their cell phones, oblivious to the soaring redwood forest surrounding them.

Braking at the stop sign and then continuing on past the student health center, I considered what to do about Grace. I had no desire to talk to her right now – not that she'd likely take my call, in any case. And given Martin's directive that I not contact any of the suspects in the case, it seemed best to comply and not risk incurring his wrath any further.

But did that directive apply to Diana, as well? Although he'd told me to stay away from the Lerici family, he'd amended this to say 'from all the *suspects*' in the case. And Diana wasn't a suspect in her son's murder. So what could it hurt if I went ahead and met her today as planned for that walk along the cliffs?

Pleased with my analytical reasoning for this obvious end-run around the detective's wishes, I shifted onto the big ring and headed once more downhill toward home.

Diana was already waiting at the surfer statue when I arrived with Buster an hour later. She was staring up at the handsome bronze figure clutching a longboard, his gaze toward Steamer Lane, where flesh-and-blood surfers were attempting to catch the choppy waves below.

'Hi!' I called out, and she turned my way.

We let the two dogs meet and check each other out, and once they'd moved from sniffing each other to jointly investigating the smells on the ground around them, the four of us started up the path toward the lighthouse.

'So what was it you wanted to talk to me about?' Diana asked.

I didn't answer immediately, using Buster's interest in a gopher hole as an excuse to gather my thoughts. I knew exactly what it was I wanted to ask. But I was afraid of what the answer might be.

Go on, Sal, just do it.

'It's about something Ernie said the day of Neil's memorial. He was talking about his childhood on the farm, and then about them not wanting him at the hospital – I think for one of your births – and then he said something odd: "He's not my son", he said.' I paused and turned to look at Diana, but she was staring out at the ocean, her face unreadable.

'Anyway,' I went on, 'so I didn't think anymore of it at the time, but then I learned the other day from Cynthia that she gave Ryan one of those DNA kits for Christmas and, well, I'm wondering if maybe the results of the test could be the reason Ryan's been so . . . out of sorts lately?'

This time when I turned to look, she not only met my gaze but stopped walking, surprising Bondo, who'd been pulling at the leash several steps ahead of her. The beefy black-and-white dog sat down in the middle of the path and cocked his head, wondering why we'd halted.

'He had his DNA done?' Diana asked in a soft voice.

'Uh, I guess so,' I answered, though in reality I had no idea if he'd ever sent in the test or not.

Diana's head drooped and she let out a soft sigh. 'I guess it was bound to happen,' she said, looking once more out toward the water. Seal Rock was crowded with the brown bodies of fat sea lions, whose hoarse barks filled the air along with the cries of the gulls wheeling overhead.

At a high-pitched *yip* from Bondo, she started forward again, and I tugged Buster away from yet another gopher mound to catch up. 'It was bound to happen that Ryan would find out . . .?' I let the unfinished question hang there, hoping she'd fill in the rest.

'I was pregnant with someone else's child when Ernie and I married.' The words came all in a rush, as if she couldn't spit them out fast enough.

'Oh.' My brain jerked into overdrive. Although I'd suspected this might be the case, to hear her actually admit it was startling. And disturbing, as well. *Could* Ryan's father be my dad?

Diana apparently hadn't noticed my distress. She continued down the path, face tight, caught up in her own personal anguish.

But then it struck me that she wasn't acting as if I was her son's half-sister. Were it true that my father was 'the guy', wouldn't she have demonstrated more nervousness when she made the admission to me? Or at least glanced my way as she said it?

But no. All I detected in her was internal strife – nothing at all related to me.

'So, this other guy . . .' I prompted.

'He was a German visiting for the summer from Hamburg. We met at a party and, well . . .' She shrugged. 'This was before Ernie and I had become serious, and it wasn't till after we got engaged that I realized I was pregnant.' She stopped again and finally turned to look at me. 'Ernie knew. But he encouraged me to keep the baby.'

'Does the real dad know he has a son in California?'

Diana frowned. 'Huh-uh. He'd already left town before I

even knew, and I had no way of contacting him. We've never been in touch since he went back home to Hamburg.'

And then I laughed. I know it was supremely inappropriate, but I simply couldn't help it.

'What?' Diana asked, confusion in her eyes.

'I'm so sorry. It's just that, well . . . Ernie also said something about a "hamburger" that day at your house, and I had assumed he was talking about his lunch or something. But now I realize . . .'

Her face relaxed as she joined in my laughter.

'But also, I guess, I'm kind of relieved, as well.'

'Relieved?' The look of confusion returned. 'How so?'

'Well, this is pretty embarrassing, actually, but I'd been just a little worried that maybe my dad was the one . . .'

I was afraid she'd be angry, but instead Diana smiled. 'No. We were indeed involved during high school and for a little while afterwards, too. But then Mario got busy with the restaurant and with fishing, and I took a job as a secretary over the hill in Santa Clara, so after a while we grew apart. And then, once he met your mom, it was obvious they were a perfect match, so I let it go.' Her expression was wistful, and I wondered if she regretted letting him go like that.

And given how my father acted every time the Lerici family came up in the conversation, I had to wonder if maybe he regretted it, too.

As I was having these confused thoughts about my family, I spied a police car heading our way along West Cliff Drive. Instinctively, I ducked my head and turned away. Which was stupid, of course, since I knew what Vargas drove, and it wasn't a black-and-white cruiser. But the incident did serve to remind me of the questionable position I was placing myself in by walking out in public with a member of the Lerici family.

With a glance over my shoulder, I started once more down the path with Buster, and Diana and Bondo followed suit. After a minute, Diana cleared her throat.

'Ernie and I made the decision not to tell anyone about Ryan's real father,' she said. 'We thought it would be easier for him if he didn't know, and the idea of his finding out from something like a DNA test never even occurred to us as a possibility back then. But I guess he must have gotten the results back and seen that he was half German and figured it out.' Diana kicked a stone that lay on the path, and it scuttled into the ice plant – now blanketed with its seasonal purple blooms – that lay between us and the cliffs.

'Ryan never said anything to you about it?'

She shook her head. 'No. But I wish he had. Because it sure seems like that must be at least part of the reason he's been so angry at me the past few months. I assumed it was all because of my not wanting to sell the farm, but this makes more sense. In fact . . .' With a snap of the fingers, she turned toward me. 'I bet this whole farm thing is just some kind of passive-aggressive way to get back at me. Oh, lord . . .'

Diana stared out to sea once more, and I did the same. In the distance, numerous white caps whipped up by the light wind sparkled in the morning sun, and closer to shore, several kayakers were making their slow way through a wide patch of dark kelp.

'I guess I'll have to talk to him,' she finally said. 'Like I should have years ago.'

We walked on in silence till we reached Woodrow Avenue and then turned around, heading back toward the lighthouse. At the sight of a young couple seated on one of the benches facing the ocean, their hands held in a tight clasp, I was reminded of Amy and her fiancé.

'So what do you think will happen after Amy gets married this fall?' I asked Diana. 'You think she'll stay on at the farm?'

'I hope so,' she said. 'It would be hard to find someone as good – and as inexpensive – as her. But I'm not holding out much hope that she'll want to stay much longer. It seems pretty obvious she's ready to move on, now that Neil's gone.'

'Well, she told me she's hoping to have the wedding at the farm, so I can't imagine her quitting before then, in any case. Have you met her fiancé?'

Diana shook her head. 'No, I haven't met him.' Then she stopped and put her hand to her mouth. 'Oh, if it is a "him", that is. Amy just told me that she and "Frankie" wanted to have their wedding at the farm. But I guess I shouldn't assume that means it's a man . . .'

'Yeah, it's a guy, all right,' I said with a laugh. 'And from what I understand, he's a real looker.'

As we continued on, gazing out to sea as we headed back the way we'd come, I considered how to phrase the last question I had for Diana. Best to simply be out with it, I decided.

'Can I ask you one more thing?' I said, breaking the silence.

'Sure,' Diana answered with a shrug. 'My life is now apparently a completely open book.'

'Well, this might sound kind of rude, but you have to believe me when I say it's important.'

She cocked her head, reminding me of Bondo. I'd piqued her interest, that was for sure.

'Okay. So, my question is, was there an issue with paying for Neil's funeral expenses?'

'There was, actually. The mortuary required payment in advance – it was over ten thousand dollars, if you can believe that – and all of Ernie's and my money is tied up in the farm and the house right now.'

'Yeah, it's amazing how expensive death is,' I said. 'My Aunt Letta's funeral ended up costing well over that amount. And they don't ever let you pay over time; it always has to be upfront.'

Diana nodded. 'Well, Neil didn't have any life insurance, being so young and not having a family, and Ryan said there was no way he had that kind of ready cash. So Grace said she'd come up with it – that she could get some money repaid that she'd used recently as an investment. It's so horrible what they do to you when you're grieving.'

'I hear ya,' I said. Though my thoughts had already moved on past the ethics of the funeral industry. For I'd just learned a couple key facts: first, notwithstanding what Cynthia had told me the other night – that she and Ryan weren't hurting for money – her husband had been unable to come up with the cash for his brother's funeral. Or perhaps he'd simply been unwilling to do so.

Moreover, I mused, I now had confirmation of what the winemaker had told me last Friday about Grace wanting to get back the money she'd invested because she wanted to pay for

Neil's funeral. Which meant that Grace hadn't needed the money until after Neil's death – *because* of it, in fact.

But I did wonder how Grace had come up with the cash, since I knew she hadn't gotten it back from the vineyard. I was about to ask Diana about this, but held off. The fact that Diana clearly thought the money *had* come from the repayment of Grace's investment meant that Grace likely didn't want her mother to know how she in fact did obtain it.

But why wouldn't she tell this to her mom? And why was she still so anxious to get her investment back from the vine-yard? Had she borrowed the money for Neil's funeral from someone who was pressing her for repayment?

These were all valid questions, I mused as we continued down the path along the cliffs, but the most important fact was that they all related to events that had occurred *after* Neil's death. In other words, not only had his death not benefitted Grace, it had ended up hurting her financially. And since I had no reason other than financial gain to suspect her of the murder, this meant I could now pretty safely strike her from my list.

What a relief. And my dad would certainly be happy to hear the news, as well. Though I'd have to figure out a way to tell him about Grace without letting on that I still suspected Ryan.

But another huge question remained: how could I make up with Grace, now that she was off the hook? There was no way I could go to Vargas with the information I'd just uncovered, given who the source had been. Even though I'd convinced myself that talking to Diana had not been a breach of the promise I'd made to the detective, I was fairly certain he'd see it otherwise.

Which meant that, for the time being at least, I'd have to accept the fact that Grace was still 'officially' a suspect in the murder, and therefore off-limits for me to contact.

Not that I held out much hope that she'd ever want to talk to me again, in any case.

SIXTEEN

'Eric wanted to hang out tonight.' I held aloft my Negroni cocktail and admired its ruby liquid, lit from behind by the late-afternoon sun.

'You should have invited him to join us,' Allison said. 'I wouldn't have minded his being here.'

'Nah, I'd rather it just be you and me. This way, we can talk about him.' Sipping from the drink, I tried in vain to discern the tart lemon and bitter Campari that served to cut the sweetness of the vermouth and potency of the gin. No such luck.

But it was good to spend the evening with my pal from high school. What with my job running a restaurant and hers as a professor up at the university – not to mention her being the mom/chauffeur to a twelve-year-old who had soccer practice, girl scout meetings, and ballet classes – we didn't get to hang out together these days nearly as much as I would have liked. But after Eric, she was my go-to person in town for fun chit-chat and gossip, as well as for deep conversation and advice.

And my number one choice when that conversation had to do with Eric.

Allison leaned forward across the picnic table in my back patio, where we were enjoying cocktail hour while waiting for my chicken to finish roasting. 'Ooooo,' she said. 'Do tell, girl-friend. Is there "something" to talk about?'

'I'm not sure. Maybe. He's pretty upset about his work these days, but I think he may be having issues with Gayle, as well. Though of course he won't admit it.'

'Huh.' She eyed me a moment, then drank from her glass of blended Scotch – a habit she'd picked up the previous year while spending her sabbatical in England. 'And this possibility makes you feel . . .?'

'Confused,' I answered quickly, my index finger tapping out a rapid cadence on the wooden table.

'I can imagine. After all this time bachin' it, and now you have *two* guys to choose from.'

'Hey, I never said Eric was wanting to split up with Gayle and get back together with me.'

'But you think that's a possibility.'

'Yeah.' I ceased my drumming with an impatient shake of the head. Allison knew me – and Eric – far too well for either of us to fool her for very long.

'And would you do it? Break it off with your hot detective to get back together with Eric?'

I laughed. Although Vargas was handsome enough in a burly, gruff sort of way, 'hot' was not the word I'd use to describe the guy.

But then I laid my head on the table and let out a moan. 'I don't know what I want. And it may not be my decision in any case, since Martin's far more likely to break up with me right about now than me, him.'

'Really? What happened?'

I realized that I hadn't told Allison about my involvement in Neil's murder investigation, so I caught her up on how Detective Vargas, on learning of my connection to Grace, had asked me to keep an ear and eye out for anything relevant I might learn about the Lerici family.

Allison stared toward the back fence, where my gnarled persimmon tree now displayed a host of large, waxy flowers. 'It's so sad,' she said. 'I didn't know Neil very well, but he seemed like a nice enough kid in high school. Even if he could be pretty snarky at times,' she added with a laugh. 'So the cops really think someone in his own family might have done it?'

'Not the parents. But Martin thinks it could have been either Ryan or Grace, among several other possibilities who aren't in the family. Though I recently got some information that I think makes Grace a pretty unlikely suspect. Which is really good, 'cause I'd have hated for it to be her. But that's the reason he's upset with me, actually. Since I kind of crossed the line by *actively* investigating, rather than merely keeping an ear out.'

'Actively, how?'

'Well, the specific thing that got me in trouble with him was that I tracked Grace's movements . . .' At Allison's open-mouthed stare, I waved her off. 'Never mind how, right now. And then I went to talk to someone at this place she'd been that day, pretending I'd come to pick up her phone which she'd left there, but which was really my phone.'

'Gee, I can't *imagine* why that would upset him.'

'Right,' I said. 'I guess I got a little too invested in it all.' I was about to tell her what had happened with my gas stove on Saturday, but then held off. There wasn't anything Allison could do about that, after all, and it would only serve to freak her out. One of us in that state of mind was plenty.

'But the thing is,' I went on, 'I now have this intel as to why it's probably not Grace, but if I tell Martin, I'll have to admit how I got the information, at which point he'll go completely ballistic on me, for sure.'

'Okay, spill. I want it all.' Allison stood. 'You can tell me while we make another round of drinks.'

Our beverages refreshed, I checked on my chicken, and as the two of us prepped the basket of Brussels sprouts I'd picked up at the farmers market, I recounted everything I could remember about the case: how Neil was killed; the split within the family over subdividing the farm; Ernie's increasing dementia; Grace having to borrow money for the funeral; Ryan recently learning he wasn't Ernie's son. 'And that's just the Lerici family. As I said, there are other suspects too.'

'It all sounds positively Shakespearean,' Allison observed.

'You think everything does. I swear you could make an argument that *SpongeBob SquarePants* is really just a remake of *The Tempest*. No, please don't,' I added as she scratched her chin and pondered the idea.

In her defense, the Bard of Avon was Allison's area of expertise as a literature professor, so it made sense that she tended to have the guy on her brain pretty much twenty-four-seven. (Though she was currently hard at work on a treatise arguing it was actually Edward de Vere, the 17th Earl of Oxford, who penned the famous plays, and not the man from Stratford.)

Allison picked up her paring knife and sliced a Brussels sprout in two, then set the knife back down. 'But seriously,' she said, 'it is kind of freaky how much the facts of this case resemble *King Lear*. Think about it: the division of the kingdom between the three siblings; the mad father; the illegitimate son. Even the names are similar: Ryan and Grace, like Regan and Goneril.' She chuckled. 'Too bad Neil's name doesn't start with a C, like Cordelia.'

And then she turned to me and brought her hand to her mouth. 'Ohmygod, Sally. And their *last name*.'

'Huh?'

Allison cocked her head at my blank look. 'Don't you get it, girl? *Leeer*-ici. Just like *Lear*!'

Forty minutes later, we sat down to our dinner of chicken roasted with tarragon and shallots, pan-fried Brussels sprouts drizzled with balsamic vinegar, and baked potatoes slathered in butter and sour cream. Big time comfort food, which – although I still couldn't taste any of it – was perfect for my current mood.

'So who are the other suspects besides Ryan and Grace?' Allison asked, sprinkling chopped chives atop her baked potato.

I ticked off the names on my fingers: 'Pete, who owns the Crab Shack out on the wharf and who ended up sharing first place in the Artichoke Cook-Off because of Neil's death; a developer who wants to turn the Lerici farm into a bunch of condos; and this woman Amy, who was helping Neil at the cook-off the day he was killed. She's been working as a sort of apprentice at the Lerici farm since last year.'

'And what about the dad as a possibility?' Allison asked. 'You said he was developing dementia, so maybe he just kind of lost it and went off on Neil.'

'But why would he want to kill his *real* son? Maybe if it had been Ryan it would make sense – jealousy or anger that he wasn't his. But Neil was the "good" kid, the one who stayed on to work at the farm.' I shook my head. 'No, I can't see it being Ernie. But now, Ryan . . .'

'Aha!' Allison grinned. 'Fratricide. Just like Claudius killing King Hamlet in order to marry his sister-in-law, Gertrude. Does Ryan by chance have the hots for Neil's girlfriend?'

'Neil didn't have any girlfriend, at least not as far as I know.

But now that you mention that . . .' I frowned, thinking back to what Cynthia had told me at the real estate mixer Friday night. 'Ryan may have been jealous of Neil, or at least worried that he was hitting on his wife.'

'Deeper and deeper into the abyss we plunge,' Allison said, then bit enthusiastically into the crispy skin of her chicken drumstick.

'Shakespeare?' I asked.

'Nah. I just made that up. So what else have you got on Ryan besides his possible suspicions of infidelity?'

'Well, if he did send in that DNA test and discover he was illegitimate, then it stands to reason he'd be jealous of Neil for that, as well. Especially given how, like I said, Neil had become kind of the golden boy in the family, since he was the one who stayed to help out at the farm. That had to have really galled, if Ryan did know his true ancestry.'

'So there's the motive. What about means and opportunity? Was Ryan there that day at the cook-off?'

'I think so. I didn't actually see him, but Grace did say she had to go meet up with her folks and with Ryan when we were talking that day. And he was also at the farm right before my horse spooked and threw me.'

Allison set down her chicken leg. 'There are horses involved, too? Next you're gonna tell me someone pulled out a sword and challenged Neil to a duel.'

'No, though that big ol' cleaver he was bashed on the head with could be the stand-in for a sword.'

I told her about going riding with Grace and how a plastic bag that was snagged on a bush had caused my horse to shy. 'Anyone who's spent much time with horses – as Ryan certainly did, growing up around the one his sister had – would know how easily they spook at things like plastic bags. So if he'd wanted to get rid of me by breaking my neck, or at least scare me off the case, he could have stuck that bag there once we'd passed by.'

'But it could just as easily have spooked Grace's horse, too, right?'

'Yeah, but she's a far more experienced rider than me. Maybe he just figured I'd be more likely to be thrown than her.'

'Maybe.' But Allison looked doubtful. 'What about that gal who helped Neil at the cook-off? You said she worked at the farm. Was she there the day you were horseback riding?'

'She was. And she also could easily have put that bag there, since we rode right past her harvesting artichokes on our way up the hill. But I just can't come up with any good reason she'd want to hurt Neil.'

Allison stood and helped herself to more chicken. 'So plenty of opportunity for her but no motive,' she said, returning to the table.

'Right. And then there's also Pete Ferrari. Did you know him in high school?'

'I did, actually. We were in the same art class when he was a sophomore and I was a senior.'

'He took art?' This surprised me, since the guy came across as more crass and coarse than the creative, bohemian type.

'Yeah, and he was a pretty talented painter, too. He had a great eye for color and even won an award for one of his pieces that year. But then I heard he'd given it up, which is sad. So why exactly is Pete a suspect?'

'Well, like I said, he ended up sharing first prize at the cook-off because of Neil's death, and according to my dad, Pete's super-competitive about his restaurant and his cooking.'

'Doesn't seem like much of a reason to kill someone,' Allison said, spearing a Brussels sprout with her fork.

'True. But Grace says there ended up being some bad blood between Pete and Neil.' I told Allison about Pete's picture being defaced in Neil's yearbook, and how two years earlier in the swim team photo they'd appeared to be close friends. 'Did you ever see Pete with Neil back when you knew Pete in school?' I asked.

Allison nodded as she finished chewing. 'I did,' she said. 'They were thick as thieves, actually – always together, it seemed like. Neil would come meet Pete after class and they'd hang out in the art studio, horsing around, during lunch. You know, playing practical jokes on the other kids, and talking in funny voices and cracking dumb jokes that only they got. They always struck me as being really goofy, but in a cute, nerdy kind of way.'

She paused. 'It's funny, but I never thought about it till this minute . . .'

'What?'

'It never occurred to me back then, but in retrospect, I wouldn't be surprised if they were gay. It would explain their hanging out together all the time and keeping kind of separate from everyone else. I wonder if they were involved back then . . .' Allison set down her fork and gazed out the window, brow creased.

After a moment she turned back to me. 'That might explain what happened to Pete that year.'

'What happened to him?'

'I'm not sure exactly what, but right before the end of the school year, Pete started missing some of our classes. Which was really weird, 'cause he *loved* art class. It was about the only thing he seemed to care about, in fact. I was actually kind of worried about him, 'cause when I did see him those last couple weeks of school, he was super morose.'

I pushed back my chair. 'Here. Lemme show you something.' I fetched my yearbook from our senior year and opened it to the photo of the junior varsity swim team. 'Check it out,' I said, pointing to Neil and Pete standing in the front row, arms about each other's shoulders, wearing wide grins. 'You think they look like two people who are romantically involved?'

She stared at the picture. 'Wow. Definitely possible, I'd say.'

'Okay, so what if Neil ended up breaking his heart?' I said, tapping my finger on Pete's smiling face. 'It could certainly explain his change in behavior from this sweet, goofy kid to being all bitter and competitive. Once you're burned like that, it can effect you for the rest of your life.' I closed the book. 'And if that is in fact what happened, I wouldn't be at all surprised if that competitiveness came out in spades with regard to Neil.'

Allison frowned. 'Yeah, but enough to murder the guy?'

SEVENTEEN

As soon as Allison left that night, the first thing I did was call my pal Nichole, up in San Francisco. We'd been friends since our law school days together, and I knew her to be a night owl, so the late hour didn't worry me.

She picked up after one ring. 'Hey, girlfriend. 'S'up?'

I caught Nichole up with what was going on in my life, then she told me about herself, and how she and her girlfriend Mei were about to embark on a long-planned trip to Singapore to visit a cousin of Mei's.

'But that's not why you're calling – just to catch up,' Nichole said.

'How'd you know?'

'Instinct. So what is it? Boyfriend troubles? A fight with Javier? Another murder case?'

When I didn't answer right away, she laughed. 'Ha! That's it, isn't it? You're as transparent as Saran Wrap, girl. So who's the dead person this time?'

'A guy I kinda knew in high school, though I was better friends with his sister.' I gave her a quick rundown of Neil's death and the various suspects, then got to the point of my call. 'So what I want to know is, are you friends with any gay men down here in Santa Cruz?'

'Yeah, I know a couple guys who live down there. So, what? Was this Neil character a "Friend of Dorothy"?'

'Maybe. And I'm trying to find out if he might have been involved with one of the suspects – this guy named Pete Ferrari, who owns the Crab Shack out on the Wharf. Any chance you could ask your friends down here if they happen to know him, and whether or not he is in fact gay?'

'Sure, I can ask around. Lemme make a few calls and get back to you.'

I put away the leftovers and washed the dishes while waiting for Nichole to call back, then plopped down onto the sofa to stream an episode of *The Good Fight*. But it only served to remind me of Martin, with whom I'd watched the same show a week earlier, so I switched off the TV and headed upstairs to my laptop to zone out on YouTube videos of Corgi puppies splashing about in swimming pools while awaiting Nichole's call.

At a quarter to midnight my cell finally rang. 'What'd you get?' I asked.

'Why, hello to you, too,' Nichole deadpanned. 'Right,' she said when I didn't respond, 'here's the skinny. My friend Paul says there is a guy named Pete who hangs out at this bar downtown who could be in the restaurant business, and he's pretty certain the dude is gay.'

'Is it a gay bar?'

She laughed. 'I don't think there are any strictly "gay" bars left in Santa Cruz any more. They're all mixed-media these days, so to speak. But I've been to this place – the Sidecar – and a lot of the LBGTQ community hangs out there, especially later at night, after the straight crowd tends to go home. Anyway, Paul doesn't know the guy's last name, but he says he's tall and lanky, with shaggy dark hair.'

'Definitely could be Pete,' I said. 'Any chance you want to come down and do reconnaissance with me?'

'No can do. We're super busy getting ready for our trip, and I have a ton to do at work before we leave on Thursday. But if you want to wait till the end of the month, I could go with you. Sounds kind of fun.'

'Nah, I don't want to wait that long. I'll find someone else to go with me.'

But after we hung up, I stared at my computer screen, wondering who the heck I could ask. 'Cause if Pete *were* in fact the murderer, it sure didn't seem wise – especially given the incident with my gas stove – to go stalking the guy all by my lonesome without any backup.

Martin was obviously out of the question, for a variety of reasons. And although Eric might go if requested, I hesitated to ask him. He might take it as a sign of interest, and I wasn't at all sure I wanted to encourage him in that way.

Allison would likely be willing, but it seemed better to get a man to accompany me, given my purpose in discovering whether or not Pete had an interest in those of the male persuasion.

My dad? Not.

But maybe Javier . . .

The next morning, I was sitting in the kitchen staring at the headlines, Buster at my feet, waiting impatiently for me to set down my plate of crumbs from my buttered toast. I'd forsaken any strawberry jam, since I wouldn't be able to taste it and figured, why add the extra calories for nothing?

The lead story in today's paper was about a suspected arson at a yoga studio out in Aptos, which made me set down my mug of coffee. *Now, who had been talking about yoga recently?* And then I remembered: It was Grace, who'd told me about her yoga teacher who'd been so helpful and sympathetic about Neil's death.

What day of the week had that been? I thought back to the days after the cook-off. It was the next night, Monday, when Vargas had asked me to keep my ears and eyes out for anything the Lerici family might have to say about Neil, so it would have been the following morning that I'd texted Grace and she'd called back. A Tuesday, then.

Just like today.

Which meant she was likely at the class again this morning. If only I could remember the name of the studio she'd said. It was some yoga-ish sounding name. Om? Mantra? Chakra? No, none of those were right.

I pulled out my phone and Googled yoga studios in Santa Cruz, and there it was: Prana Studio, on Center Street – only about a block from Gauguin. So I'd have good reason to be down there and just 'happen' to run across her as her class let out.

Searching my recent calls, I found the one from Grace two weeks ago, at 9:05 a.m. *What time was it now?* Eight forty-five. *Damn.* I'd have to get going.

Gulping down my coffee, I dashed to the bedroom for a jacket, grabbed a treat for Buster, my wallet, and my keys, and ran out the door to the T-Bird.

Ten minutes later, I parked in the Gauguin lot and hustled to the yoga studio. It was next door to a boutique clothing store, so I stood gazing at the spring display in the window of Madras-print shirts and brightly-colored sundresses, keeping one eye on the door to the yoga studio.

After five minutes, a group of chattering women exited the studio, followed by several others, all clutching rolled-up yoga pads. But no Grace.

By nine fifteen, I was starting to think maybe she'd skipped class today and was studying my phone, trying to decide whether to head back to my car, when I looked up to find my quarry standing but six feet away. She was staring at me as if my body were covered in grotesque boils and lesions.

'What are you doing here?' Grace's voice was so cold I felt the urge to zip my fleece sweater all the way up to my chin. 'Are you *still* following me?'

'What? No! I was just on my way to the restaurant.' I gestured down Cedar Street toward the block which housed Gauguin.

'Uh-huh.' I could tell she didn't believe me. Which made perfect sense, since it was in fact a complete lie. With a shake of the head, she started across the street.

'Grace, wait. I can explain.'

I don't know if it was because of my pleading tone or out of simple curiosity, but she stopped and turned back. Head tilted, her hard eyes boring into me, she waited.

'You're right; I was following you.'

This produced a smug smile.

'I've been trying to help Detective Vargas with his investigation into Neil's death, but before coming clean to you about what I was doing, I had to rule you out as a suspect first. Which I've now done.'

I was trying to read her expression, but couldn't tell if it was one of anger, relief, or disbelief. A combination of all three, I decided.

'You truly thought I might have murdered my own *brother*?' Grace's face had gone slack and the yoga mat started to slip from her hands. Grasping hold of it more firmly, she shook her head. 'I . . . I can't believe you'd think—'

'No, I never believed that,' I cut in. 'But I needed to get the proof to convince Vargas. Which is why I followed you up to the vineyard. But now that I know you needed that money for Neil's funeral, and not for some reason that pre-dated his death, it's clear that Vargas's theory – that you had a financial motive for killing Neil – just doesn't fly. 'Cause, well, his death actually *hurt* you financially.'

She was staring dully at the ground, her body wavering, and I was afraid she might collapse and keel over onto the sidewalk.

'Here, why don't we go sit somewhere and I can explain it all to you. How 'bout that place over there?'

Grace followed me into the coffee shop across the street, and we took a seat at a small table by the window. I was fully aware that I was going against Vargas's directive, but at this point I no longer cared. He was already so angry that it didn't much matter what I did from here on out. And I felt I owed it to Grace to come clean. Especially if I had any hope of remaining her friend after all this was over.

Our drinks ordered, I cleared my throat and considered how best to approach the situation. But Grace spoke first, deciding for me.

'You said that *I* was no longer a suspect, but what about Ryan?'

And there it was: my own personal Rubicon. Did I cross it? Because if I answered her question honestly, there would be no going back. Up till now, I'd been able to at least pretend I was merely making up with a friend – someone I truly believed was not guilty of the crime under investigation – so I had good reason to say what I had to her.

But if I continued down this path and told Grace our theories regarding other suspects, including her own brother, I'd in effect be bringing her into the investigation as a fellow sleuth – something guaranteed to send Vargas into paroxysms of rage if he ever found out. And something which could also subject me to serious retribution, legal as well as personal.

The server approached with our drinks, and I used the opportunity to consider my options, stirring cream into my coffee and taking a sip.

It was a sure bet Vargas wasn't going to keep me in the loop any longer, and it occurred to me that Grace had all sorts of inside information neither Vargas or I could possibly hope to discover on our own. She could end up being the key to solving the murder.

I'd just have to make damn sure no one ever learned of her involvement.

With a glance around the room to see if anyone else was in earshot, I leaned across our table. 'Can I trust you to keep this to yourself?'

'Sure,' she answered quickly.

I looked her in the eye. 'I'm serious. This could get both of us into a big time trouble if it ever got out that I told you. So I need to be sure you won't tell *anyone* – including Ryan – what I'm about to say. Because, well, we *have* uncovered a possible motive for him. A couple, actually.'

'You *have*?' She sat back, eyes wide. 'Wha . . . what are they?'

I continued to hold her gaze, still unsure whether to proceed.

After a moment, Grace swallowed, then said in a soft voice, 'If it's true Ryan had *anything* to do with Neil's death, then he deserves whatever he gets.'

The combination of anger and pain in her eyes convinced me. 'Okay, then. So here it is. First, there's a financial motive for Ryan to have wanted Neil gone, since Neil was the one kid opposed to subdividing the farm and selling it to that developer. I gather Ryan didn't have the cash to pay for Neil's funeral, which was why you ended up having to do so . . .'

Grace nodded agreement.

'So maybe he really, really needed that money from the sale for some reason. Cynthia told me they weren't hurting for money, but it's possible she just doesn't know the truth. But also, it sounds like Ryan might have been jealous of Neil. Cynthia also told me he'd accused her of being interested in Neil, though she pooh-poohed the idea. But it would also make sense that he might be hurt over Neil being so obviously the favorite. You know, since he's the one who stayed on to work the farm.'

'I'm sorry,' Grace said, shaking her head, 'but I can't see any of that being enough for Ryan to want to hurt . . .' She leaned forward and lowered her voice. 'To *kill* his own brother. Huh-uh, I just don't believe it.'

'But there's more,' I said. 'I found out something from your mom yesterday that could explain a lot: why Ryan's been in such a foul mood the past few months; why he was so bent on selling the farm; and why he might have all of a sudden just completely lost it and done something crazy.'

I had Grace's complete attention now, her dark eyes full of questions and fear.

'Diana told me that Ryan isn't Ernie's son. His dad is some German guy she knew before she and your dad got married.'

'*What?*'

'And it looks like Ryan must have discovered the truth about his ancestry only a few months ago, after Cynthia gave him one of those DNA test kits for Christmas.'

Grace blinked a few times, then turned to stare out the window, jaw tight. 'He must have felt absolutely shattered,' she said after a moment. 'Not only to learn something like that, but also that Mom and Dad had kept if from him all these years?'

'I know. I can't even imagine how I'd feel in his position.'

'And then to have Neil – the "real" son – be the one insisting we not subdivide the property . . .' She turned toward me with a frown. 'But Neil had always been the one who was totally into the artichokes and the farm, so it couldn't have been any big surprise to Ryan that he wouldn't want to sell. When we were kids, it was Neil who'd go out into the fields with Dad, ride around with him on the tractor, hang out with the farmhands . . .'

Grace picked up her latte and sipped from its foamy top. 'And in the rainy season, he'd drag me with him down to the marshy area below the stable to collect pollywogs. We'd keep them in water in mayonnaise jars till they grew into frogs, and then they'd escape and we'd find them all over the house. Mom hated that,' she said with a laugh.

But then she let out a sigh and her face again grew sad. 'Even as an adult he still loved those frogs,' she said. 'Only a month ago I was with him down at that same spot, and when he saw one, I swear he got just as excited as he had when we were little kids. He was going on and on about how the tadpoles had turned into this particular kind of frog, and something about the sequence of it all and how great it was, but I was barely even paying attention and just made fun of him for never growing up.'

Grace's voice caught in a sob. 'And now he never will,' she said.

EIGHTEEN

've got to hand it to Javier. The guy is most definitely straight, and was raised Catholic in a tiny village in Michoacán, but he seems to have none of the 'gay panic' I see in some of my other straight male friends. Even Eric, who's pretty darn secure in his masculinity, can be a little uncomfortable around gay guys, especially if he's completely outnumbered.

But when I asked Javier that night if he'd be willing to go with me to the Sidecar after work, he readily agreed. 'You know it's a gay hangout after-hours, right?' I'd said, and he'd merely shrugged.

'Whatever. I don't care, as long as they stock good Scotch. But I am curious why this sudden desire to hang out at a gay bar. You thinking of switching teams?'

'Nah. Though given the state of my love life right about now, it might not be a bad idea. But I think it's actually gonna be more guys than gals there tonight. Which is why I want to go.'

'Oh yeah?' Javier looked up from the rainbow chard he had sautéing in his pan. 'How come?'

'You know Pete Ferrari, the guy who runs the Crab Shack next door to Solari's?'

'I don't know him personally, but I know his name.'

'Well, this friend of mine is interested in Pete, but he's not sure if he's gay or not, so I said I'd find out for him.'

'Why doesn't he just find out himself? It's not like it's all that hard to tell if a guy's into you or not.'

I briefly pondered how much experience Javier had with men flirting with him. It wouldn't surprise me, given the chef's delicate features, gorgeous brown eyes, and easy smile. He'd be quite the catch – for someone of either persuasion.

'Oh . . . well, I guess he's just shy,' I replied. Javier had a good point, but since I was inventing this entire story, I didn't have much of an answer.

This seemed to satisfy him, however, and he laughed. 'So I gather you want me to be the bait.'

'No, no, that's not it. I just don't want to go there alone, is all.'

'Right.' Javier continued to chuckle as he plated up his chard next to the order of grilled salmon Kris had sent over from the charbroiler. 'No worries,' he said. 'It's all good. But you're buying tonight.'

It was almost midnight by the time we got to the Sidecar, but although it was only a Tuesday night, the place was still crowded. Grace Jones was blasting from the speakers, and about a dozen people were showing off their moves on the small dance floor.

Javier and I waited several minutes for the busy bartender to come our way, then, drinks in hand, found a table in the corner. The booming techno music made any real conversation impossible, so I sat back and studied the bar patrons, looking for Pete. Several guys were huddled together at the far end of the bar, and when one stepped aside momentarily I spotted a familiar figure sitting on a stool, a bottle of beer before him.

'He's here!' I shouted over the music.

'What?' Javier leaned forward and cupped his ear.

I repeated my statement, pointing across the room, and he turned to look. 'Oh, right,' he said. 'That guy. I've seen him at the Restaurant Owners Association meetings.'

'You want to go chat him up?'

'I guess so, since that's why we're here, right?' Javier picked up his highball glass and stood, while I did my best to shrink down into my chair and become invisible. Not that any of the guys in the bar were paying the least bit of attention to me. They were far too busy watching Javier as he sauntered across the room wearing an enigmatic smile.

But instead of approaching the group containing Pete, Javier walked past the men and headed down the hallway toward the restrooms. Had he chickened out at the last minute?

I sipped from my bourbon, keeping one eye on the hallway and the other on a pair slow dancing to Lady Gaga's 'Million Reasons'. As the song drew to a close, Javier emerged from the hallway and went to stand at the far end of the bar, right next to Pete. He'd left his glass behind, and as I watched, he leaned over to speak to the bartender, who nodded and poured him another Scotch-rocks.

Javier paid for his drink, then turned as if to survey the scene. Pete glanced his way, sipped from his beer, and glanced again. After a moment, he turned to Javier and said something. Javier responded with a grin – I could see the flash of his white teeth from all the way across the room – and said something in return, prompting Pete to swivel in his chair so that he was facing Javier, his back now to me.

They talked for a while, at times leaning in close to speak into each other's ear. At one point, Pete reached out to lay a hand on Javier's arm, but Javier made no move to step back or brush it off. After what seemed like forever – though it was probably only five minutes – both men laughed, and Javier raised his glass to clink it with Pete's beer bottle. He drank down the rest of his Scotch and set the glass on the bar, then said something else to Pete and, with a nod, started back toward me.

Afraid that Pete might turn to see where Javier was headed and spot me at the table, I bolted out the front door to wait for Javier.

'Well, that was interesting,' he said, joining me outside. 'And to answer your question, I'd say that's a for sure "yes". He was most definitely coming on to me. But you might warn your friend that the guy stinks of cigarettes.' Javier made a fanning motion with his hand, as if waving away imaginary smoke. 'But then again, I'm super sensitive to the smell these days. You know, ever since quitting.'

So Allison's hunch was right. Pete *was* gay. Which begged the next set of questions: *had* he and Neil been involved during high school and then had a bad break-up and, if so, had Pete held a grudge against Neil because of that for all these years? A grudge serious enough to end in murder?

'So what'd you two talk about all that time?' I asked as we set off down the street toward my car.

'It wasn't all *that* long,' Javier said. 'Though I do have to say it was kind of nice being on the receiving end of all that attention. Too bad I don't get the same reaction from the women I meet in bars.'

'Don't be so sure you don't. They're just maybe a little more subtle, is all.'

Javier considered this a moment, then chuckled. 'Maybe. Anyway, to answer your question, I was kind of surprised Pete didn't recognize me like I had him, but once I told him I was the chef at Gauguin, he started asking me all these questions about the restaurant.'

I stopped in my tracks. 'What? You told him where you worked?'

'Why shouldn't I?' Javier looked at me with a frown, and I realized I'd better change tack, lest he figure out that the story about my 'friend' was pure fabrication.

'No, it's okay,' I said quickly. 'I was just worried about Pete knowing I'd put you up to it, which could be awkward if he and my friend do end up getting together, is all. That's why I ran out of there so fast. I didn't want Pete to see me. But no worries; I'm sure they can work it out themselves if it ever comes to that.'

'Ah, got it. Sorry.' Javier started down the sidewalk once more and I trotted to catch up.

'So what exactly did he want to know about Gauguin?'

Javier glanced my way. 'Well, what's funny is that he actually seemed pretty curious about *you*. If the guy hadn't been so obviously flirting with me, I'd have thought maybe you were the one he was interested in. But hey, maybe he swings both ways.'

It was my turn to frown. *Why would Pete be interested in me?* Had he seen me in the bar tonight and figured out what it was I was doing? A shiver passed over me, and I shook it off.

'Curious . . . how?' I asked.

'Like, he wanted to know how I liked having you as a boss. Though of course I immediately let him know that you weren't in fact my boss any longer, that I'm now half owner of Gauguin. And he also asked if we'd been doing better or worse ever since you inherited the place.'

Javier paused and chewed his lip. 'You know, he seemed really interested in the financial aspect of the restaurant, come to think of it. So maybe it was that more than you he was interested in. Huh. I wonder if his place is having problems . . .'

'Interesting,' I said. 'Maybe you're right. He certainly wouldn't be the first restaurant owner to run into financial difficulties.'

And if that were the case, I realized, it would explain his competitiveness with my father. Since Solari's – which catered to pretty much the exact same clientele as the Crab Shack – was doing just fine, Pete could easily find my dad's success galling if his place was in the red.

But even more relevant to my immediate concern was the fact that Pete likely hadn't seen me tonight, after all. *You're just being paranoid*, I chided myself as Javier and I continued down the street. *There's no way Pete could know I suspect him of killing Neil.*

I'd been hoping my dad would email or call to make some sort of gesture of reconciliation, but when Wednesday morning arrived with still no contact, I decided it would have to be me who reached out to him. I'm not keen on interactions involving conflict, but unresolved conflict is even worse.

A face-to-face meeting seemed best, so after my morning coffee and dog walk, I clipped into the pedals of my trusty two-wheeled steed and pedaled down to the wharf. Solari's didn't open for another hour, but I knew Dad would already be there, simmering the red sauce and filleting whatever the catch of the day happened to be.

He was at the long counter opposite the range top sorting through several bunches of basil when I clomped into the kitchen in my cycling cleats. 'I don't know why they even bother delivering produce that's clearly past its time,' Dad groused, tossing a handful of blackened leaves into the garbage can next to him. 'Maybe it's time to change vendors.'

At least he wasn't directing his ire at me.

'Yeah, that's no good,' I said, coming to stand by his side.

He glanced my way, then went back to picking through the wilted basil. Dad had to know why I was there, but stubborn as he was, he was going to make me speak first.

Fine. I could play that game. 'So I wanted to apologize . . .'

A shrug from my father.

'I know you asked me to lay off the Lerici family, but truly, it wouldn't have made any difference even if I had, since Detective Vargas was still going to investigate them, no matter what.'

Dad made a *huffing* sound and threw another handful of herbs into the garbage.

'But it turns out my continuing to look into the Lerici siblings was actually a good thing, because I discovered evidence that pretty much disproves Vargas's theory for Grace being involved.'

'Glad to hear it,' Dad muttered, finally breaking his silence. 'And Ryan?'

'I haven't been so fortunate with him. But I haven't found anything to show he *was* involved, either.'

'Because he *couldn't* have been.' Dad smacked his hand on the cutting board, then tipped the rest of the basil into the trash can. He took several deep breaths before turning to face me, his eyes sad. 'I just know in my heart it couldn't be him. Not Diana's son.'

'I know why you care so much about the family,' I said quietly. 'Diana told me about the two of you.'

His shoulders sank and he let out another long sigh. 'Oh, honey,' he said, stepping forward to give me a hug.

'It's okay, Dad. I know it was before you and Mom got together, and I like her. You have good taste.'

With a laugh, he released me from his arms. 'I don't know why I felt like I needed to keep it from you, us having dated back in high school. It was just so odd, having you become such good friends with Grace, is all.'

'And you really liked Diana.'

He smiled, but didn't answer.

'She felt the same, you know. I could tell, when we talked.'

Dad carried the cutting board to the sink and wiped it down with a side towel.

'Do you ever regret it?' I asked, following him across the kitchen. 'Not marrying her?'

'Not for a second. I loved your mother more than anything on this blessed Earth.' He set the board on the counter and lay a hand on my shoulder. 'And she also gave me you.'

We were interrupted by the sound of a surf guitar ringing out from the back pocket of my cycling jersey. 'Go ahead and take that, hon,' Dad said. 'I've gotta get back to work.'

'So are we okay?'

'We're always okay, *bambina*.'

With a reassuring smile, he headed for the walk-in fridge as I pulled out my phone. 'Hey, Eric. What's up?'

'Not much. I just got out of court and was wondering if you'd be up for meeting for coffee here at the cafeteria.'

Whatever it was he wanted to talk about, he wasn't letting up. I glanced at the time on my phone. Ten twenty. I'd promised Javier I'd meet him at the restaurant at one to go over the tax forms before sending them off to our accountant, but that gave me time to meet Eric before going home to shower and change clothes.

'Sure,' I said. 'I'm just leaving Solari's on my bike, so I'll meet you there in about ten minutes.'

NINETEEN

B ack when I still worked as an attorney, I used to spend a lot of time at the County Building, consulting court documents in the county clerk's office and doing research in the law library. Since Eric worked in the same building, we'd often meet for coffee and donuts in the building's basement cafeteria – a spot popular with cops waiting to testify in court and harried government workers in need of a caffeine and sugar pick-me-up.

Bicycles aren't technically allowed in the building, but I snuck in the downstairs back entrance and wheeled down the fluorescent-lit hallway without being yelled at by anyone. Eric was already there, a cup of coffee and half-eaten bear claw before him. I leaned my bike against the wall, set my helmet on the table, and headed to the counter for my own coffee and a croissant.

'So how was court?' I asked, setting down my booty and pulling out a chair.

Eric shrugged. 'Annoying. Just more of the same.'

'Uh, huh.' I kept my eyes on him as I sipped from my cup.

He avoided my gaze, shifting in his seat, taking off his glasses to wipe them on his shirttail, then finally looked up. 'Is everything okay with Vargas?' he asked. 'I could tell you were having a bit of a tiff there, the other day at your *nonna*'s . . .'

'More than a tiff, I'd say. He barely spoke to me all the way home, and what he did say wasn't much fun.'

Eric was watching me closely. 'And that was . . .?' he prompted.

I didn't much relish the idea of reliving the conversation, but I knew it would be good to talk it all through with someone. And Eric had always been my go-to guy for spilling my guts.

'Okay,' I said, splaying my fingers on the vinyl tabletop. 'So Martin's pissed 'cause he thinks I kind of went overboard on this whole Neil Lerici thing. He'd asked me to keep my ears and eyes out about anything that might be interesting, you know, since I was friends with Neil's sister, Grace, which I agreed to do. But then, when he found out I'd been *actively* looking into the death, well . . .'

'I gather that was the news he got during Sunday dinner?'

'Right. So now he's forbidden me to talk to anyone in the family, and I'm pretty sure he doesn't ever want to talk to *me* again, either.'

Eric lay his hand atop mine. 'I'm sorry,' he said. 'You don't need that right now. What with losing your sense of smell an' all. Has it by any chance returned?'

I shook my head.

'And I know I haven't been much of a friend lately . . .' He stared at the remnants of his pastry, jaw tight, then raised his eyes to mine. 'Look, I feel really bad about the way I've been acting the past few months. Which is the main reason I've been wanting to get together and talk. I realize now I shouldn't have let my relationship with Gayle affect ours like it did.'

'Did? That sounds like the past tense.'

'Yeah, well . . .' Eric shifted again in his chair and cleared his throat. '*She* seems to think everything's just hunky-dory, but I'm not so sure. She just doesn't seem to get me, like, you know . . .'

Like I do, is what I figured he was thinking. But I wasn't going to finish the sentence for him.

He shook his head impatiently. 'Okay, so take what happened this morning, for instance. Gayle was in court waiting for her case to be called, and I was up there trying to convince the judge that my stupid little fraud case shouldn't be dismissed. And then afterwards in the hallway, when I was griping to her about how I keep getting assigned all these piddly-ass files, she says to me, "You know, those CEQA cases are really important. If that guy's EIR truly was fraudulent, you're doing us all a huge favor by—"'

'Wait, what did you just say?' I interrupted. 'See-quah?'

'Right. CEQA, the California Environmental Quality Act. You know, for protecting groundwater and animal habitats? We're prosecuting this scummy two-bit consultant who sub-mitted a totally bogus Environmental Impact Report for his client. Yet one more big-time important case that I've been assigned by my boss.' Eric's voice oozed with sarcasm.

'Ohmygod,' I said.

'What?'

'It all makes sense now. It was CEQA he was talking about.'

Eric stared at me, confusion in his eyes. '*Who* was?'

'Neil Lerici, the guy who was murdered during the Artichoke Cook-Off. His sister told me he'd gotten super excited about a specific kind of frog he found on the property recently, and said he was going on and on about some "sequence" and how important it was. Which didn't make a whole lot of sense to me when she told the story. But I just realized he must have been saying "CEQA" not "sequence".'

'Whoa, hold on, girl.' Eric made a T with his hands. 'Back up a little and tell me what the heck you're talking about.'

I explained about Ernie Lerici wanting to subdivide the farm and how Neil and Diana had been holdouts on the sale to a developer. 'And when you were talking about CEQA just now, it reminded me of a case our law firm had a few years back, where this client who wanted to build a house up near Davenport ended up having to jump through a gazillion governmental hoops because they'd found a few red-legged frogs on his land.'

Eric was nodding understanding. Anyone involved in the legal or construction business in our area is well aware of the stringent protections those endangered amphibians enjoy. Their presence on a property can mean years of studies, reports, and other red tape before any construction will be allowed – if it ever is.

'So can you imagine how excited Neil would have been if he'd discovered a red-legged frog on the farm?' I pushed back my chair and stood, too antsy now to sit still. 'It would have seemed like an answer to his prayers, manna from heaven.'

'An apparition of *la Virgen de Guadalupe*, disguised as a frog prince with red stockings,' Eric added with a laugh. 'Because those suckers'll put the kibosh on a planned development faster than anything I know.'

'Totally.'

But my exhilaration changed quickly to melancholy as I had

another thought. 'I wonder who else he told about his discovery,' I said. 'Since the existence of those frogs may very well be what got him killed.'

My first thought when I got home after my coffee date with Eric was to call Detective Vargas and tell him about my revelation. But then I remembered all the reasons I couldn't.

Glaring at my cell phone as if it were to blame for my many woes, I set the device on the kitchen counter and started down the hall for my shower. But then I stopped. If Martin was going to refuse to speak with me, then why shouldn't I talk to someone else instead? Someone like Grace.

I punched in her number and she picked up after one ring. 'Sally. Did you find out something new about' – she lowered her voice – 'the case?'

'I did, as a matter of fact, which is why I'm calling. You got a minute?'

'Absolutely. I was just going over the quarterly statements for Jack's business, but it can wait. Any news you have about Neil's death is far more important than filing stupid tax returns.'

'Well, I won't keep you long. I just wanted to tell you I had coffee this morning with my friend Eric, who's a district attorney, and he was talking about this case he has involving CEQA, the California Environmental Quality Act, and it made me remember what you'd said yesterday about Neil getting all excited about finding the frog at the farm.'

'Uh-huh . . .?'

I could tell she had no idea what I was getting at. 'You told me that Neil was talking about some "sequence" after he discovered the frog, right?'

'Right.'

'Well, is it possible he said "see-*quah*" rather than "se-*quence*"?'

'Sure, I guess so . . . But I wasn't paying all that much attention to exactly what he said. I mostly just remember how excited he was, and how silly it seemed to me to act that way because of some frog.'

'Well, that frog could actually be really important.' I explained to her about the protections afforded the red-legged frog, and how CEQA was the regulatory scheme setting forth all the red tape developers had to go through if it were suspected the land might contain an endangered species habitat. 'So if it was in fact a red-legged frog that Neil found, its presence could very well prevent any development from happening on the farm property, or at least drag out the permitting process so long that no one would want to get involved in it.'

'Ohmygod,' Grace said. 'Do you think it *was* that kind of frog?'

'It makes sense to me. I know they live in marshy places like where you described. And it would certainly explain why Neil was so excited. I wouldn't be surprised if he'd done research about ways to prevent the development, and if so, CEQA would have been one of the first things to come up for a Google search about environmental protections.'

Grace was silent.

'So the next question,' I went on, 'is who would he have told about the frog?'

This got her going. 'I know what you're thinking, but I still can't believe Ryan would have attacked Neil, even if he did tell him about it.'

'He was there at the cook-off that day, though, right?' I asked.

'Yeah . . .'

'Which Vargas for sure has to know. So if he gets wind of this red-legged frog thing, it's only gonna add fuel to his fire about Ryan.'

'Well, what about that Sumner guy – the developer? Neil could have told him about the frog.'

'True. And believe me, he's just gone way up on my list of suspects. But unlike Ryan, we have no way of placing him at the scene of the crime that day.'

'Okay, so we just need to prove Ryan's innocent, then. Because I know he is.' Grace's voice was now full of impatience. 'What if we could show that Neil never told him about the frog?'

'Well, that wouldn't prove he didn't kill Neil, but it would be a start. Too bad we can't check Neil's emails and texts, but the cops for sure have taken away all his computers and stuff.'

'We could search his room, though,' Grace said. 'Maybe he left something there that would help – something the police didn't think was important. You wanna meet me up at the farm this afternoon?'

I consulted the time. 'No can do. I have to be at Gauguin in an hour. But how about tomorrow morning?'

'Sounds good. Say ten o'clock?'

'Perfect.'

'He what?' I strained to hear the voice on the other end of my phone, which was competing with the kitchen fan and the Robot Coupe Javier was using to shred Brussels sprouts for tonight's salad special. 'Here, lemme go to another room.' Pushing through the door into the wait station, I let it swing back into place. 'Okay, much better. Now say that again?'

The call came from our line cook Brian's cell, but his girl-friend Roxanne was the one on the line. 'I'm at the ER with Brian,' she said. 'He fell off his mountain bike and hit his head on a stump, so I wanted to have him checked out to make sure he doesn't have a concussion.'

'Oh, no. Does he seem okay? Was he wearing a helmet?'

'Yes and yes. And he's super mad at me for dragging him down here, since he's supposed to be at work in a half hour, but—'

'No, you did the right thing. You don't want to mess around with head injuries. Tell him not to worry, and if he can come in later tonight, that's great, but if not, it'll be fine. We'll figure out something.'

When I walked back into the kitchen, Javier looked up from the mound of shredded sprouts he was now tossing with a citrus vinaigrette. 'What was that about?'

'Brian fell off his bike and is at the hospital getting checked out. Which could take a while, given what I know from my past experience at the ER. So what do you wanna do? You think Tomás could handle the line if you were there with him to help?'

'I say let's ask him.' Javier pulled off his vinyl gloves and threw them into the trash, and I followed him into the *garde manger.*

'Hey guys. What's up?' The prep cook set his knife down next to a pile of black cod steaks.

'Brian's at the ER,' I said, 'and Kris is out of town, so it's your lucky day. You're being promoted.'

'Really? That's gr— I mean, what happened to Brian? Is he all right?'

'I'm sure he'll be fine. He fell off his bike and Roxanne just wanted to have him checked out to be safe. He may even come in later tonight. But for the time being, we need another set of hands in the kitchen. How would you feel about helping Javier on the hot line?'

Tomás thought a moment. 'Well, I'd totally love to learn the line some time, but just being thrown out there all of a sudden seems kind of scary . . .' He glanced nervously from me to Javier. 'But I can totally do it if you want.'

'Do you have much experience grilling?' I asked.

'Definitely. I'm king of the barbecue at all our family get-togethers. I could totally handle the charbroiler.'

'All right then. Once you finish with that sablefish, come on out and I'll give you a primer on the grill station. And don't worry, Javier and I are definitely planning on teaching you the hot line sometime very soon.'

'Awesome!' With a broad grin, Tomás attacked his fish with renewed vigor.

While Javier finished prepping his salad, toasting the pine nuts, shaving the Pecorino cheese, and filling a bowl with dried cranberries, I set to work on the *mise en place* for the line. I'd just dropped a metal pan of chopped walnuts into the row of inserts running along the back of the stove when Javier came up behind me.

'You think he'll be okay at the charbroiler?' the chef asked.

'I hope so. It's not like we have much choice. But he's a smart kid, and a hard worker. And I'll be sure to give him the drill about how to tell when the steaks are done.'

Grill station cooks all know the 'touch trick' for gauging the doneness of meat: if the steak feels like the fleshy part of your hand below the thumb while touching your index finger to your thumb, then it's rare. If the meat feels like that same part of your hand with your middle finger pressed against your thumb, then it's medium rare. And you can work your way down the other fingers – ring, then pinkie – to test for medium- and well-done steaks.

Javier nodded and reached for a sauce pot. 'So is your friend going to ask Pete out on a date?' he asked.

'Oh. I, uh, haven't talked to him yet. But I will.'

With all the excitement about the red-legged frog and wondering about Ryan and the developer as suspects, I hadn't given any thought to Pete today. *But*, I mused as I headed to the walk-in for a pound of butter, *I really do need to consider what it might mean, now that I know he is in fact gay.*

My pal Nichole liked to say that when there's been a crime of passion it's always most likely the lover who did it, and she'd been right before.

Could it be that Neil's death was the result of jilting a boyfriend all the way back in his sophomore year of high school? And if so, how could I find out?

TWENTY

I beat Grace to the farm the next morning, but as soon as I pulled up in front of the old Victorian house, Bondo's egg-shaped head appeared at the window, barking his announcement of my arrival. A minute later, Diana opened the front door and, seeing it was me, came out onto the porch.

'Oh, hello, Sally,' she said as I climbed out of the T-Bird. 'What brings you here today?'

'I'm meeting Grace and we're going to . . . uh . . .' *Oh, boy.* What could I tell her? That we wanted to search her dead son's room to try to find something to prove that her other son wasn't the one who killed him?

I was saved from having to come up with an answer by the sound of tires crunching their way up the gravel drive. 'Oh, look, here she is now.'

Joining Diana on the porch, I glanced her way as I waited for Grace to park, but then did a double-take. 'What happened to your eye?'

Diana let out an embarrassed laugh as she reached up to touch the swollen black-and-blue area below her left eye. 'Oh, it's nothing. I just knocked myself in the face with a cupboard door, is all. So stupid.'

It didn't look like 'nothing' to me, but I wasn't going to press the point.

Grace had the exact same reaction as me. 'Ohmygod, Mom, what happened to your eye?' she said as she came up the front steps.

Diana waved her off with a shake of the head. 'It's nothing, *truly*. Now I really have to get back to my lemon curd and scones. I'm making dessert for my book club tonight.' And with that, she turned and walked back into the house.

'I'll tell you later,' I whispered to Grace, and the two of us followed Diana inside and then headed up the stairs. Once in

Neil's room with the door closed, I recounted to Grace what her mother had said to me.

'I guess it's possible,' she said, taking a seat on one of the twin beds. 'I banged my head on my car door a few weeks ago and gave myself a big ol' bruise. But I do kind of worry that maybe Dad had one of his angry spells and could have . . .' Grace trailed off and chewed her lip.

'Has he ever shown any violence in the past?' I asked.

She shook her head. 'Not that I know of. All I've ever seen him do is yell, and then he'll sometimes stomp out of the room afterwards. I've never actually seen him do anything physical.'

'Well what about Ryan, then? He seems pretty pissed off at your mother these days.'

'What?' Grace's voice was sharp. 'No way. He would never do something like that to Mom.'

But both of us knew damn well there was a chance it *could* have been Ryan – or Ernie – and as I stared at a poster of seasonal vegetables that had been tacked to the bedroom wall, I had a vision of the Shakespeare performance I'd seen several years earlier, and the bloody eyes of the Earl of Gloucester, mutilated by the wrathful Cornwall.

How weird was this. I was itching to tell Allison that the case had yet one more similarity to *King Lear*.

'Well,' Grace said, startling me from my literary musings, 'I guess we should get to it,' and opened the drawer of the bedside table. 'You wanna look through his desk?'

'Sure.'

I had pulled out a stack of papers and was sifting through them one by one, when a sharp intake of breath made me look up. 'Did you find something?'

'What the . . .?' Grace was staring at a magazine, her eyes growing wider by the second, then turned it around to face me.

OUT, the cover read in large block letters, and featured a hunky guy in a tight red tank top.

'So Neil was gay? Wow.' Grace studied the cover once more, then let the magazine fall onto her lap. 'Though I guess I shouldn't be that surprised . . . It's not like he ever had a girl-friend that I knew of.'

'Yeah,' I said. 'I thought he might be.'

She turned to me with a frown. 'How long have you known? Did you suspect back in high school?'

'No way. It never even occurred to me way back then. But after seeing that photo of him and Pete in our yearbook on the swim team, and then talking to my friend Allison – you know, she was our year in school?'

Grace shook her head. 'I never really knew her that well, but I know who she is.'

'Well, anyway, Allison was in art class with Pete Ferrari and says he and Neil were really close when they were sopho-mores, but then at the end of the school year, Pete got super depressed. She thinks they might have been involved, and given what you told me about their having a falling out, I'm thinking it must have been more than that – you know, a romantic break-up. And if it was Neil who was the one who broke it off . . .'

'Then Pete could've held it against Neil ever since then.' Grace stood up from the bed, knocking the glossy magazine to the floor. 'So *he's* our best suspect, then, not Ryan.'

'Don't worry; Pete's definitely on the list. Not only was he obviously there that day of the cook-off, but he ended up winning first prize solely because of Neil's death. And my father says he's a real hothead, to boot.'

Grace pulled the drawer all the way out from the bedside table and dumped its contents on the floor. 'Well, let's see, then, if we can find anything here that has to do with Pete.'

While she examined the contents of the drawer, I went back to my stack of papers. They were mostly farm-related: brochures about tractors and harvesters; seed catalogues; a journal detailing the pruning, spraying, flowering, fruiting, and harvesting of the apple orchard above the stable; and sheets of paper with miscellaneous notes scrawled on them about what I took to be varieties of artichokes and their growing season and yields.

Shoving the stack back in the drawer, I opened the next one down. At the very top lay a sheaf of papers stapled together.

'Eureka! I've found something,' I said, and read aloud the title on the first page: 'Site Assessment for the California

Red-Legged Frog: Gray Hawk Housing Project, Shasta County, California.'

Grace dropped the postcard she'd been examining and came to look over my shoulder. 'So it *was* a red-legged frog,' she said. '*And* he was researching it.'

'Yep.' I scanned the table of contents on the next page, then turned to page four to read the section on Legal Status. 'It says the frog was designated a threatened subspecies in 1996 and that critical habitat was proposed for it in 2000. And just look at the size of this report.' I flipped through the pages with my thumb as if it were a deck of cards. 'Forty-two pages long, most of which are about all the studies and site inspections they did on the land. Can you imagine the amount of money this must have cost? And it probably took years to do.'

'Wait, what's that?' Grace asked as I continued to leaf through the report.

'Looks like he's highlighted some text. Lemme see . . . It's in the section about reporting the results of field surveys. And there's a handwritten note that says "specimen spotted near pond below horse barn. Gotta get photo". Here, is this Neil's handwriting?'

Grace studied the page and nodded. 'Uh-huh, that's for sure his writing. And that spot he's talking about is where we were the day he got so excited about finding that frog.'

'Well, I guess this proves he was stockpiling ammunition to fight the development,' I said as the two of us stared at the pages in my hand. 'So the next question is, had he told anyone?'

'Let's keep looking,' Grace said, and headed for Neil's closet.

We found nothing else of interest in Neil's room. Frustrated to have discovered that report and then not a hint of anything suggesting whom he might have told about the frog, we retired to the kitchen for coffee and some of the scones Diana had just taken out of the oven.

'This is terrific,' I said, spreading more lemon curd atop the half-eaten pastry. 'It's so chewy.' Notwithstanding my lack of taste, I could tell from the mouth feel that the scone had the perfect balance of shortening and cream. And was that maybe just a hint of citrus that I was detecting in the curd?

'Oh, thanks,' Diane said with a grin. 'Would you like the recipe?'

'Sure. Maybe we could serve them at Gauguin as a part of a dessert special.'

Diana pulled an old wooden box out of the cupboard and, as she did so, I noticed that the bottom corner of the door came to exactly eye-level. So perhaps she did in fact give herself that black eye.

She flipped through the index cards in the box and extracted one. 'Here. It's my mother's recipe. They're made with cream cheese, which is what makes them so moist.' Diana grabbed her purse off the kitchen counter and rummaged around for her keys. 'Just leave the card on the table when you're done,' she said. 'I've got to head into town to pick up some groceries for tonight.'

'Where's Dad?' Grace asked. 'Should I lock up when we leave?'

'He's down by the fields, I think, so no need.' Leaning over to kiss her daughter goodbye, she waved goodbye to me and headed out the door.

While I pulled out my phone to snap a photo of the recipe card, Grace stood and looked out the kitchen window. 'She's right; Dad's down there with Amy,' she said, letting the curtain fall back into place. She sat back down and flashed me a conspiratorial look. 'So what do you think we should do now?'

I set my phone on the farmhouse table. 'Who knows? Vargas is treating me as if I have the bubonic plague, so I can't tell him what we know.'

'Wait. But aren't you two dating?'

'Not at the moment we're not. It's hard to date someone who won't even talk to you.'

She eyed me for a moment with a frown. 'I guess I can imagine how this could all be pretty tricky for a relationship.'

I dabbed at the lemon curd on my plate with my finger. 'Just a little.'

'Okay, so what if I told him?'

'No way. If he even suspected I've been talking to you about the case he'd probably send out someone to arrest me for interfering with an investigation or some such thing.'

Grace stood once more and started pacing back and forth between the kitchen window and the enormous porcelain sink. 'Well, we have to do *something*. We can't just sit here and wait for him to haul Ryan off to jail for a crime he didn't commit. We have to prove it was Pete. Or . . . who else did you say he suspected?'

'Well, you for one. Since he doesn't yet know about your reason for needing that money – that it was for Neil's funeral.'

'Great.' Plopping back down onto her chair, she lay her head on the wood tabletop.

'But there's also Amy, who was with Neil most of that day. And, of course, the developer, Sumner. If we could prove that Neil told *him* about the frog, that would be great. Though, of course, he's the one person we can't place at the scene of the crime. Plus, I have no idea how I could get any information about him, in any case.'

I took another bite of scone and as I chewed – that cream cheese truly did impart a tender, moist texture – I thought about what I'd seen that day in the dumpster enclosure out on the wharf.

'I wonder why the heck whoever did it shoved that artichoke in his mouth,' I mused out loud.

'Huh?' Grace raised her head. 'I never heard about that.'

'That's 'cause it wasn't in any of the news stories. I guess they didn't want it to get out, in case it ends up being an important piece of evidence. But I saw it there, its pointy end sticking out of Neil's mouth. And it just seems weird that someone would do that.'

'Maybe the artichoke *is* a clue,' Grace said. 'What if it was Pete, and he didn't realize he'd actually killed Neil. He could have been, I don't know . . . taunting him about the cook-off by shoving an artichoke in his mouth.' She stood and started pacing once more. 'Because it sure doesn't sound like something Ryan would have done. He grew up on an artichoke farm, so why would he use one in such an aggressive way?'

But then she stopped and stood still, gazing out the window toward the rows of artichoke fields.

We both knew the answer to her rhetorical question: Ryan had every reason to resent the crop grown on the farm that his brother – whom he now knew to be but a half-brother – had been so keen to keep from being sold. And the crop that Neil had appeared to care about more than any human, including the members of his own family.

'I need to talk to Ryan,' she said. 'Find out if Neil told him about the frog.'

'No, you can't, Grace. Promise me you won't.'

She turned to glare at me, and I got the feeling we were now engaged in some kind of stand-off. 'You can't prevent me, you know. And since both me and my brother are apparently looking at possible arrest for murder, I don't see why he and I shouldn't band together to fight this thing.'

Exactly what I'd feared might happen. *Why, oh why, did I confide in Grace?*

'Please, just give me a little more time,' I said, my voice rising almost a full octave. I shoved back my chair and hurried across the kitchen to take her by the hand. 'I'm sure I can figure this all out. Or we can, *together*.'

I don't know if it was the pleading look in my eyes or the prospect of getting to solve her brother's murder along with 'Sally, the Sleuth of Santa Cruz', as the local newspaper had taken to calling me, but I could tell from the way her face and shoulders relaxed that she was on the verge of caving.

'You and me – as a team again, just like in high school,' I coaxed.

Grace pursed her lips in thought, then glanced out the window again at her father, who was now trudging up the path from the fields toward the farmhouse.

'I have a key to Ryan's house,' she said, turning back to me with a sly smile. 'Let's go snoop around.'

TWENTY-ONE

A half hour later, Grace rapped loudly on the front door of Ryan and Cynthia's house. When no one answered, she used a key to let herself in, and the two of us stood for a moment in the entranceway. It was one of those gingerbready Victorian homes right downtown, and I could tell the building had undergone quite a bit of restoration. The paint job in the living room was exquisite – a pastel shade reminiscent of orange sherbet set off by a creamy white – and the crown molding along the edge of the ceiling appeared brand new.

'How long ago did they buy this place?' I asked, crossing the room to lay a hand on an elaborately carved wood staircase. Walnut, I guessed.

'About five years ago, right before Jason was born. They decided to move up to a bigger house once they found out Cynthia was pregnant.'

'I'll say they moved up, all right. This place must be worth a bundle.'

'Yep.' Was all Grace had to say in response to that.

I wandered toward the back of the house and into the kitchen. This room boasted pale yellow walls and a Wedgewood stove that I'd be willing to trade my firstborn for, if I had one. And the floor looked to have been recently relaid with 1920s-style linoleum in a retro black-and-white checkered pattern.

On the counter next to the stove I spotted a stack of papers. 'I can go through these,' I said to Grace, 'if you want to look in the other rooms.'

'Sure. I'll check out the study.'

The pile turned out to be all real estate related paperwork: sales and lease agreements; buyer's disclosure statements; flyers for properties now on the market; and several business cards from local realtors.

After setting the papers back on the counter in what I hoped was more or less the same arrangement they'd been in before,

I walked over to the stove and examined its enameled surface. I'd been an old stove aficionado ever since first cooking on my Aunt Letta's vintage O'Keefe and Merritt when I was still in law school. This beauty was unusual, however, in that it sported red highlights on its handles and knobs.

Leaning over to examine the stove's pristine black metal burners, I felt the skin on the back of my neck prickle as I flashed on what had happened at my house the previous Saturday. Only someone familiar with an old-style stove – the kind you needed a match to ignite – would be conscious of how dangerous it would be to turn on the gas to my stove without lighting the burner.

And I now knew that Ryan was familiar with that kind of stove.

The sound of a slamming door made me jump. I turned, expecting to see Grace, and was startled again by who it was instead.

'What are *you* doing here?'

Ryan stood glaring at me from across the kitchen.

'I . . . uh . . .'

'And how the hell did you even get inside?' He continued to stare, his nostrils flaring like an angry bull, and I glanced around to see if there was another exit besides the doorway he was blocking. None. 'It sure is strange the way you keep turning up at our family homes,' he said in almost a growl. 'First the farm and now my kitchen? What kind of game are you playing at, anyway?'

As Ryan started across the room, I reached behind me for the cast iron skillet that sat upon the Wedgewood stove.

'She's with me,' Grace said, coming up behind him. 'I just stopped by to get my phone, which I forgot last night when I was sitting for Jason.'

'Oh.' He turned to face his sister, who held up the phone as evidence of her statement.

I let go of the skillet along with the breath I'd been holding.

Grace touched Ryan on the arm. 'Sorry to startle you. I didn't expect you to be here, or I would have called first.' And then she laughed. 'Not that I could have, of course, without my phone.'

But Ryan wasn't smiling.

'Okay, we'll get out of your hair now.' Grace nodded toward

the front door, and I hurried past Ryan and followed her across the living room, her brother's dark eyes tracking us all the way outside.

Once in her car, we burst into a fit of the giggles – me more from relief than anything else. 'Well *that* was certainly bad timing,' I said.

'Yeah, good thing I had a ready-made excuse to use.' Grace flashed an ironic smile. 'I figured if it worked for you at the vineyard, it could work for me, as well.'

'Right.' I cleared my throat, not loving the direction this conversation was going. 'Just too bad he came home before we got to really look around and find anything useful.'

'Ah, but I did.' Grace leaned forward and pulled something from the small of her back that had been tucked into the top of her slacks. 'I found this,' she said, waving a white business-sized envelope in front of my face.

'What is it?'

'His last bank statement, I'm pretty sure. You said one of the main reasons Detective Vargas suspects Ryan is because he thinks he really needed money from the sale of the farm, right? And this could prove that Ryan has plenty of money.'

Or the opposite, was my thought.

'So we need to steam it open to see. And then I can sneak it back into the house next time I'm there.' Grace handed the envelope to me and started the car.

'Gauguin's just a few blocks from here,' I said. 'Let's do it there.'

'Good idea.'

As she pulled away from the curb, I saw Ryan come outside and climb into his white BMW, which was parked in the driveway. While I watched, he swiveled around in the seat to back out, and our eyes met.

With a shiver, I looked quickly away.

Grace drove two blocks down Chestnut, turned right, and then left onto Cedar Street. She pulled into the Gauguin parking lot, and as I opened the door to get out, I observed Ryan's car driving slowly past the restaurant.

'I think Ryan followed us,' I said after he'd gone by.

Grace turned to look, then shook her head. 'He's probably

just on his way back to work,' she said. 'His office isn't too far from here.'

'Maybe.' But I wasn't convinced.

I unlocked the side door and we headed through the *garde manger* and kitchen to the wait station, where I filled the electric kettle the servers used for heating tea water, and switched it on.

'He's your brother, so you can do the breaking and entering,' I said once the water was boiling and a steady flow of steam was piping out of the spout.

Grace held the envelope over the kettle, testing the flap periodically to see if the glue had started to come unstuck.

'So, does Ryan have any investments you know about?' I asked as we waited for the steam to do its magic.

'Yeah, I think so. I heard him talking to Cynthia the other day about some CDs that were coming due and had to be rolled over.'

'How about that house? Do they have a big mortgage on it?'

'No, they paid it off last year. I remember, because they had a party to celebrate and "burn the mortgage". Although Ryan made sure everyone knew it wasn't really a "mortgage", but a "deed of trust",' Grace added with a snort. 'But of course you would know that, being a lawyer an' all.'

'Ex-lawyer. But yeah, we learned about all that stuff in law school.'

Once the glue started to loosen, I handed Grace a butter knife, which she gently wedged under the edge of the flap. After another minute or so over the steam, it finally came free.

I leaned over her shoulder to look as she spread the enclosed sheet out on one of the dining room tables. It was indeed a bank statement. At the top of the page I read the opening and closing balances for the month: $107,087.13 and $112,905.39.

'Whoa. That's a *lot* of money to have in a savings account,' I said, 'since you're gonna make almost no interest on it.'

Grace stared at the paper without speaking, then folded it up and slid it back into the envelope.

'But the important point,' I went on, 'is that we now know Ryan clearly has plenty of dough. So much that he doesn't even worry about making any interest on over a hundred grand. Which means Vargas's "financial gain" theory for the guy doesn't hold a whole lot of water.'

Grace didn't appear to be listening, however. She was now staring out the window, disbelief in her eyes. 'He had the money,' she said after a bit. 'He told me he didn't have any liquid cash to pay for Neil's funeral, but he *had* the money.'

'True, but that's good news, right?' And then I remembered that Grace had been the one who'd ended up having to pay the mortuary expenses since Ryan had refused.

'That son of a bitch,' she growled. 'He made me borrow the money at an *astronomical* interest rate, and all the time he had over a hundred grand just sitting in his bank account.' Grace shook the envelope for emphasis, then crumpled it in her hand.

'No, wait! We don't want him to know—'

She stood still for a moment, her shoulders rising and falling, then turned to face me. 'I have to go,' Grace said, and nearly ran back through the kitchen and out the door to her car.

Great, I thought once she'd swept out of the *garde manger*. That was all I needed – for her to go storming off in anger to Ryan, and in the process let him know what we'd really been up to at his house that morning. Notwithstanding Grace's certainty that her brother had merely been driving back to work when he'd followed us to Gauguin earlier, it seemed pretty clear to me that he was, at the very least, exceedingly unhappy with my behavior. And now that unhappiness would no doubt escalate to something more akin to out-and-out anger – or worse.

But now I knew why Grace was so anxious to get repaid by the vineyard. If she'd had to pay for Neil's funeral expenses by taking out a loan on short notice or getting cashback on her credit card, that could mean an interest rate of as much as eighteen percent – or even higher. And I could also understand how, out of shame, she might want to keep the fact of her bad investment in the vineyard from anyone else. And also how she'd want to prevent her parents from feeling guilty about her being saddled with such exorbitant interest because of their inability to pay. Which was why Grace had seemed so startled when she'd realized someone might have overheard her phone conversation that day at the farmhouse.

Family dynamics could be so damn complicated.

With a sympathetic sigh, I unplugged the tea kettle and headed up the stairs behind the reach-in refrigerator to the restaurant office. Taking a seat at the desk, I ran my finger over the red Bakelite telephone that sat on its oak surface. My Aunt Letta had purchased the treasure from the owner of a popular Chinese restaurant downtown that had been destroyed during the big earthquake of 1989, and I often made calls on it simply for the pleasure of cradling its heavy receiver in my hand.

I reached out for the phone, but then stopped as I realized I had no idea who I could call.

Dad would be too busy with the lunch service at Solari's to want to chat with his daughter right now. And no way, Martin. Though I fervently wished I could hear his soothing voice and tell him everything I'd learned over the past few days. Nichole was leaving for Singapore today, and Allison, I knew, was teaching all day.

As for Grace, she was likely screaming bloody murder at Ryan at this very moment and would not be inclined to pick up her phone to take my call.

What about Eric? He often worked through lunch, reviewing case files and police reports at his desk while munching on a tuna fish sandwich. And given our conversation the day before, I guessed he'd be happy to hear from me. But did I want to talk to *him*?

It sure seemed as if Eric was testing the waters with me about perhaps rekindling our relationship – the way he'd asked about me and Vargas and then talked about the problems he'd been having with Gayle. Would my calling him now be seen as encouragement in that department? Did I *want* it to be seen as encouragement?

I wasn't sure. And that itself was a revelation.

Picking up the receiver, I used my index finger to dial his number on the rotary phone.

It went directly to voicemail. *Oh, well. Probably just as well.*

I left Eric a message saying I'd just wanted to call someone from the Gauguin telephone and that there was no need to return the call. As I set the vintage handset on its cradle, a buzzing from the cell phone in my pocket brought me back to the twenty-first century.

It was a text from Javier: *can U go to farmers mkt today? something came up & I cant go.*

Sure, I wrote back. *Anything in particular you want?*

chard baby lettuce aspar & anything you think looks good, he answered.

I texted him a thumbs up emoji, fetched several large cloth shopping bags from the storage closet downstairs, and headed to the weekly market two blocks away.

The place was already bustling, although it had only officially opened fifteen minutes earlier. I made my way through the section devoted to live music and cooked food, past vendors hawking grilled-cauliflower-and-pulled-pork tacos, spicy red curry with tandoor-baked naan, and rotisserie chickens spilling their luscious fat atop mounds of tiny fingerling potatoes roasting underneath.

But something didn't seem right. With a frown, I gazed about me, trying to pinpoint what was different today. And then, walking through the cloud of smoke rising from a grill covered with succulent Hawaiian-glazed pork ribs, I realized what it was.

I couldn't smell a thing.

At least I won't be tempted by the deep-fried churros today, I thought, doing my best to quell the wave of sadness quickly overtaking me. With a huff of impatience, I quickened my step and hurried down a row of vendors selling jams, baked goods, sauerkraut and kimchee, cheese, and flowers. But as I passed the seafood seller at the end of the row, deftly shucking oysters for eager buyers to slurp from their shells, I stopped.

Wait. Was that a whiff of fish I detected? Stepping up to the cooler displaying fillets of halibut glistening atop mounds of ice, I leaned over and took a deep breath. Nothing.

Had I imagined it? The smell had been fleeting, but I felt certain that it had been there – if only for a moment. Then again, perhaps it was only wishful thinking. *Or rather, wishful smelling*, I thought bitterly as I continued on toward the produce section of the market.

This being April, the height of the growing season was not yet upon us, but the selection of produce was still impressive: asparagus, radishes, peas, carrots, lemons and grapefruit, broccolini and cauliflower, artichokes, lettuces and greens, kale, chard, avocados, leeks and onions, strawberries, fennel, and more.

I consulted the text Javier had sent and made for the woman selling asparagus and chard. Then, the greens I'd purchased nestled lightly atop the bundles of delicate spears, I wandered down the row in search of baby lettuces and anything else that might strike my fancy for one of the specials tonight.

As I turned the corner to head down the next row, I spied a tall, lanky man loading artichokes into a cardboard box. It was Pete Ferrari.

I sidled up next to him. 'Haven't had enough of artichokes lately?' I said in a mock-critical voice.

He glanced my way, then went back to choosing his specimens, examining each for blemishes and then squeezing it to ensure the proper weight and firmness.

I tried another tack. 'Whatcha gonna make with them?'

'The same thing I did for the cook-off, since it was such a big winner. And these are a great deal.' He nodded toward a pink placard reading: 'Baby Artichokes 5 x $1.00'.

'That *is* a good price. Maybe I'll get some for Gauguin.'

Did he react to the name of the restaurant? Was he thinking about Javier? I couldn't tell.

Opening one of my shopping bags, I started dropping artichokes inside, inspecting them carefully as Pete was doing. 'So what dish was it you won that prize for, anyway? I don't think I ever heard.'

'Braised artichokes stuffed with crab and fennel,' he said, finally showing some interest in the conversation. 'You pan-fry the chokes, then simmer 'em with wine, some *mirepoix* and a bunch of other herbs, and stuff them with crabmeat and fennel salad. But I'm not gonna give you the details or anything,' he added with a smirk. 'Wouldn't want to see the dish show up on the Gauguin menu.'

He left me to pay for his artichokes, and as he counted them out for the cashier and then dumped them back in his box, my eye was caught again by the bright pink sign advertising the thorny vegetables he'd used for his winning recipe at the cook-off. '*Baby* artichokes', it read.

The same variety that had been stuffed into Neil's mouth after he was killed.

TWENTY-TWO

Javier came into the Gauguin kitchen as I was organizing the produce I'd bought at the farmers market. 'These baby artichokes were a great deal, so I bought a few dozen for a special tonight. Maybe roasted and topped with feta and pine nuts?'

'Sounds good.' Javier washed his hands, then set about prepping the asparagus by snapping off the ends and filling a large pot with water in which to blanch them. 'Sorry for the late notice about the farmers market,' he said, 'but a friend needed a ride to the airport at the last minute, so I offered to take her.'

'A *friend*?' I waggled my eyebrows suggestively.

'Actually, it may be working into something a little more than that,' he said with a shy smile. 'We'll see when she gets back from Portland.'

The pot now full, he hefted it to the Wolf range and turned on the burner knob to light the flame underneath. But nothing happened.

'*Me lleva,*' he growled, then dragged the pot to the other side of the stove so he could peer at the offending burner. 'There's gunk spilled all over it. Must have clogged the holes in the head.'

Continuing to swear under his breath in Spanish, Javier left the kitchen and returned a minute later, brandishing a paper clip. He unfolded the metal so it became a thin prong, which he inserted into each hole one by one. 'We really have to make sure everyone cleans up their spills before they get cooked on,' he said, reaching once more for the knob. But it still didn't light.

I bent over to listen, then stood back up. 'There's no gas,' I said. 'That's the problem. Here, try the other burners.'

None of them worked. Nor did the oven.

'Oh, no.' Javier slumped, his face sagging like a fallen soufflé. 'I bet it's the thermocouple. We better get Dan here ASAP,' he said, then ran back upstairs to the office where we kept our list of important phone numbers, such as that for the appliance repair guy.

I was slicing my artichokes in half, pondering what it was with me and dramas involving gas stoves of late, when Javier came back down. 'He's out on another call and won't be here for at least an hour, probably more,' he said. 'What the hell are we gonna do?'

I thought a moment. We wouldn't need the oven for another couple hours when we opened, but we needed the stove pretty much immediately, to make the sauces and *roux* and to blanch all the side-dish vegetables so they'd be ready for a quick sauté once ordered.

'I know,' I said. 'I can run down to Solari's and borrow my dad's portable stove – the one I used for the cook-off. It's only got two burners, but it's better than nothing.'

'Great.' Javier grinned. But when I didn't instantly set down my knife, he waved me off as if I were some pesky insect he was scooting out the door. '¡*Órale, ya vete*!'

I went quickly, as directed, making it to Solari's in record time, grateful that none of Vargas's traffic cop cohorts were out and about to see me speeding through the roundabout at the entrance to the wharf.

Dad was in the storage room, unboxing cans of San Marzano tomatoes. 'Hi, hon,' he said when I came in. 'What brings you here?'

'I need to borrow your portable stove. The Gauguin one's on the blink and the repairman might not get there for a couple hours.'

'That's no fun,' Dad said. 'Did you check to see if the line's clogged?'

'The gas isn't coming on at all, not even in the stove.'

I followed my father across the room and helped him lift the stove from the shelf to the floor. 'Sounds like the thermocouple,' he said. 'That happened to us last year. But at least it's an easy fix – as long as they have the part.'

'Yeah, that's what Javier thought, too.' I leaned down to pick up the stove but then stopped. 'Oh, wait. Before I go, I should catch you up real quick on what I found out since we last talked. You know,' I added with a glance down the hall, 'about the case?'

'Oh?'

I recounted what I'd learned from Grace about Neil getting so excited about finding a frog down by the stable, how we'd found that site assessment paperwork in Neil's room, and what it would mean if the farmland was a red-legged frog habitat.

'So I'm thinking,' I said in a hushed voice, 'that Neil might have told that developer, Francis Sumner, about the frog, and that he was going to use it to fight any proposed development of the property.'

'Which sure would have given the guy good reason to want Neil out of the picture before he could tell anyone else,' Dad said.

'Right.' I didn't mention that this same theory could, of course, apply equally well to Ryan. But, concentrating as he was on this new lead, my father luckily didn't go there. 'And I also got some more info about Pete. It looks like he and Neil might have been more than good friends during high school. I think they might actually have been involved and then had a nasty—'

'Pete gay?' my dad interrupted. 'I don't think so. No way.' Although he lived in a hip, left coast kind of town, my father was surprisingly naïve when it came to things like LGBTQ culture.

I let out the sort of sigh only an exasperated daughter can produce. 'C'mon, Dad. Just 'cause he puts on this macho bravado doesn't mean anything. You don't have to be all wimpy or femme to be a gay man. Look at Rock Hudson.'

He shrugged. 'Yeah, I guess you're right. Nonna had a *huge* crush on him back in the day.'

'Before she switched allegiance to Hugh Jackman,' I said, and he laughed. 'Anyway,' I went on, 'if it's true they were involved and then had an ugly break-up, that's a good reason Pete might have had for holding a grudge against Neil all these years. And get this. I saw Pete today at the farmers market, and he was buying a bunch of baby artichokes, which he said were for the same dish he made at the cook-off.'

Dad looked at me with blank eyes, as if to say, 'So?'

'Which means he was using baby artichokes that day – the same kind that was stuffed in Neil's mouth after he was killed.'

'Pfhhhh,' Dad said with a wave of the hand. 'Much as I wouldn't mind it being Pete, I don't think that proves anything. A ton of people were using those artichokes that day. You're just gonna have to come up with something more concrete, is all.'

Easy for you to say, I thought as I hefted the stove and headed out to my car.

The appliance repairman didn't show up till fifteen minutes before Gauguin was due to open, and as Brian – who'd been given a clean bill of health at the ER the previous night – set out squirt bottles of orange juice and crème fraîche and filled the stainless steel inserts with sliced onions, brandied apricots, and chopped cilantro, he had to step over Dan's tall body sprawled out on the floor in front of the hot line.

'Yep, it's the thermocouple all right,' he said, shutting off his flash light and extracting his head from the guts of the oven. 'Lemme go see if I have one with me.'

'Didn't you tell him you suspected that was what it was?' I asked Javier after he'd left the kitchen.

'I did,' he said. 'But I think he came straight here from his last job, so he wouldn't have been able to stop and get one from the shop.'

'Well, let's just hope there's one in his truck.'

We were in luck. Dan did have the part and was able to swap it out within twenty minutes. Bullet dodged.

But not a half hour later another one came zinging my way.

I don't normally answer my phone at work, and I leave the device up in the restaurant office during the dinner service. But I'd run upstairs to fetch a business card for a customer when I happened to hear it ring. 'Martin Vargas' the name on the screen read.

Could he finally be calling to apologize? I picked up the phone and swiped right.

Bad idea.

'Have you completely lost your *mind*?' he bellowed before I could get out a 'hello'. 'Are you incapable of even following the *simplest* of instructions?'

'I . . .'

'I just got a message from dispatch that Ryan Lerici called the station to complain, and it was about you – *again*. He said you and Grace broke into his house and stole a piece of mail, and I'm afraid to even ask if it's true.'

I made no response to this implied question. After all, having worked as an attorney for many years, I was well aware of my Fifth Amendment right not to incriminate myself.

The detective, however, clearly expected an answer. 'Well, *did* you?' he demanded when I continued to hold my silence.

'Look, I don't see what the big deal is,' I parried. 'Grace goes into her brother's house all the time. He even gave her a key so she could get in when he wasn't home.'

It was Martin's turn to say nothing. But I knew it was only because he was counting to ten or doing some kind of breathing exercise to try to keep from throwing the phone across the room.

Yep, breathing exercise for sure. It now sounded like a tropical force wind storm on the other end of the line.

'Okay . . .' he finally managed to articulate. 'I'm gonna take that as a yes. Which means you're guilty of breaking and entering and, I'm guessing, theft as well, since you didn't deny taking that bank statement.'

Uh-oh. Ryan must have told them everything. Which meant Vargas also knew we'd opened the mail, which had to be some sort of federal crime added to the mix. *Great.*

I was trying to come up with something to say that wouldn't merely serve to make him even more angry, but he saved me from having to do so by continuing on with his rant.

'I'm not really sure what to say, Sally.' (That made two of us.) 'I know I explicitly told you *not* to speak to *any* of the Lerici family.' (Not technically true, but I wasn't going to pick that particular bone with him right at this moment.) 'And when I told you that – though you may not believe it – I was mostly worried about *your* safety. But now, I have to say, I've become far more concerned with you completely screwing up this case.'

'Look, I'm—'

But he again cut me off. 'And as if I didn't need even more

to worry about, Ryan is insisting he wants to press charges against you, which places me in an extremely awkward position, to say the least.'

Martin finally stopped talking, but I no longer had the desire to try to defend myself.

He was right. I'd made a total mess of everything. I'd recklessly disregarded his very clear and very sensible directive, and now at least one of the prime suspects in Neil's murder – and perhaps more, since there was a good chance Pete was on to the fact that I was sniffing at his door – was aware of his status as 'person of interest'. Not only that, but I'd taken Grace, whom Vargas still considered a suspect in the case, into my confidence and had divulged to her all sorts of private and sensitive information.

I was lucky he'd merely called, rather than arriving unannounced at Gauguin bearing a pair of handcuffs and a warrant with my name on it.

Was there any way to explain my actions to him? To make him at least see that my intentions had been good, even if they'd been utterly ill-advised?

I had to at least try.

I took a deep breath. 'Okay, you're absolutely right. I was completely out of line, and I'm so, *so* sorry. But you have to understand—'

'No, Sally. There's nothing for me to understand. I'm going to make this absolutely clear – so clear that even you can comprehend. Do. Not. Contact. *Any* of the Lerici family or anyone else *at all* connected with the case. And if I get wind of anything to suggest that you are within even a mile of any of those people, I will personally come arrest you for obstruction of justice and escort you to the county jail.'

And before I could say anything in response, he ended the call.

TWENTY-THREE

I t shouldn't come as any surprise that I didn't sleep well that night. I'd been distracted throughout the evening at Gauguin after Vargas's call, and on two occasions Javier had to remind me to pull out orders of our Broccoli and Gruyère Gratin special that I had browning in the salamander before they burned.

And then after I got home, I'd spent almost an hour looking up Penal Code statutes online to see which of its provisions I'd violated over the past two weeks. Several, apparently, including at least one that could result in a hefty fine as well as imprisonment for up to a year.

By now supremely jittery, I'd poured myself a Maker's Mark and then sat down to scroll through old texts from Martin to remind myself of the time when I hadn't been his public enemy number one. But this only served to make me depressed as well as anxious, and a second helping of bourbon hadn't helped.

So when I finally awoke the next morning, groggy from lack of sleep and my jaw aching from having spent what little time I did doze off with my teeth tightly clenched, I was not in a good mood.

As soon as Buster realized I was awake, he hopped onto the bed and stood with his face so close to me that I could feel his hot breath on my cheeks.

'Okay, fine.' I shoved him aside and climbed out of bed, causing the dog to jump back down, then race to the door. When I didn't immediately follow after him, he stopped and turned to stare at me.

Are you coming? his eyes said.

'You gotta wait till I get dressed,' I responded.

At the word 'wait', Buster's ears deflated, and he obediently sank to the hallway carpet. But the anxious dog continued to track my every move as I pulled on jeans and a sloppy sweater and headed to the bathroom to brush my teeth and wash the sleep from my eyes.

During our walk around the neighborhood, I did my best to focus on the world about me: a neighbor's pale pink climbing rose just beginning to burst with the first blooms of the season; the trio of crows who squawked scornfully at Buster and me as we passed underneath the power line upon which they perched; a brown paper bag skipping down the street, then being cast aloft by the wind as if executing a ballet dancer's *grand jeté*.

But it didn't work. The roses brought to mind the flowers I'd seen at Neil's celebration of life; the noisy crows reminded me of the three squabbling Lerici siblings; and the paper bag just made me think of the plastic one that had spooked my horse that day up at the farm.

Once back at home, after giving Buster his breakfast and brewing a pot of coffee for myself, I settled down to review the stack of finalized tax documents for Gauguin that our accountant had sent over the day before. The task required close attention and, as a result, finally succeeded in allowing me to at least temporarily forget the Lericis, Amy, Pete, Sumner, Vargas, and everyone else associated with both the murder investigation and my floundering love life.

After eating a lunch of baby spinach, cottage cheese, and sliced pickled beets, I changed into my cycling clothes. I had a couple hours before I needed to be at Gauguin, and a ride up the coast to Davenport seemed like a good way to try to shake off my nervous energy. I'd just pulled on my gloves and clipped my helmet strap snugly under my chin when my cell rang.

'Oh, good,' Dad's voice boomed over the phone. 'I'm glad I got you. I only have a sec, 'cause an eight-top just sent in their orders, but I had to call and tell you something real quick.'

'Okay . . .'

'So, when I went out front just now to change one of the specials on our board, I saw that woman Amy who works at the Lerici farm, and she was with the same guy she was with that night at the bar. I watched to see where they were headed and they went next door into the Crab Shack.'

'Really? Huh. I wonder if I could get down there before they leave. 'Cause I'd sure love to get a look at the guy.'

'Depends on if they're getting their food to go or eating in,'

Dad said, stating the obvious. 'Sorry I can't run over there to
see or try to snap a photo of them, but I gotta get back to work.
Emilio's over at the stove right now giving me the evil eye.'

'I understand. Thanks for calling to let me know.'

Maybe, even if they were only getting take-out, I'd arrive in
time to at least get a glimpse of the pair before they left.

I was able to ride down there just as quickly as if I'd driven,
given the traffic that had backed up from the roundabout at the
start of Beach Street all the way to the Dream Inn at the top
of the hill. Making the turn onto the wharf, I sped toward its
end, and as I bounced along the asphalt-coated planks set atop
the ancient pier's wooden pilings, I considered what little I
knew about Amy's fiancé: the good-looking, fair-haired guy
who'd agreed to have their wedding at the Lerici farm, even
though he'd apparently never met either Diana or Ernie or set
foot on the property.

And that's when I realized who he must be – and how it all
fit into the case.

I freewheeled up to the Solari's side door into the dish
room, then stowed my bike and helmet in the restaurant
office. Waving to my dad, who was at the stove tossing a
pan of mussels and shrimp, I hurried back outside and down
the passageway between Solari's and Pete's place. Then, once
around the corner, I ambled past the Crab Shack's picture
window that faces out toward the road. As I did my best to
feign disinterest, I glanced inside, searching for someone in
an Oakland A's baseball cap.

And there she was, at a booth right next to the window. If
she hadn't been swiveled the other way to listen to the server,
Amy would have looked right into my eyes.

But who was she with?

Betting she wouldn't turn away from the waiter while he was
talking, I risked taking another moment to check out her lunch
partner.

Whoa. It was a shock, the confirmation that I'd been right.
The face was one I'd seen before, on a glossy pamphlet with
an orange hardhat covering his styled blond hair. And it wore
the same toothy grin that had smiled out from the flyer I'd
spotted atop the pile of mail in Amy's car.

It was the developer, Francis A. Sumner. Also known as Frankie – just like the young Sinatra in his teen idol years.

Darting to the far side of the window out of the couple's view, I leaned back against the wall, my brain churning. *So Amy's engaged to the guy who wants to build condos on the Lerici farm.*

It seemed to explain so much. Neil could easily have told Amy about finding the frog on the property, and then she, in turn, could have mentioned it to her fiancé. Did she know he was interested in developing the farm? *Or could she even be in on the plan with him?* It seemed likely, but then again, there was a possibility he hadn't told her, given her connection to the place and her relationship with Neil.

Plus, I thought as I stole another glance at the couple through the window, *if she* was *aware of her fiancé's plans for the property, wouldn't she want to keep her relationship with him a secret from the Lerici family?* The fact that she'd happily told Diana the guy's name seemed to indicate she wasn't aware of his intentions. Not to mention her enthusiasm about having their wedding at the farmhouse this coming autumn – even though, if Sumner got his way, the place would likely have been transformed into a construction site by that time.

No, I decided, *I bet she doesn't know.* And given that Frankie Sumner surely knew of her desire to have the wedding at the property, that would be a good reason not to tell her until the deal was firm. Why rock the nuptial-planning boat unless absolutely necessary?

Which meant she could easily have told her fiancé about the frog, not realizing the import of that information to him.

Then again, I mused, watching an old man heft a canvas bocce ball case from the back seat of his car, Ryan could have told Sumner about the red-legged frog – especially if his brother had threatened Ryan with fighting the project based on its protected status. Or Neil himself could have told the developer. But no matter how it had occurred, Frankie Sumner would not have been happy to learn about the presence of that frog.

I peeked around the edge of the window for another quick look at the couple. The server had now left and, as I watched,

Sumner reached his arm across the table and Amy took his hand in hers. She had her back to me, but I could see that he was laughing about something.

Returning to my protected spot against the Crab Shack wall, I considered the possibilities. Assuming Francis Sumner *had* learned about the red-legged frog, could he have decided he wanted to silence the younger Lerici brother and make sure he never told anyone else about its presence on the property? Did the other facts mesh with the developer having killed Neil – and then subsequently gone after me, once he got wind of the fact that I was interested in the case?

I had no evidence that he was at the farm the day my horse had spooked, but then again, there was little other than my own paranoia to suggest the incident was anything but an unfortunate accident.

But what about the gas on my stove being turned on? It only made sense for it to have been someone who knew about my loss of smell, but could either Amy or Ryan have mentioned that to the developer? I couldn't think of any reason they would have done so but, as Evelyn had said that day at my house, you never know what might come up in a conversation. Especially between two lovers.

One major sticking point with regard to Sumner, however, was opportunity. He was the only one of my suspects I couldn't place at the Artichoke Cook-Off.

But then I had a twinge of memory – that day in the Lerici farmhouse kitchen, when I'd found the pamphlet with his photo on it. At the time, I'd thought his face seemed somehow familiar . . .

And then it hit me: Francis Sumner was the tall, blond guy Amy had been standing next to in line at the judges' tent. I'd assumed he was simply another contestant, but now that I really thought about it, I couldn't remember him holding a plate of food in his hands. I did remember him having a sour expression, however, which I'd attributed to the long line. But what if his foul mood had been the result of an argument with Neil? *Or worse?*

Without thinking, I pulled my phone from the back pocket of my cycling jersey and scrolled to Vargas's number in my contacts. I was about to punch 'call' when I remembered I wasn't supposed to be within a mile of either Amy or Francis Sumner. *Damn.*

I could always tell Martin I just 'happened' to see the pair while coming to visit my dad, but I was pretty sure he'd see through the lie. With a silent curse, I shoved the phone back in my pocket and kicked at a crumpled cigarette packet some idiot had thrown on the ground. Then, feeling responsible for the piece of trash now that I'd interacted with it, I walked over to pick up the packet and deposit it in a nearby waste bin.

A wooden bench sat near the trash can along the far side of the Crab Shack building. Shooing a brazen seagull from its back, I took a seat while I pondered what to do with this new information I had.

I could ask my father to call Vargas. But I immediately realized what a bad idea that was. Dad was the worst person I knew for being able to keep a secret. The second the detective started to query him about any details, he'd get nervous and spill the fact that he'd told me about Amy and her fiancé being down here, and that I was the one who'd actually discovered the guy's identity and asked him to call.

A movement in front of the Crab Shack caught my eye. Pete strode toward the parking area, keys in hand, and made for his car – one of those cute little Mini Coopers, with a sky blue paint job. He popped the hatchback and extracted a large bag from which poked about a dozen loaves of French bread. Catching sight of me as he started back to the restaurant, he nodded in greeting and continued on inside.

Well, if I continued to sit here, Amy and her fiancé would likewise eventually emerge and spot me as Pete had done. Probably not a great idea. And what more could I do, anyway? Trying to follow the pair after they finished their meal wouldn't do any good. The important thing was that I now knew how Sumner could have learned both about the frog and my recent contact with the Lerici family. Best to get out of there now, before they discovered I'd been spying on them.

Clomping in my cycling cleats down the passageway back to Solari's, however, my plan went awry. I was just about to open the screen door into the dish room when Amy emerged from the restroom across the way. 'Oh, hi, Sally,' she said. 'What brings you out to the wharf?'

'Uh, well . . .' I nodded toward the Solari's door.

'Oh, right. Duh. You must be visiting your dad. I'm embarrassed to say my fiancé and I are having lunch at the Crab Shack. Sorry we didn't go to Solari's, but Frankie was really jonesing for one of Pete's famous crab sandwiches.'

'Right.'

I was torn. Part of me wanted to get the hell out of there, since I was in flagrant violation of Vargas's clear and emphatic mandate. But another part was aching to warn Amy that her betrothed was at the very least a sleazeball, and that he might possibly be a murderer, as well.

'So, have you two set a date for the wedding yet?' The devil balancing on my left shoulder was digging in and gaining traction.

'Sometime in late September, most likely. The weather's always great around here that time of year, and since I'd like it to be an outdoor ceremony—'

'At the farm,' I filled in.

'Yeah, that's my hope, anyway.'

She'd just provided me with an opening I couldn't resist. Glancing around to make sure Sumner hadn't come outside to join her, I took a step forward. 'Uh, there's something I think you should know,' I said in a low voice. 'About your fiancé. Were you aware he's actually in the process of trying to buy the Lerici farm, and that he wants turn it into a block of condominiums?'

It was hard to tell what her taut jaw and narrowed eyes conveyed. Disbelief? Confirmation of something she'd suspected but hoped wasn't true?

'So, anyway,' I went on, 'you may want to rethink your plans of having the wedding there, since the property could well have turned into a construction site come autumn. You know, if he gets his way.'

'How do you know . . .?' Amy began, but didn't finish the question. It was now her turn to glance back toward the restaurant, as if Sumner might be listening in.

'And I think there may be some other things he's not telling you, as well,' I said, then immediately wished the words back.

I had to get out of there before I broke down and told her everything. As it was, I'd already stepped way over the line. I backed up to the Solari's door and reached for the handle. 'Look, I'm sorry. I wish I could stay and talk more, but I really need to get going.'

Amy looked as if she wanted to ask something – which made sense. I'd certainly want to know more after what I'd just told her. But instead, she merely nodded, then licked her lips and blinked several times before turning to head back inside the Crab Shack.

Stupid, stupid! Letting the screen door slam shut behind me, I strode through the dish room and kitchen, causing Emilio to look up from the hot line in surprise. Would Amy tell her fiancé what I'd said? If so, I really needed to watch my back.

Once again I considered calling Vargas. He needed to know what I'd learned – about the red-legged frog, about Amy being engaged to Francis Sumner, and about Pete's previous relationship with Neil.

Wheeling my bike back through the dish room, I came to a decision. I'd phone the detective as soon as I got home and come completely clean, no matter what it meant for me. This had become far too big to keep to myself any longer, no matter what the consequences.

'Hey, hon,' Dad called out from the pot washing sink. He shut off the hose he'd been using to spray down a stainless steel hotel pan. 'So did you see the guy Amy's with?'

'I did,' I said. 'And I think it might be an important key to the case. I'm gonna call Vargas and tell him all about it when I get home.'

We chatted for another couple of minutes and then, after strapping on my helmet, I waved goodbye to my dad – who immediately turned on the hose again full blast – and pushed my bike through the screen door.

I'd taken only a few steps down the passageway when I felt a sharp blow to the head.

TWENTY-FOUR

My helmet took the brunt of the impact, but I nevertheless staggered to maintain my balance as the bike clattered to the ground. *What the . . .?* Turning to see who my aggressor might be, I was prevented from doing so when the person shoved me hard on the back of the head. As if in slow motion, I fell forward, arms outstretched in an automatic response to cushion the fall.

It didn't work.

Some time later – I don't know if it was seconds or minutes – I came to. I was lying face down, and the first thing I became conscious of was the sticky substance beneath me. Had I fallen into a pool of spilled cooking oil . . . or something worse?

But as my eyes slowly regained their ability to focus, I realized the substance was a dark red. *Blood.*

My own blood? I didn't feel any pain. But then again, I'd heard that the body can go into a kind of shock and not register pain after sustaining an injury. Javier had told me about the one time he'd been involved in a fight, and how he hadn't felt a thing right after the other guy punched him in the face – though he sure did later on.

I was about to try to push myself off the ground when a pair of hands grabbed me from behind.

Oh, no. They were still here.

'No!' I shrieked. 'Get off me!'

And then, as I struggled to free myself, I was hit by the acrid reek of stale cigarettes.

Pete! It was him all along.

'Sally, it's okay,' the man responded, and immediately released his grip on my shoulders.

I rolled over and sat up. It was indeed Pete, who'd now sat back on his heels and was staring at me as if it was he, rather than I, who had suffered the shock.

'Ohmygod,' he said, 'you're bleeding like crazy!'

I reached up to touch my face, and my fingers came away stained crimson.

'What on earth is going on out here!' my father's voice bellowed through the screen door. And then he let out a gasp. 'Sally! What happened!' Dad threw open the door and ran to where I sat, then turned to Pete, rage in his eyes. 'What the hell have you *done*?'

Pete held out both hands as he scrambled to his feet. 'Nothing! I just came out here for a cigarette and saw her lying there. I was trying to help.'

Dad turned to me for confirmation, but I could only shrug. 'I dunno,' I said. 'Someone whacked me on the head with something and then shoved me onto my face. But I don't know who it was.' I looked into Pete's eyes. 'It could have been him . . . But I lost consciousness and have no idea how long I was out for.'

Dad frowned, unsure whether to slug Pete or thank him for coming to my aid. 'Well, it's been a few minutes since you left, so . . .' He shook his head in frustration. 'You,' he said to Pete, 'don't go anywhere.' And then he knelt next to me and gazed into my face. 'You okay, honey? You think you have a concussion?'

'I doubt it. Whoever it was,' I said with a glance at Pete, 'obviously didn't expect me to be wearing a helmet, so it protected me from the blow. They must have heard me talking to you in the dish room and just walloped me as soon as I came outside, without realizing I had the helmet on. And then when that didn't work, they shoved me to the ground and took off. Or didn't,' I added with another look toward the Crab Shack owner.

'Well, I'm calling the cops,' Dad said, and pulled his phone from his black-and-white checked chef's pants.

'Good idea,' said Pete. 'But I have to get back to work. They can come find me there.'

I waited till Dad had ended the call, then asked him to help me up.

'Why don't you come into the restaurant so we can get that face cleaned up to see what the damage is,' he said. 'Looks like you might have broken your nose.'

And then I laughed.

'What?' I could tell he was starting to think maybe I had in fact sustained a concussion, after all.

'That would explain it,' I said, and grabbed the yellow-stained side towel from his apron string. Lifting the fabric to my nose, I inhaled deeply. 'Clam sauce with garlic!' I exclaimed, then laughed again.

Dad continued to stare at me, his eyes taking on an even more worried expression.

'Don't you get it?' I said. 'I can smell again! It's not super strong, but it's *there*.'

'Ah.' He smiled, then patted me on the shoulder. 'That's great, hon. Now c'mon. Let's get you cleaned up.'

'No.' I used Dad's towel to wipe some of the blood off my face, surprised at how little sense of feeling I still had. 'I just had an idea.' I picked up my bike and wheeled it into the Solari's dish room, then unstrapped my helmet and set it atop a high shelf next to a seldom-used fish kettle. 'I need to go over to the Crab Shack.'

Dad protested, but there was little he could do to stop me. So instead of trying, he followed me back outside, down the passageway, and into Pete's restaurant.

I stood at the entrance for a moment, letting my eyes adjust to the bright sun streaming through the picture window across the room. Several dozen eyes looked up at the woman with the bloody face standing at the door, but I ignored all but four of them.

Striding across the room, I came to a stop in front of the table at which Amy and Francis Sumner still sat. The two gaped at me. In front of them were half-eaten crab sandwiches, made with fat wedges of what I suspected was the bread I'd seen Pete bring in from his car earlier.

'Wha . . . what happened to your face?' Amy asked after a few beats.

I glanced at her partner, but his face was unreadable, with the hint of a frown and his mouth slightly open in what could have been either astonishment or trepidation.

'Someone jumped me in the passageway as I came out of Solari's.'

'No way. Really?' Amy stood and reached out a hand to my

arm. 'Are you okay? Did they steal anything? Not your bike, I hope!'

Wait. How did she know I had my bike? And then I realized that would be an obvious guess to anyone, given my multi-colored spandex outfit and cycling gloves.

'No, they didn't take anything,' I said. 'And I'll be fine. I was wearing my helmet, so when they whacked me on the head with whatever it was, it just made me momentarily loopy. Until they shoved me to the ground. Which is how I got this.' I reached up once more to touch my nose and was startled by the flash of pain I now experienced.

'Ohmygod.' Amy sat back down and turned to Sumner, whose frown had now deepened.

'But I'm pretty sure we'll be able to figure out who it was who attacked me.'

Francis Sumner now finally spoke. 'Oh, yeah? And how's that?'

'Because they shoved me on the back of my bike helmet, which I'm thinking will make for a pretty good surface for fingerprints.'

My dad, who'd been standing next to me during this whole exchange, let out a little 'Ah . . .' of understanding.

'So, I'm sure Pete won't mind if I borrow some of his glass-ware for a few days.' Unfolding one of the paper napkins that sat on the table, I held it in my hand as I reached across the table.

'Hey, wait,' the developer said. 'You can't just come in here and—'

A crashing sound, followed immediately by the sensation of a swarm of insects pelting my bare calves, prevented me from answering. I looked down to see Amy's water glass, now shattered, on the tile floor. 'Oh,' she said. 'So sorry!'

I stared at her, and she returned my gaze, innocence shining from those baby blues.

She'd clearly assumed I was going for *her* glass.

Which is when I realized how naïve I'd been. Of *course* she'd known about her fiancé's plans for the farm. And she'd likely been in on the whole thing from the start. I just hadn't wanted to believe it.

Snatching her butter knife – whose telltale mayonnaise sheen identified it as having been handled by her – I wrapped it in the napkin, then used another to whisk Sumner's glass off the table.

Amy jumped up from her chair, but her fiancé grabbed her by the wrist and shook his head. The eyes of all the other restaurant patrons had once more turned our way, and I nodded and smiled sweetly through my blood-smeared face as I swept past them toward the door.

And then I saw Pete, staring at Amy and Sumner's table as he twisted the bar towel he held so hard that his knuckles had turned white. He shook his head, then hurried after my father and me out the door and into the passageway.

'Did that mean what I think it does?' the Crab Shack owner asked. 'That *she's* also the one who killed Neil?'

'I'm guessing it does,' I answered. 'But these items should help provide at least a partial answer to that question.'

Pete gazed through the door at the couple, now hunched over their table, arguing. There was a fury in his eyes I'd never witnessed before, but then he blinked and his shoulders sagged. When he looked back toward me, I saw only sadness there.

'Well, I hope she rots in jail. Neil was . . .' Pete paused as his voice cracked. 'He was a really good man.' With a quick wipe to the corner of his eye, he turned and headed back into the restaurant.

'Whoa,' Dad said, crossing the passageway to Solari's and opening the screen door for me. 'What was that all about?'

'It's kind of complicated. I'll tell you later.'

I set the glass and knife on the shelf next to my helmet, then smiled at the sound of an approaching siren, its wail growing louder by the second.

'He caved as soon as her prints came back positive for your helmet. Said he wanted a deal, and then he'd tell all.'

It was the following Monday, and Martin and I had returned to Cruzin' Coffee for a morning fix of caffeine – along with a dose of debriefing and apologies. My nose had been reset and was now plastered with bandages, and my bruised forehead and cheeks gave me the appearance of the losing party in a prize fight – though the ER doctor had assured me I'd make a full recovery within a few weeks.

'So did he get that deal?' I asked.

Vargas nodded as he stirred sugar into his espresso. 'But it took some convincing. Between you and me and the wall, that new DA is a piece of work.'

'Yeah, Eric's not too keen on him, either,' I said.

'His attorney did finally get him the plea bargain they wanted, though – which was to avoid a homicide rap – after which Sumner spilled the entire story, at least as far as he knows.'

Martin leaned against the tall back separating our booth from the others and eyeballed me as I savored the luscious, creamy deliciousness of my cappuccino. *Flavor!* I was still getting used to the fact that my sense of smell was returning, and I could once again actually *taste* my food and drink.

'And?' I prompted. 'Are you at liberty to say?'

He chewed his lip, then leaned across the table. 'Sure, I guess I owe you that much.'

'Since I did, after all, break the case for you.' My smile was coy, but inside I was still feeling anxious about his reaction to my – yet again – having completely ignored his directive to stay away from the suspects in the investigation.

'Yeah, well,' he replied with a dry cough, 'we'll get to that in a bit. But here's the scoop: it turns out Amy has a significant investment in Sumner's development firm, and she was in with him from the start, trying to get the Lericis to sell the farm to his company.'

Setting down my cup, I licked the foam from my upper lip. 'I figured it was something like that. And she got the gig working there as a way to ingratiate herself to the family.'

'Right. The two of them were hoping that once she got close to Neil, she'd be able to talk him into selling.'

'But she must not have pressured him so much that he realized she was on Ryan and Grace's side,' I said, 'because I'm guessing he told her about finding that red-legged frog.'

Vargas shot me a hard look. 'You *knew* about the frog?'

'Uh . . . yeah. That's why Grace and I went to Ryan's house: to see if we could find anything proving that he knew about it – or didn't know.'

The detective closed his eyes as he shook his head and let out a long, noisy breath. And if he could have exhibited any other clichéd signals to demonstrate just how exasperated he was with me at the moment, I'm sure he would have done so.

I ignored his theatrics. 'And I'm also guessing that once the two of them knew about Neil finding the frog, that upped the stakes big time. Amy would have been frantic to convince him that selling the property was the best thing to do, before he told anyone else about the frog.'

'Uh-huh,' Vargas agreed. 'Sumner said they discussed it and decided she should try to persuade him that selling would be best for his parents – that the dad was getting senile and wouldn't be able to handle living at the farm anymore, and so keeping it was just selfishness on his part.'

'I bet that went over like a lead balloon.'

'No kidding. And apparently she and Neil ended up having a big blow-up about the whole thing during the Artichoke Cook-Off.'

'Oh, wow . . .' I thought back to when I'd seen Amy that day with the blond guy I now knew to be Francis Sumner. 'I think I must have run into her right after that happened,' I said. 'She was with Sumner, and neither of them looked the least bit happy. She must have just told him about her fight with Neil.'

'When exactly was this?' Vargas asked. His eyes were eager with anticipation. 'It could be important, since a lot of what Sumner told me will for sure be inadmissible in court.'

'Right, hearsay,' I said with a nod. 'So it was after I'd dropped off my food sample to the judges that I saw them. They were in line waiting to turn in Neil's sample, and they both looked pretty upset. Now, what time would that have been . . .?'

I frowned in concentration, causing a spasm of pain to shoot across my cheeks and nose. *Okay*, I thought, *I'm going to have to try to remember to limit my facial expressions till my wounds heal.*

'My sample was due at one fifty,' I went on once the pain subsided, 'so it must have been a little before two o'clock when I saw them.'

'And when was it that you saw Amy return to the booth and discover the food burning?'

'Lemme see . . . I stopped to talk to my dad for a while, and then she didn't come back to Neil's booth for another few minutes, so . . . two fifteen? Two twenty?'

'Good,' Vargas said, sipping his espresso. 'That all matches what Sumner says – that Amy told him she saw Neil heading for the dumpster area when she got back from the judges' tent and followed him there, where they continued their argument. She claims that he all of a sudden just lost it and pulled the cleaver from his apron pocket and threatened her, at which point she grabbed the knife and whacked him on the head with its blunt side. According to Sumner, she swears she didn't mean to kill him – that it was just an instinctive reaction to his pulling the knife on her.'

'She sure didn't shout for anyone to come help or call nine-one-one, though,' I said. 'She just left him there, bleeding behind the dumpsters.'

'Yup.' Vargas shook his head in disgust.

Frowning, I stirred my foamy coffee as I tried to make sense of it all. 'But why,' I asked after a bit, 'would Neil just lose it like that – enough to pull a cleaver on her? That doesn't seem to jibe at all with what I know about the guy's personality.' And then I looked up at Martin. 'He found out, didn't he? About Amy and Sumner being in cahoots.'

'Bingo,' said the detective with the sort of smile a proud tutor might award a promising student. 'Sumner told me the only reason Amy agreed to help Neil out at the cook-off was because he'd promised that he'd talk to his parents about selling the farm if she'd do so. But then, once all the prep work was done that day, he told her he never meant what he'd said – that he'd figured out that she and Sumner were involved and that her coming to work at the farm was all simply a ruse to try to get the family to sell the property.'

'So how'd he figure out the connection between the two?' I asked, and Vargas shrugged.

'He must have seen them together or something. But the important thing is, Neil made it clear to Amy that he only made the promise he did as a way to get back at her and yank her chain. And then, when he finally told her the truth that day, he apparently just laughed about how she'd been such a sucker to fall for his ploy.'

'Which explains both the argument he and Amy had right before I saw her with Sumner at the judges' tent, and why Neil would be angry enough at Amy to threaten her with the cleaver – given how she'd totally lied about why she wanted to work at the farm.' I licked my spoon thoughtfully before dipping it back in the cup. 'But I do still wonder what was the deal with that artichoke that was stuffed in his mouth.'

'I asked Sumner the same thing,' Vargas said, 'and according to him, when Amy saw it lying on the ground after she'd clobbered Neil, she was still so pissed off about what he'd done that she just shoved it into his mouth on impulse. I guess she must have thought of it as some kind of payback statement or joke.'

I snorted. 'Some joke. So you said the fingerprints on my helmet were Amy's.'

'Right. Which is why she's now a guest at our lovely detention center down on Water Street awaiting arraignment. *And* they got a partial at your house on Saturday. Thanks for letting my guys come over to try again, by the way. Guess I should stick to thinking and leave the CSI stuff to the experts.' Vargas chuckled as he drank down the contents of his tiny cup.

'So it *was* her who turned the gas on.' I shivered at the memory of how close I'd come to lighting that match and blowing myself – along with Evelyn and our two dogs – sky high. 'Did Sumner know about that, too?'

'He swears he didn't – that she never told him. And he didn't know anything about that plastic bag that spooked your horse, either. But given what you've told me, I've gotta believe it just snagged there on its own. Doesn't much matter at this point, in any case, since we've got Amy for the gas stove incident.'

I watched as the barista floated steamed milk atop a cappuccino, waggling the pitcher back and forth to create a floral design like the one that had graced my own. 'You think they have enough to nail her for Neil's death?' I asked.

'I do,' Martin replied quickly. 'I'm betting she'll cop to

bashing him with the cleaver once she knows Sumner has spilled it already – especially if the DA agrees to limit the charge to second degree murder or manslaughter. And along with what we already have regarding the two attacks on you, I'd be surprised if she didn't get some serious prison time.'

I started to nod, then caught myself before causing any further pain to my poor face. 'One other thing I do wonder, though, is why Amy kept talking about having their wedding there at the farm, since she knew he wanted to knock the place down to build condos.' But then I answered my own question. 'I guess she must just have hoped he'd delay the demolition till after the wedding. Of course it's all moot now, since that's a wedding that is surely never gonna happen.'

With a wry smile, I spooned up the last of my milky foam and lifted it to my lips. But when I looked up at Martin, his face was serious.

'Uh-oh,' I said, setting the spoon back down. 'Time for the reckoning. Look, I really am sorry about everything. I know I should have listened to you and kept out of all this.'

He reached across the table and lay his hand on mine. 'Sally, the thing I care about most right now is that you're okay. That was always my main concern. But . . .'

I'd known there would be a 'but' and waited for it.

He withdrew the hand, which began to tap out a rapid rhythm on the tabletop. 'Here's the thing,' he said. 'I care for you, Sally, I really do. But I simply can't see this working.' The tapping ceased. 'Us. We're just too different. I'm a by-the-book, over-protective, rules kind of guy, and you're . . .'

'*Not* like that,' I finished for him. 'I know. And I agree. But it has been fun, right?'

He finally flashed a smile. 'It has, indeed.'

TWENTY-FIVE

Notwithstanding it was a Monday, Kalo's was still popping that night, so Eric and I ordered drinks and hung out in the bar while waiting for a table. He'd called soon after my coffee date – no, make that a definite *not*-date – with Vargas, to see how I was doing.

'You heard,' I said when Eric asked. 'Sorry I didn't let you know myself, but it's been a weird past few days.'

'No worries. I understand. And I gotta say, it was all the talk this morning at work. No keeping any secrets from us district attorneys.'

Eric had invited me to dinner and I'd readily agreed. 'But let's make it someplace with lots of zesty flavors, 'cause apparently the up-side to having your nose broken is that it can bring back a lost sense of smell.'

This wasn't technically true. The ER doc had told me my smell had likely come back all on its own – that after almost three weeks, the nerves had finally started to regenerate, which was why I'd been having fleeting moments of late where I'd been able to sense aromas and flavors. And the good news was that she'd also told me that, since I'd now recovered some of my sense of smell, there was a decent chance it would continue to improve.

But the broken nose made for a far better story.

In any case, here we were at Kalo's, and my mouth was watering at the thought of their crab-and-cream-cheese wontons and lamb kebobs with coconut-lime dipping sauce.

Once we were seated, Eric raised his Mai Tai in a toast. 'To our celebrity sleuth – oh, boy, don't try to say *that* after more than one drink – who has yet again matched wits with Santa Cruz's finest and come out on top.'

'Or rather on the bottom, in this instance,' I said, reaching up to touch the bandages on my face. 'And I didn't really figure it all out till the very end, when Amy smashed that glass.'

'In other words, you didn't solve it till you solved it. Kinda the way it always works, no?'

His boyish grin was infectious and I joined in his laughter, only to immediately regret it. 'Ow,' I said, then drank down the rest of my bourbon to soothe the pain.

'So how'd Vargas take it, anyway?' Eric asked. 'You solving his case for him – again.'

I picked up the menu, even though I knew exactly what I wanted to order. It was how exactly I wanted to respond to Eric's question that I wasn't sure of.

'What, was he angry?'

Letting the menu fall back to the table, I leaned back in my chair. 'I think more frustrated than angry. And he broke up with me. Not that there was really all that much to break up *from*,' I added. 'He said he thought we were too different to ever work out as a couple.'

Eric didn't speak, but he was giving me his full attention.

'Which of course is absolutely true.' Swiveling in my seat, I tried to catch the eye of the server to request another drink. But I admit it was also to avoid Eric's scrutiny.

Our next round ordered, we sat in silence as Eric perused and I pretended to peruse the menu. 'And how's it going with Gayle?' I asked after a bit. 'Since we're on the subject of our love lives – or lack thereof.'

'Lack thereof is pretty much it,' Eric said with a dry laugh. 'We broke up, too. Friday night, probably at the exact same moment you were at the ER getting patched up. Interesting timing, that.'

Interesting, indeed. Had it been prompted by what Eric had witnessed between Vargas and me during Nonna's Sunday dinner?

Before I could offer any response to Eric's announcement, the server arrived with our cocktails and took our food orders. Once she'd left, he cleared his throat, tasted his Mai Tai, and looked up at me. 'What Vargas said about you two being different . . .'

I met his gaze. 'Uh, huh?'

'Seems like that's what we have going for us. I mean, yeah, we're different in lots of ways, but in all the ways that really count I think we're actually pretty similar – or at least compatible.'

When I didn't respond right away, he took me by the hand. 'So what do you think, Sal? Wanna give it another shot?'

I studied his face for signs of . . . I'm not quite sure what. Doubt? Cynicism? But all I could discern was absolute earnestness. I squeezed his hand. 'Yeah, okay. I'm game if you are.'

Eric looked as if he might have been about to lean forward to give me a kiss, but if so, he was stopped by a voice calling out at that moment, 'Oooo, look at the little love birds!'

It was Grace, with her mother in tow. 'Oh, hi,' I said, withdrawing my hand from Eric's and feeling my body grow warm. Hot flash? I thought not.

'I was going to suggest we join you for a few minutes – we're meeting Jack, my dad, and Ryan and Cynthia here at seven – but perhaps you'd rather be alone?' Grace turned to wink at me, then did a double-take as she noticed my bandages.

'No, no, it's fine. We'd love to have you join us,' I said with a glance across the table. 'Right?'

Eric didn't seem eager to have company, but he smiled graciously as he stood and pulled out a chair for Diana. 'Please.'

'Are you okay?' Grace asked as she took the seat next to mine. 'I heard what happened, but you look *awful*.'

'Gee, thanks,' I said. 'It's actually not as bad as it looks. But how did you? Oh, right . . .'

'Detective Vargas interviewed the whole family this morning,' Diana said, confirming what I'd surmised. 'And he told us how Amy attacked you. I'm so sorry. I feel somehow responsible, since she was our employee.'

I shook my head. *Ouch. Again.* 'It's not your fault. She had us all fooled, including me, up till the end. Did Vargas tell you why she . . . did what she did?'

'No need to dance around the subject,' Diana said with a grim smile. 'Yes, he told us that she's accused of killing Neil – and why.' She stared down at the polished wood tabletop for a moment, and when she looked up her eyes were moist. 'I can't believe I didn't see through her ruse.'

'None of us did,' Grace said. 'There was nothing any of us could have done.'

The server arrived with Eric's and my dinners and, after setting down our plates, went to fetch menus for the two newcomers.

'What'd you order?' Diana asked Eric, dabbing at her eyes with her napkin. 'It looks delicious.'

'It is. It's the hanger steak special. Here, you want a taste?' He cut a slice of his beef, coated with a thick sesame-ginger glaze, and offered Diana the fork.

'Oh, yum. I think that's what I'll have, too. Don't put the order in yet, though,' she told the hovering server. 'We're waiting for a table for six. But I wouldn't mind a glass of Chardonnay in the meantime.'

'And a Longboard lager for me,' Grace said, returning the menus.

'So what's going to happen to the farm now,' I asked once we were again alone. 'You gonna hire someone else to work it?'

Grace glanced at Diana, who shrugged. 'I see no reason not to tell her,' the mother said, then turned to me. 'We had a family meeting this afternoon, after the detective finished interviewing us all. It was partly so I could make peace with Ryan about . . . everything.' She bit her lip. 'I think he's okay. Hurt, but better now that we talked. And we'll definitely have to keep working through it all. It'll take some time.'

'Ryan apologized for not stepping up to pay for Neil's funeral,' Grace said. 'And for being such a jerk of late. He was just in a really bad place emotionally after getting the results of that DNA test, he said, and ended up taking it out on everyone else. He did offer to take over that loan I got, though, so that's nice.'

Diana was nodding, her eyes sad. 'But we also talked about the future of the farm,' she said. 'Ernie was having one of his good days today, thank goodness, which made it easier. I asked what everyone wanted to do, now that Neil was no longer here to manage the place . . .'

'. . . and I said we should try to keep it,' Grace put in.

'Really?' I lowered my lamb-laden fork. 'But I thought you wanted to sell?'

'I did. But that was before all this.' She waved her hand vaguely, as if to indicate the world at large, almost knocking the beer and wine off the tray our server had just brought to the table.

'And Ryan said he felt the same way,' Grace went on once she and Diana had their drinks. 'So I talked to Jack, and he's on board for us moving out to the farm. It's way bigger than the condo we now rent, and he'll be able to use the tack room as his shop. And that way I can help Mom and Dad around the house – though we'll have to hire someone to manage the farm itself, since I know virtually nothing about artichokes.'

Diana smiled at her daughter. 'It's not a permanent fix, of course. It won't be too much longer before Ernie and I have to move anyway – to some place like the income property we own, that's single story and closer to town. But for the time being, I think this will be the perfect solution.'

'And given everything that's happened over the past few months,' Grace said, 'we all agreed that it seemed best to try to keep things the same as much as possible. The family doesn't need any more big changes right now.'

'Well, I'm truly happy for you. Here, let's toast.' I raised my glass, and Grace, Diana, and Eric followed suit.

'To us, and to the Lerici farm,' Diana said. 'Cornelio would be so happy to know it's going to stay in the family.'

'Cornelio?' I frowned and looked toward Grace for explanation.

'That's Neil's full name,' she said. 'He was named after my uncle, Dad's brother, Cornelio. But everyone always just called him Neil to avoid confusion.'

Ha! So his name *did* start with a C, after all – just like Cordelia in *King Lear*. The parallel was complete. I couldn't wait to tell Allison the news.

But more than that, I thought, catching Eric's smiling eyes on mine, *I can't wait for this dinner to be over.*

RECIPES

'Rogue' Negroni Cocktail
(serves 1)

The classic version of this cocktail calls for equal parts of the three liquors, which makes for a beverage that – at least to my taste – is far too sweet. So I've come up with a drier version employing a higher percentage of gin. And although traditionalists may turn up their nose at the splash of lemon juice and soda added at the end, I find their inclusion makes for a lively and refreshing finish to the cocktail. *Cin cin!*

Ingredients

2 oz. (¼ cup) dry gin
½ oz. (1 tablespoon) Campari liqueur
½ oz. (1 tablespoon) sweet red vermouth
splash (about 1 teaspoon) lemon juice
splash (about 2 teaspoons) soda water
1 lemon or orange slice, for garnish

Directions

Place 4-5 ice cubes into a cocktail shaker, then add the gin, Campari, and vermouth. Shake vigorously until frothy, then pour everything – including the ice – into an Old Fashioned (or similar 10-oz.) glass. Add a splash of lemon juice and of soda, stir, and garnish with the slice of lemon or orange.

Artichoke Soup with Potatoes and Cream
(serves 4)

This is the dish that earned my father, Mario, top honors from the judges at the Santa Cruz Artichoke Cook-Off. And it truly is a winner, with the addition of garlic and shallots, Parmesan cheese, and white wine to balance the flavorful artichokes and make for a silky, savory soup.

Dad made his award-winning soup with fresh artichokes, but this version substitutes the canned or jarred variety, which tastes great and is far easier to prepare. Just be sure to choose artichoke hearts packed in water – not the marinated variety. Or, if you can find them, feel free to use frozen hearts.

If you don't have any Parmesan cheese rind, this ingredient may be omitted, but you might want to add more shaved cheese to the garnish to make up for its absence.

Ingredients for Soup

2 tablespoons olive oil
¾ lb. Yukon gold or other yellow potatoes (about 6 smallish ones)
4 large shallots
3 large garlic cloves
1 14 oz. can/jar artichoke heart pieces packed in water (about 8.5 oz. drained)
½ teaspoon herbes de Provence (may substitute dried thyme)
1 cup dry white wine
4 cups chicken stock
3" rind Parmesan cheese

½ cup heavy cream
1 teaspoon salt
½ teaspoon black pepper

Ingredients for Garnish

3 tablespoons extra virgin olive oil, plus more for drizzling
5-6 artichoke heart pieces, reserved from can or jar
salt, to taste
½ cup shaved Parmesan cheese

Directions for Soup

Peel the potatoes and cut them into ½ inch pieces. Heat the oil in a large saucepan over moderate heat until shimmering, then add the potatoes. Peel, then cut the shallots and garlic in half, and add them to the pan. Sauté the vegetables over medium heat, stirring occasionally, until they start to brown – about 5 minutes. Drain the artichoke heart pieces, set aside five or six for the garnish, and add the rest to the pan.

Sprinkle the vegetables with the herbes de Provence, then pour in the wine and simmer until the liquid has mostly cooked away – about 8 minutes. Add the chicken stock and cheese rinds and simmer, partly covered, until the vegetables are tender – about 20 minutes.

Let the vegetables and broth cool, then remove and discard the cheese rinds. Purée the soup with an immersion blender (or use a regular blender, working in batches, and pour back in the pan). Add the cream and the salt and pepper, and – if serving immediately – bring back up to a simmer over medium heat.

The soup can be prepared up to this point and refrigerated for a day (which is recommended, as it will help the flavors meld).

<u>Directions for Garnish</u>

Squeeze the retained artichoke hearts dry with a cloth or paper towel, then slice them lengthwise into thin strips.

Heat the olive oil in a skillet over moderate heat until shimmering, then scatter the artichoke strips into the hot oil. Stirring often, fry until crispy and golden brown, which will take only a minute or so. *Watch them carefully, as they can quickly burn.* Remove with a slotted spoon to a paper towel to drain, then sprinkle lightly with salt.

Reheat the soup, if necessary, then ladle into bowls and drizzle each with about a teaspoon of olive oil. Place a mound of shaved cheese in the middle of each bowl, then scatter the frizzled artichokes on top.

Brussels Sprout Salad with Citrus Vinaigrette
(serves 6)

It may strike some as odd to eat Brussels sprouts raw, but the citrus vinaigrette in this recipe serves to tenderize the shredded vegetables by breaking down their fiber, much in the same way the marinade 'cooks' the fish in ceviche. For this reason, it's best to dress the salad an hour or two before serving it, so the vinaigrette can have time to work its magic. Which, of course, makes this the perfect dish for a restaurant such as Gauguin – or for that dinner party you're hosting, when you don't want to spend the entire evening in the kitchen.

Ingredients for Salad

4 cups whole Brussels sprouts (about 1 lb.)
½ cup dried cranberries
½ cup raw pine nuts
½ cup shaved or coarsely-grated Pecorino cheese (about 2 oz. by weight)

Ingredients for Vinaigrette

3 tablespoons orange juice (½ an orange, squeezed)
2 tablespoons lemon juice (½ a lemon, squeezed)
1 med. clove garlic, peeled and minced (about 1 teaspoon)
1 tablespoon Dijon mustard
2 tablespoons honey
2 tablespoons extra virgin olive oil
¼ teaspoon salt
⅛ teaspoon black pepper

Directions

Slice the bottom (stem end) off the Brussels sprouts and remove any discolored leaves. Shred the sprouts, either in a food processor or with a sharp knife. Place the shredded sprouts in a large bowl along with the dried cranberries and set aside.

Set a large skillet over medium-high heat and when hot, add the pine nuts. Tossing or stirring the nuts frequently, toast them until golden brown – about 1 minute. (Some may turn dark brown, which is fine – *just be careful not let them burn!*) Remove the pan from the heat and pour the nuts into a bowl. Once they have cooled, store them in a sealed plastic bag until needed.

Combine all the vinaigrette ingredients in either a glass jar or a medium-size bowl. If in a jar, screw on the lid and shake until well-blended; if in a bowl, use a whisk to blend. Pour the vinaigrette over the Brussels sprouts and cranberries, and toss until the salad is evenly-coated. Cover the salad and store in the fridge for up to three hours.

To serve, plate up the dressed salad, then top with the shaved/ grated cheese and the toasted pine nuts.

Steak Diane
(serves 2)

The name of this dish – which recalls the Roman goddess of the hunt – is deliciously appropriate, given its history as a romantic 'date night' meal, traditionally served by candlelight atop a white tablecloth. Having a hi-fi playing smooth jazz in the background doesn't hurt, either.

When Martin prepared Steak Diane for me, he used tenderloins (aka filet mignon), which are typically used for the dish. But I prefer a more flavorful cut of beef such as rib eye, or even a well-marbled tri-tip steak. Feel free to use whatever kind of steak you like, as long as it's a tender cut that can pan-fry quickly. For a medium-rare steak (which I like), use an insta-read thermometer and remove it from the pan when the center of the thickest part reads 130° F. For a rare steak, remove at 125° F.

The trick to making this *à la minute* dish is to have all the ingredients prepped and at hand before you start to cook, as it all comes together quite quickly. Which is also a good reason to pair the dish with something simple – as did Martin – such as baked or roast potatoes and a tossed green salad.

Ingredients

2 boneless beef steaks, about 8 oz. each, at room temperature
salt and freshly ground pepper
1 tablespoon olive oil
1 tablespoon butter
1 large shallot, finely chopped (about 2 tablespoons)

2 tablespoons brandy or Cognac
1 tablespoon Dijon mustard
1 teaspoon Worcestershire sauce
½ cup heavy cream
1 teaspoon fresh-squeezed lemon juice (or to taste)
1 tablespoon chopped parsley or green onions, for garnish

Directions

Finely chop the shallots and coarsely chop the parsley/green onions, and set aside.

Sprinkle the steaks lightly with salt and season them generously with freshly-ground black pepper.

Heat a heavy skillet (cast iron is good), large enough to hold the steaks without crowding them, over medium-high heat, then add the olive oil and butter. Once the foam in the butter has subsided, lay the steaks in the pan and fry until nicely browned on the bottom. Flip them over and continue cooking until done to your taste. Remove from the pan to a plate and cover with foil to keep warm while you prepare the sauce.

Turn the heat down to medium and add the shallots to the pan, sautéing them till they start to soften. Add the brandy, mustard, and Worcestershire sauce and stir until well-blended. Pour in the cream and let the sauce come to a simmer. Turn off the heat, then add lemon juice, salt, and freshly-ground pepper to taste.

Spoon the sauce over the steaks, garnish with the chopped parsley or green onions, set the needle down on that Frank Sinatra disc you have on the turntable, and enjoy!

Sally's Decadent Blondies
(makes one 9" x 13" pan)

These blondies are *extremely* rich. So rich that one 3" x 3" piece is likely all you'll want to eat in one sitting.

Or not. Because the combination of the chewy bar, crunchy nuts, sweet chips, and salt is pretty darn addicting. So go ahead; just try to limit yourself to one square.

Ingredients

½ lb. (2 sticks) unsalted butter, melted
2 cups brown sugar
2 eggs
2 teaspoons vanilla
1 teaspoon salt
2 cups flour
1 cup chopped macadamia nuts
1 cup white chocolate chips
1 tablespoon vegetable oil, for greasing pan

Directions

Heat oven to 350° F.

In a large bowl, use a mixer to combine the melted butter and brown sugar, blending until the sugar has completely dissolved. Add the eggs and vanilla and mix until smooth. Switching to a wooden spoon (because the batter will become too stiff for a mixer), add the salt and flour and stir until no streaks remain. Stir in the macadamia nuts and chocolate chips.

Grease a 9" x 13" baking pan with the vegetable oil. Dump the batter into the pan, smooth flat, and bake until the edges start to brown and a toothpick inserted into the middle comes out clean (25-30 minutes). Let cool, then cut into squares.

ACKNOWLEDGMENTS

Although writing is indeed a solitary activity, producing the best book possible and getting the final, polished version into the hands of readers involves far more people than simply the author.

I am indebted to my terrific beta readers, Robin McDuff, Nancy Lundblad, Ellen Byron, and Becky Clark, whose honesty and eagle-eyes I truly appreciate.

Thanks also to Robin McDuff for her advice about oven and stove repairs, to Fernando Traba for providing me with authentic and colorful Mexican slang, and to Shirley Tessler for once again acting as my recipe editor.

I'm eternally grateful to my fabulous agent, Erin Niumata, for her hard work and persistent belief in me and my books, to Maggie Auffarth, and to everyone else at Folio Literary Management who helped make this fifth Sally Solari mystery a reality. Enormous thanks go out also to my editor, Rachel Slatter, to Natasha Bell, Anna Harrisson, Martin Brown and all the others at Severn House. And *grazie mille* to my marvelous publicist, Maryglenn Warnock.

Finally, here's to all the generous and hard-working folks involved in Sisters in Crime and Mystery Writers of America; to my fellow food bloggers at Mystery Lovers' Kitchen (Leslie Budewitz, Lucy Burdette, Valerie Burns, Peg Cochran, Maya Corrigan, Cleo Coyle, Maddie Day, Vicki Delany, Tina Kashian, Molly MacRae, and Mia Manansala); and to my besties at Chicks on the Case (Ellen Byron, Jennifer J. Chow, Becky Clark, Marla Cooper, Vickie Fee, Kellye Garrett, Cynthia Kuhn, Lisa Q. Mathews, and Kathleen Valenti).